MONSTROUS

Book One

SAWYER BLACK

DAVID W. WRIGHT

STERLING & STONE

To YOU, the reader.
Thank you for taking a chance on us.
Thank you for your support.
Thank you for the emails.
Thank you for the reviews.
Thank you for reading and joining us on this road.

MONSTROUS

Chapter One

"WILL IT BE SCARY?" Amélie asked.

"No." Henry laughed. "Definitely not."

"Then I don't wanna hear it."

"What? That's crazy talk! Last night you begged me to stop because you said I was scaring you. This morning you practically *yelled* at me, saying I should know better than to tell you stories that give you nightmares."

"It's okay, I don't mind right now."

Henry rolled his eyes, leaned past his daughter, grabbed the e-reader from her nightstand, then flicked to *ForNevermore*, the story he'd been reading aloud for the last week. He never should've started. It wasn't appropriate for children, at least not a ten-year-old. But after he'd spent nine of Amélie's first decade alive on the road, touring at every club with an opening and trying to build a name that might eventually mean something, Henry had a difficult, if not impossible, time saying 'no' to his baby girl.

"It's too scary. I'm not giving you any more nightmares."

"It's not too scary. I promise." She folded her fingers

together and made her eyes wider. "Actually, Daddy, it's scarier if you don't read it, since I'll have to make up the story in my head. The real bad stuff can't be as bad as whatever I'll make up, and then you'll really be in trouble."

Henry laughed again. With all there was to love about Amélie, an ability to craft a winning argument was certainly one of her finest qualities. Truth was, he *did* want to finish the story. He loved it when her face froze, as he whispered the scariest parts, and how she clung to his body the moment he tried to leave.

Now that Henry was mostly home, days stretched differently. They were shorter when Amélie was around and longer when she wasn't. There were endless afternoons when Henry felt like he waited all day to read to his daughter. At ten, Amélie was growing too fast, or at least not slow enough to help Henry shed the pounds of guilt he carried for being away so much during the years that mattered most. He hated how time always flew, never needing fuel. He fell asleep each night thinking of the hours with Amélie he never had, and woke in the mornings counting ways he could fix what was broken or fill what was missing.

Days turned into weeks and months to years, barely breathing through the hours on their way. Amélie would be eighteen before he knew it. All the money in the world couldn't stop time from bleeding or allow him to hold Amélie closer once it came time for her to leave the nest.

It's not fair.

Part of Henry wanted to pull his baby girl from school and get her a full-time tutor so he could see her when he wanted. But that wasn't fair, either, and he didn't want to make his shit hers. Because he had only so much time with Amélie, Henry celebrated stories, knowing they were one of the best ways to stretch minutes and make them easier to remember.

"Okay, then. One more night. But if you have nightmares, we're reading *Clifford* tomorrow."

Amélie laughed. "No. Way."

"You're assuming it won't be good, but that's a faulty assumption," Henry said, his face stone-serious. "I picked up a new *Clifford* just today, and I was planning to read that since you were so scared last night. In this one, Clifford eats some bad dog food after Emily Elizabeth tries to save money by buying it in bulk. Poor Clifford ends up going nuts and eating every kid on Birdwell Island."

Still giggling, Amélie said, "I haven't read *Clifford* in five years, but *that* sounds like one worth reading. Maybe after *ForNevermore*."

Henry smiled, then tapped the e-reader's screen, opening the book to where they'd left off the evening before. "Ready?"

"Ready!"

Henry cleared just one sentence from the story before something moved his attention from the words to the door. He lowered the e-reader and turned to Amélie. "Did you hear that?"

The sound wasn't especially loud, nowhere near a crash. It was barely there. Unworthy of intrusion into his story. Yet, in that narrow margin between blinks, Henry *knew* something was wrong.

Amélie shrugged. "Maybe? It sounded like something might've fallen. Mommy's probably home and carrying too much stuff. Keep reading." She smiled, quietly begging for Henry to finish and turn his back on distraction, which he often found so hard to do.

He started the second sentence as his inner whisper

insisted that he stand and investigate. Then he finished the paragraph, with his stomach churning.

Their new home still made Henry uncomfortable. If there was such a thing as too much house, Henry had bought it. Sure, it was grand to have a pool, a movie room, and a dishwasher big enough to rinse a flying saucer, but the place was so goddamned massive it felt more like a museum, especially at night. There were many things he missed about their old house — being able to run to the front door and help Samantha when she came home late with groceries was only one.

Not feeling guilty for his everyday extravagance was like a hundred of the other.

Henry shook the discomfort from his shoulders, then returned to the story, making it one more sentence before he was interrupted by a far-off crash. "I think Mommy's home, honey. Mind if I go check?"

"Why do you need to see if she's home? She'll be up in a minute, just like always."

"Yes, but she might forget to bring your surprise."

Amélie smiled. "What surprise?"

"You know the rule about spoiling surprises," Henry whispered. "I'll be back in a second, okay?"

"One. … It's been a second."

"Amélie …"

"Okay, Daddy."

"Be right back." Henry leaned in, kissed her on the cheek, then set the e-reader on Amélie's nightstand and left the room, wondering what sort of surprise he'd be able to find and bring back upstairs.

He stepped into the hallway, calling to Sam, a panic he couldn't explain getting worse with every step.

"Sam! Are you home? Samantha!"

Once Henry stopped touring, getting Amélie down at

bedtime had become *his thing.* Sam capitalized on the final part of the evening by using it to finish lingering errands. But she always had most of the day, too, which made Henry hate it that she left the house so late, when stores started closing and lights went dim. The hours bad shit started to happen. Sam said his needless worry, fueled by paranoia, was a fair trade for a mostly-empty supermarket.

Henry reached the end of the hallway, stepped onto the winding stairway, and cast his eyes down into the foyer as he began his descent. He froze halfway down, a second before the scream that was loud enough to peel paper from the walls — a scream that would surely bring his daughter to the stairs.

"I said, don't make a fucking sound." One of two men on either side of Samantha was gripping her hair with one hand, pressing the gun in his other hard into her temple. He was thin and bald, wearing all black. His eyes were tiny but fierce.

Who the fuck are these people?

For a second, Henry figured they were burglars. They were dressed identically in black pants, shirts, and gloves. But no masks. Henry wished he'd not let Sam talk him out of buying a gun. Now he was standing at the top of the stairs, helpless.

Sam looked like she was doing everything possible to hold her whimper inside, but it fell out anyway. The second thug was a barrel of a man, with a keg for a body and a bulldog's face. He raised a fist dyed blue with tattoo ink and pointed at Samantha's face. "I'd shut the fuck up if I were you. Loud sounds make my friend here jumpy."

Henry raised his hands, palms facing the front door, then started descending the stairs, his heart beating harder with every step.

He could stop this from happening, maybe make everything okay.

There were two thugs, and they didn't know about Amélie upstairs … yet.

He had to keep it that way.

"Stop it right there." Tiny Eyes moved his gun from Sam's temple, then shoved her toward the bulldog, who drew his pistol and jammed it under her chin while Tiny Eyes turned his weapon on Henry.

Henry stopped, four stairs from the bottom, eyes flitting from the bulldog to his partner as he wrestled with the odds of chancing another step. "Let's all stay cool, okay? You can have whatever you want." He lowered his body a stair. "Help me help you. You want it, I can give it to you. You just gotta let me know what it is you're looking for. Let my wife go so we can talk."

Henry took another step, suddenly realizing the depth of their danger. The men weren't wearing masks, and that meant witnesses.

Samantha looked up, quiet tears streaking her face, eyes shining on Henry with the same belief that had brightened his darkest moments, the faith that he would always make everything right. The light of unflinching confidence kept them trucking through a dozen years of struggle, from back when they barely had a buck to buy milk for Amélie or to pay bills that had hung above them like a water-rotted roof.

Like always, Sam expected him to fix things. Because he always *had*. But it was only because of *her* that he had succeeded. She always believed in him, even if he didn't.

He didn't believe he could do it, not this time.

Maybe this time her faith meant nothing.

This time there were two men, and they were both holding guns.

Henry took another two steps.

"Stop right there, asshole!" Tiny Eyes yelled, aiming his gun at Henry's forehead.

Bulldog's giant fist disappeared into Sam's hair. "One more step, Punchline, and Mrs. Punchline gets it."

So, it's not random. They know who I am.

Sam whimpered.

Henry was too slow and out of shape to fight, but assholes could often be bought. "Just let me get to the safe. You can't open it without me. There's enough in there to keep you happy for a long, long time."

As Henry's right foot landed on the polished marble floor at the bottom of the stairs, his attention was yanked back by a barely-there voice from behind and above him. "Daddy?"

He turned and saw Amélie standing at the top of the staircase. Another "Daddy!" But this one was a scream. Henry spun toward the front door to follow her gaze, just as the blow slammed into the back of his head.

Henry dropped to his hands and knees, his teeth slamming together on his tongue.

His mouth filled with copper, and blood warmed his neck, gushing from the split in his skull, spreading in a pool under his sagging head. At first, his shadow made the blood appear black.

Behind him, Amélie screamed.

Henry gasped, sucking air through his teeth as the world shook around him, turning dark at the edges as pints of crimson syrup spilled across the pristine floor. Sam screamed. Amélie's voice joined her mother's in an alarming harmony.

Bulldog said, "Somebody shut these bitches up!"

All I have to do is force myself to stand. I've been standing up for years.

Pain is only temporary.

Despite the gunman standing over him, Henry struggled to push himself up. He caught a glimpse of the third man rushing up the stairs toward Amélie.

Stay the fuck away from her!

His fingers slipped in his own blood, and his hands shot out from under him. His forehead cracked against the heavy tile, and his vision turned to white light.

Amélie shrieked.

Oh God, no!

He tried to get up again, blood from a cut over his eyebrow pattering into the smeared puddle beneath him.

He turned his head toward the approaching footsteps, rolling his eyes up to see who it was. Nausea twisted his gut, vomit rising into his throat. Tiny Eyes knelt with his knee next to Henry's shoulder. "Who said you could get up?"

The gun against the back of his head made his shoulders draw up, a chill spreading across his chest.

A sudden flash of pain and thunder, and Henry's world went dark.

Chapter Two

HENRY OPENED his eyes to his brilliantly lit home.

Except it *wasn't* his house. At least, not like he remembered or could have imagined it. There was too much light to make sense. Fuzzy shapes of walls and furniture. Familiar but fluid, toying with geometry, as if there was no gravity to ground them.

He rose from the marble, trying to focus through the blur. His throat was desert-dry, and his entire body tingled. Like the house around him, he barely felt there.

"Samantha!" he called out. "Amélie!"

The words echoed oddly. The thick air left his lungs, and his voice whistled in the emptiness, twisting itself into a sound that returned as something else, as unintelligible as the shapes.

The house was as silent as it was bright. He crossed the foyer and stepped into a hallway that had never been there before. The corridor stretched into shadow, growing darker by the inch, until it crashed into a midnight horizon. For a flickering moment, Henry saw the long hall lined with countless tall figures in long black robes, fabric fluttering in a wind that he could neither hear nor feel. The shadowy figures disappeared almost immediately after he saw them, as did the sprawling length of the hall.

Henry emerged from the other end and stepped into the living room. It was big as an auditorium, many times its usual size. And on the wrong side of the house. Everything was exaggerated, as things often were in dreams.

Henry tried to wake himself, first by screaming for Sam and Amélie until his voice broke from the effort, then by pinching his arm. Finally, he raked his fingernails against his forearms, trying to draw blood. Pain flared into his shoulder, but he couldn't break the skin.

The best and worst of everything always happened in the snug nucleus of a dream. Nightmares had haunted Henry since he was four, when he witnessed his mother's murder after she had refused to surrender her purse to a mugger. Shot twice, her tiny chest had collapsed from the bullets. She hit the sidewalk, finally letting go of the strap. The man had snatched it up, running around the corner with some wadded tissues and a buck sixty-nine in pennies.

She'd been holding his hand, pulling him down Radford on the way to get a pack of Tareyton 100s. He couldn't remember her face, but in the haze before slumber, Henry would see the blood on her lips. Hear the crack of her head as it bounced off the concrete. It didn't get better until Samantha moved in. Rocking him on the squealing springs of his cheap bed until his heart had finally slowed.

But even though his surroundings were muddled like the memory of his mother's face, Henry knew this was something different. Or if it *was* a dream, it was one buried inside another.

Maybe I'm dead?

He remembered the attackers, yet only as if the incident had happened years instead of seconds ago. He thought of the anguish on Sam's face, and the deafening scream of "Daddy!" behind him.

Then the *THWAP!* on the back of his head before everything went black.

Panic pounded in Henry's heart. Maybe he *was* dead. Maybe he even *deserved* to be dead. But no matter what, he had unfinished business. They had taken Sam and Amélie. His family was alone and unprotected. They needed him, and Samantha was waiting for him to make things right.

But here Henry stood, in front of his living room door, trying to inhale this reality. In Henry's home, the large door before him opened to a short hallway leading to the game room. His second favorite room in the house. But here, in the ugly eternity of whatever *this* was, that door would surely open to Hell.

His hand hovered above the doorknob, wanting to turn it and find his family was on the other side, but he somehow *knew* it was something far worse waiting instead.

Still, if going through Hell was the only way to reach his family, the journey was worth it.

Henry opened the door, crossed the threshold, and found himself standing in the middle of an endless road, his house no longer behind him. He took a few steps, then the road twisted into a vacuum of black with nothing above, below, or around him. Just as quickly, he took another two steps and the world began to fill itself in, like a video game slowly rendering his surroundings.

A broken city sprawled across his vision, crumbling to the right, left, and everywhere around him. It was worse than ruined, and unlike anything Henry had ever seen. The city didn't seem old or new, it simply looked destroyed, as if that was how it had been forever and would be for always.

Thousands of mountainous buildings lay fallen and crumbled, collapsed in countless stages of decay. Angry black clouds churned in the charcoal sky. As they stirred, Henry felt like the air above was somehow sucking every cell of hope from his body. Maybe it was the city itself.

A million shades of gray and black sent Henry to his knees.

If he was already dead, then he was ready to perish again.

He could never save his family, so why even try?

Giving up was the easiest thing in the world. He'd done it hundreds of times. An encore meant nothing.

Henry rocked back and forth, staring out at an endless landscape of broken city, as a stark loneliness deeper than anything he had ever felt before swelled inside him. He tried thinking of Sam and Amélie. There was something he was supposed to do, some sort of danger to keep them from. Without him, everything was lost.

He ignored the charcoal world and closed his eyes, trying to remember.

Henry lifted his eyelids and looked at the city from under his brow. Gasping as he stood, Henry turned in a helpless circle, looking at the countless mangled faces staring back at him from a million broken windows. Dark creatures that weren't quite people, hiding in buildings that weren't quite buildings, all of them fixing their awful eyes upon on him, the weight of their collective gaze adding a blaze to his despair.

He had to get away, or he'd surely forget everything and wind up with them, staring from a decayed window for all of eternity. Henry ran down the broken road.

Fire licked his blood as he pushed his body to race harder and faster toward the horizon. Lit with the thinnest seam of light, just bright enough to seed his hope. Henry's lungs seemed one wrong breath from collapse, until it dawned on him that the fatigue was only in his head.

After running for what felt like hours, Henry realized there were no limits in this place.

He ran faster, and the crumbled city started to fade, eaten by the growing light. As Henry moved closer, the brilliant shining was sucked into a deep blue horizon, wide and open enough to shame Montana.

But even the skies were nothing compared to the Tree.

The Tree, taller than the broken towers behind him, pulled Henry into itself. His churning feet rose from the road, and he let himself go, holding his arms out so his body was a cross as he floated toward the most beautiful thing he had ever seen.

The Tree's grace was enough to make Henry cry. He floated into the same breeze that kissed its bark, and when he saw the damage marring its surface, his lips parted with a sob that shook his shoulders.

Chocolate-colored limbs lay in brittle piles of decay scattered around the base. Each broken branch seemed to scream. Fresh green tendrils bloomed from the trunk, crying for light. Farther up, small buds blossomed into larger blooms and murmured to Henry: *Hope isn't dead.*

He floated closer to the Tree and remembered everything. The pain of having Samantha and Amélie ripped from his life closed his throat, and he dared to believe he was inside a dream for the first time since opening the door to the certainty of Hell.

Maybe he *wasn't* dead. Maybe this was something else. Something *better*. Something he could still wake from. Maybe Henry could still save his family because there were no intruders in his home, and his family was safe and snoring.

Henry raced toward the possible truth, trying to

convince himself that it was only a dream. Something as beautiful and tragic as the Tree would *have* to be. Searching for any false thread that might unravel his nocturnal facade, Henry rounded the trunk before falling to his feet on the other side of the Tree. And there he encountered a magnificent clearing.

The grass was especially green against the azure sky. A long stone table rested in the center. It could have sat a hundred, though it held only two. The table was an icy gray, except for where two men sat across from each other, staring, a chessboard between them.

After being alone for what felt like so long, Henry was grateful to find others inside his dream. His loneliness began to ebb away. Maybe *they* could help him wake up.

As Henry approached the table, the world grew more colorful still. Another thousand trees thickened the distance while miles of fresh lavender rippled the grassy slopes in purple rows.

Neither man turned to Henry, though he could feel them certain of his presence. He took another small, tentative step, feeling almost as if he were invading some tranquil ceremony. A ritual with importance. Religious fear tingled his body. He felt eyes on his back, a scrutiny that begged him to run.

He almost longed for the figures in the windows.

He turned, but the dark city behind him had grown into teeth, darkening the horizon like an inky grin, as if threatening to grow and encroach on the beautiful life thriving in the garden. He flinched back, his ass running into the table's edge. He spun with an indrawn hiss of embarrassment.

Neither man looked away from their game. Each player had only two pieces. A king and a knight.

"Hello?" Henry said, quietly at first, then again but louder.

His third cry, nearly as loud as the second, but half as timid, drew the attention of the gentleman on Henry's side of the table. The man turned to Henry, his wavy hair a dirty pewter, nuzzling his shoulders. His skin was the color of bark, and wrinkled like an old tree. His eyes were marbles, both snow white like his robes.

Across from him sat a sun-kissed Spaniard, with hair thick and dark as coal, though not nearly as black as his robes. He looked up at Henry and nodded, staring with sky-blue eyes, no pupils, and a smile like a crescent moon.

"Where am I?" Henry asked, trembling.

The man in white stared. Henry heard the man's voice in his head.

Why ask what you already know?

Henry swallowed. "Am I …"

"Dead? Yes." The dark-haired man rose from the table, floated over it, and moved toward Henry, leaving the game and the glow around it.

"No." Henry shook his head, arguing mostly with himself. "This isn't possible. Not you or *any* of this."

"You're right," said the man in black.

"Where am I? Where are Sam and Amélie?"

The man in black said nothing.

"Where am I?" Henry repeated.

The man in black ignored him as their world faded into a roiling mist, smearing their surroundings into something hazy and white. He smiled. "You're in Nowhere. Now pay attention. This is the best part of the show so far, where we get to see all your personal *demons*."

Henry peered into the mist, squinting until everything blurred. He blinked as color started to swallow its absence.

But the colors were wrong.

Every horrible shade from Henry's abbreviated life appeared everywhere at once. Memories spilled onto the fog like three-dimensional film. It seemed as if Henry could step into every frame, if he only knew how.

Henry watched as his past self took the stage for the first time, hunched and painted in sweat, standing with a microphone a foot above the ground, knees shaking through the joke. Then, as a sophomore, paired with Cheryl Johnson for lab. Getting partnered with Cheryl was the best thing that could ever happen to a fat piece of shit like him. He bent over and sneezed, sending a long anal salute out of his ass and into the air. Cheryl laughed, and the entire class followed.

Memories fell. Beatings. Humiliations. Personal atrocities. Splattering like rain from a cloud.

Good things and glad moments. Triumphs and victories. They blurred in and out of his quickly-collapsing world, the little bit of happiness left barely bleeding through the thick seams of misery.

"What is this place?" Everything about it made him want to cry. "You said *Nowhere*, but what the Hell does that mean?"

"This is where we wait," said the man in white from his spot at the table. He pinched the knight between his pointer and thumb, then moved it two spaces up and one across.

"Wait for what?"

"To go one place or the other."

"What the Hell are you talking about?"

"Bingo!" said the man in black with a smile, still standing, but no longer looking at Henry.

"What?"

"No, the part after," said the man in white.

"After what?"

The man in black turned to Henry, his blue eyes heavy with fatigue. "You said *what the Hell.* He said *one place or the other.* Heaven or Hell, this is where we wait."

"You mean … Purgatory?"

"Yes." The man in white smiled at Henry as if he'd won a prize.

"No, this is some sorta fucking dream. A bad trip or something."

"No, it's quite real," the man in white said. "You *are* dead. This is where we wait. You've known this since before you arrived and are only feigning ignorance now." He stared into Henry's eyes with his creepy all-white gaze, then gestured toward the table. "Have a seat."

Henry sat. The man in black sighed and sat beside him.

Henry looked at the board. Still four pieces. "Do you know if my wife and daughter are okay?"

"I do not." The man in white shook his head.

"Do you know how I get back?"

"You *don't,*" he said, eyes still on his pieces, like it was his move instead of the Spaniard's.

"I have to know what happened to my family. If I'm dead, then they might be, too. They were in danger when—"

"Danger?"

"Yes. Three men broke into our fucking house. I don't know what happened after I was shot."

Henry smashed his fist into the stone table as he imagined, or *remembered,* Sam getting dragged through the foyer by her beautiful black hair, then up the stairs toward the bedrooms, past a still-screaming Amélie. Henry shook whatever it was from his mind. Fantasy or memory, it didn't matter.

"This is a dream. I have to wake up!"

The man in black said, "No, definitely not a dream."

"It is!" Henry roared, willing to murder to make it so, if only someone would show him who to kill. "There's no such thing as Purgatory! You're all figments of my fucked-up imagination, a result of some bad acid in high school or something. So, do me a favor and tell me how to get the fuck out of Oz."

The man in white shook his head. "Worrying makes things worse. You're safe now. And that's all that matters." He stood, smiled, and gently set his hands on Henry's shoulders. "Relax. In Nowhere, patience is *everything*."

"No." Henry shook the man's hands away. "Fuck that! Three men came into my house to hurt my family! I have to get back and help them." His voice crumbled into a choke. "I have to *know*."

"No." The man in white shook his head. "Worrying makes things worse. It brings out the Lost. And we don't want the Lost, do we? You're safe. That's all that matters now. Patience is—"

"They're in danger *now*!" Henry yelled, wondering if someone had laced his weed.

That is the last time I buy from the dude with the purple hair. Didn't someone once say you should never buy your shit from a dude with purple hair? If not, that NEEDS to be a fucking T-shirt.

"You've been gone too long to help them now." The man in white still had a lunatic's smile.

"What do you mean, *too long?*"

"You've been dead at least seven hours."

"Wait," Henry said. "You said I've been gone *too long*. Does that mean I *can* go back?"

The man in white turned and looked up, gazing at the Tree with wide eyes as though it had just appeared.

"Henry wants to know if he can return," said the man in black. "Should we tell him?"

"Wait. How do you know my name?"

The man in black sighed. "Really, Henry? With your family and all of *this?*" He waved his hand through the memories and misfortune still raining behind them. "And *that's* what you want to know? Mountains or minutia, Henry. You must focus."

He wanted to hate the man in black, but the man had answers. "Can I go home?"

"Yes," said the man in black, smiling wide as he offered Henry his hand.

Henry, not knowing what else to do, took it. The man in black's robe was replaced by a shiny black suit with a perfectly knotted raspberry tie. "What the …?"

"Now, now." The man wrapped an arm gently around Henry's shoulders. He led him away from the long stone table, farther from the Tree and back toward the road. The buildings were no longer broken or crumbled. Lush orchards now lined either side, bookending a cobbled path paved with freshly scrubbed brick.

The man in black pulled Henry close, as if about to reveal a secret.

"Come. I'm going to tell you how to get back home."

Chapter Three

"NAME'S BOOTHE. That's booth with an *e* if you're adding me to your correspondents." The man in black smiled like he was selling toothpaste.

Before Henry could respond, his attention was pulled to a scampering from behind. He turned, surprised to see the man in white falling in stride beside them.

Boothe turned to the man in white, irritated. "Do you *really* need to be here, Randall?"

"Do you really need an answer?"

Boothe ignored Randall and turned back to Henry. "You're here because you aren't ready for anywhere else. Does that make sense?"

Henry was surprised that it *did* make sense, even if he was confused and feeling mildly disoriented as the man in black spoke.

He nodded. This was where he was supposed to be.

"Good, then this will be easy to understand. You're not quite ready for up there." He pointed to the now nearly periwinkle sky. "And you certainly aren't going to want to go down there." His pointer dangled above the grass. "And no one wants to stay *here*, even though it's arguably better than down there."

"Don't listen to him," Randall said.

Boothe laughed as though the other man were stupid. "There are two ways to break boredom in Nowhere." He jerked his thumb toward Randall's scowl. "Play with him, or help people like you. I'm forced by circumstance to play with him no matter what."

"Don't listen to him. He's trying to manipulate you. He's a demon."

Boothe laughed, bending over and clutching his stomach. Then he stumbled to a halt and caught his breath. He stood with a sigh, wiping the tears from his eyes. "You have no idea how long the two of us have been at this, Henry. Some days, it really does feel like forever. *Of course* I am trying to manipulate you. Have you ever managed to get one thing you wanted in life without manipulating the situation?" He gave Henry a second to answer, then went ahead and did it for him. "Of course not! That doesn't preclude my goals and yours from intersection. Would you like to go home, Henry?"

"Why would you help me get home?" Henry asked, dizzy.

"That's need-to-know information," Boothe said. "And you don't. Would you like to go home or not? If *yes*, I can help. If *no*, please leave so I can return to the table and take Randall's knight."

Randall stopped walking, took Henry by the arm, and pulled his eyes toward him. He seemed ages older than Boothe, and his voice was shaky and frail. "Henry, please listen."

A hundred million colors disappeared. Randall's world was nothing but white.

"You want to get up there?" He glanced at the empty

above. "If you take what he's offering, you'll be in Nowhere forever, like him." He scowled, slightly turning his head. "Or, you'll end up down there."

"Are you telling me that I shouldn't make a deal with the Devil?"

Boothe laughed. "*Devil?* Hah! I wish."

Randall shot Boothe a nasty look. "Something like that."

"I don't know *what* to believe. I'm probably tripping my balls off, standing on 45th and screaming at a lamppost. But if this is somehow real, and my wife and daughter are in danger, then I need to get back."

"I can help you with that," Boothe cooed. "You come with me, and I'll bring you home. You can see your wife and child right away."

"Don't trust him," Randall said.

Henry turned to Randall. "Can *you* tell me if my family is safe?"

He stared back at Henry, quietly pleading with him to not be a fool. Henry said nothing, waiting until Randall shook his head. "No. Of *course* I can't say that."

"Then sorry," Henry said. "But circle gets the square."

"He's going to trick you, Henry. You already know this. It's *when,* not *if.*"

"If this is real, fine. He's welcome to trick me after he helps me find my family."

"Don't mind him," Boothe said. "He gets fussy because he doesn't know how to get people to play with him."

Henry turned to Boothe. "It's true, right? You *are* trying to trick me."

"No," Boothe said. "Don't be ridiculous. Technically, I am a demon. But that particular word is *absurd* for my character, though I can do nothing to alter your interpretation, entirely misinformed as it is, constantly reinforced by a lifetime of cartoon dogma. I am *not* the Devil, and you've signed no contract, or done *anything* binding. Your eternal soul is yours to keep. Best of luck with it. I'm tricking you like a well-crafted television commercial tricks you into buying exactly what you want."

"What's the trick?"

Randall sighed, looking up with a dramatic roll of his eyes. "He can't tell you that."

"There *is* no trick." Boothe kept his eyes on Henry. "The arrangement is simple. Something for you, and something for me. What I want is none of your business, because it has nothing to do with you."

"I'm assuming you're playing a trick no matter what you say, but I'm already dead so what can it matter? Either way, I get back to my family first, right?"

"Randall's making you paranoid." Boothe smiled. "There is no trick, and you will get exactly what you're asking for. A return trip to see your family. I suggest we go. Time is different down there and we've already lost twelve hours."

"Twelve hours! I thought you said seven? You mean … are they okay?"

"It's a long story, and seconds are minutes. Why have me tell you when you can see for yourself? Just say, *I'm ready* and you can go back."

"Turn away," Randall warned. "Don't follow him. You've given him too much permission already."

Henry ignored Randall, despite the man's apparent intentions. He turned to Boothe and said, "I'm ready."

Boothe smiled like a cat with a mouthful of yellow feathers, but Henry didn't care. He was going home.

Chapter Four

HENRY OPENED his eyes to an impossible darkness.

The world was darker than black, as if his eyes had been ripped from their sockets.

He was freezing. And like his sight, Henry's body felt broad and indistinct. His orbit blurred. He blinked, but batting his eyelids did nothing. He focused on the pins and needles in his hands and imagined it spreading like fire through his frame. A variation on a meditation technique he'd finally tried at Sam's insistence. He only lasted four days, but the visualization of fire had worked to calm him and now often led him into sleep. And if Samantha ever asked if he still meditated, he could say *yes* without feeling like he was lying.

Life returned to his fingers, and Henry's hands moved over his nude midsection.

What the fuck?

Why am I naked?

Where the fuck am I?

His mind was stacked high with horrifying pictures of himself naked and passed out, spread through the internet.

He imagined Perez Hilton drawing a sarcastic comment with a pink arrow aimed at his smallish dick.

Then he remembered the men in his house. The blood on the floor. The screams and pain.

Samantha! Amélie!

He was back, or at least he thought he was. He had to get up and look around. Blind, he could only guess his location. The surface below him was cold and hard. Henry wondered if he was still in his home, where finding his wife and daughter would be as simple as standing and turning on a light.

Maybe I'm still at the bottom of the stairs.

A dull sound rang above his head, like someone throwing back the deadbolt on the front door.

I fell down in the foyer, and Sam's opening the door for the paramedics.

Then the shadow was split by bright light as Henry's body slid out of the dark.

What the Hell?

Henry gasped in surprise. Boothe leaned over him, still in his dapper black suit.

Oh God, I'm still dreaming.

Henry reached down to cover his crotch. Boothe, paying no particular attention to his nudity, smiled down at Henry as he absorbed his surroundings — a white room, with silver doors lining two walls.

"Is this a ... hospital?"

Boothe smiled. "Yes."

"Why does it look like a morgue?"

"Is this the part where you realize that death has found you, like I said all along, and this wasn't some *bad trip* as you were fool to believe? Because, Dear Henry, we don't have time for that if you wish to get out of here."

Boothe pointed toward a door. "Would you prefer to

run out on your own, or would you like me to blink us out?"

"*Blink* us out?"

"Yes, astral transportation. I blink, we teleport away."

"Teleport like in *Star Trek*, or like Nightcrawler in *X-Men?*"

Boothe looked at him, annoyed. "What?"

"How are we going to teleport? Is—"

Boothe grabbed Henry's hand, and they were gone.

In a flash of brightness and tingling, Henry stood, legs wobbly, stark naked in painful daylight, in the middle of a filthy alley between two tall apartment buildings. Holding his hands over his heaving gut, he swallowed bile and squinted toward the street.

He spun, looking for Boothe, but the demon was gone.

You motherfucker!

Though he didn't recognize the location, Henry figured he was in downtown Burg. Thankfully, the alley was small, with no road traffic and nobody presently on the street. Hundreds of windows glimmered above. Surely someone would look out at any minute and see a naked pasty fat guy, mistake him for a pervert, and call the cops.

He ran to the first dumpster in sight and threw open the lid, hoping to find something to wear, even if it was filthy. Like characters often did in movies with glaring plot holes and conveniently placed clothes, weapons, and whatever else the hero might need.

But Henry found nothing but trash. Wet magazines and newspapers. An ungodly amount of half-eaten food with a universe of insects feasting on the decay. The reek clung to his skin as he moved to the next one. After the third dumpster, he ran from the alley and straight onto what had to be the busiest street in the fucking world.

At first, Henry only heard the laughter. Then came the

screams. He turned to the people pointing, some of them looking downright horrified. Cars passed in blurs, eyes wide behind windows, hands on horns.

What? It's not that small!

Henry ran, certain he was still dreaming, *knowing* he'd open his eyes if he could only keep running. He ducked down another alley, relieved to find another dumpster overflowing with cardboard boxes. He hoped to stumble across some clean garbage, maybe from people who had to move overnight, forced to toss a pair of perfectly serviceable size 42 pants and an XXL shirt.

He raced toward the dumpster. A siren blurted behind him.

Oh shit.

A commanding voice crackled through the speaker. "Stop right there! Put your hands up!"

Henry ignored the command and ran instead. A second cop car appeared in front of him, blocking his escape.

Shit, these fuckers are fast! Someone must've told 'em a naked guy was passing out donuts.

The tabloids had been reasonably kind to his career, but Henry couldn't afford being caught running around naked, and likely high on who knew what. He ran straight for the cruiser, covering his face in the crook of his elbow, hoping his flabby arm would keep him disguised.

Following a new instinct telling him it was cool to launch himself at a squad car, he leapt on the hood, then back to the ground. He raced through the alley's asshole and onto a connecting street, faster than he'd ever run and with more grace than should have been possible. A disorienting fog settled across his mind. Pins and needles rising back up to stab his fingers and sting his toes.

He ran without thought, down four city streets and

through six alleys, past God knew how many people. They were pointing. Laughing and screaming. Snapping photos with their goddamned smartphones. Until Henry no longer heard sirens, though it was impossible to believe he'd outrun a couple of cop cars.

Still, it was easier than believing he was back from the dead.

Henry slowed to a walk, winded and hunched over. He ducked into another alley, hoping for a rest. Bad luck laughed in his face. He wasn't alone.

Three bald guys looking like they were headed to a neo-Nazi convention filed from the exit of a seemingly closed business. Passing boxes like buckets in a fire brigade, the first one loaded them into the back door of a waiting van. They weren't wearing all black like the men who had broken into Henry's home. They had jeans and regular shirts but were clearly up to no good.

The tallest, a heavyset guy in a Jets jersey, saw him first. "Whoa, holy shit. What the fuck, bro?"

Henry stepped back, near certain he had interrupted a crime in progress. His body bristled, noting his extreme disadvantage. Unarmed and naked against three men who likely lived at the perpetual edge of violence.

"You lost, freak?" said a second man in a black hoodie. He looked mixed race, Hispanic and Black, maybe Filipino, so maybe they *weren't* on their way to a Klan meeting.

Black Hoodie laughed, inviting laughter from the others. Jets Jersey reached into his pocket, and Henry couldn't tell if he grabbed a phone or camera. He snapped a picture, and all three of them were laughing by the time he finished the shot.

Ah, perfect!

Henry was embarrassed, but for a second he was also

thankful for his fame. The snapping pics meant they recognized him. They might be fans, or at least cool enough to help him out.

"Hey guys, yeah, I'm lost. I got into some bad shit, I don't even know." He ignored the likely crime and continued, playing dumb. "Can you help me out? Maybe sell me your hoodie? Something, so I'm not naked, and can get home? I don't have any money on me, but I can send you something. Anything, if you can help me out."

Jets Jersey burst into laughter. "What are you, dude? Some sorta elephant man?"

Henry knew he wasn't pretty, but that seemed harsh. He decided to ignore them, try walking by. He managed nearly three feet, when the men took turns looking startled. Then they each drew a gun, one at a time.

"Yo," Henry said, raising his palms to complete the picture of a nonthreatening pasty white guy. "I'm just leaving and I didn't see nothin' — okay?"

"The fuck you are, freak!" Jets Jersey said. "You gonna get in the van."

"What?" Henry said, confused.

Why do they wanna kidnap me?

They're gonna kill me just because I saw them doing some shit?

"Get in!" Black Hoodie shook his pistol at Henry.

Henry *flared.*

At least that's the only word he could think of for a feeling he'd never had before. Every part of him expanded away from a compression of rage. A beastly anger he hadn't even been aware of. Fire crackled beneath his skin, and without thought, he opened his mouth and screamed. No, not a scream. This was a lion's roar.

Jets Jersey's eyes went wide and he pulled the trigger.

The bullet sailed by, traveling through the air like

rippling water and crashing into the brick wall behind him with a *kachunk*.

What the Hell?

Henry reached out, grabbed Jets Jersey's hand, and twisted the gun so it caught the thug's finger in the guard. It snapped like a Twix. Jets Jersey screamed, and Henry twisted the pistol back up into his neck, then squeezed the man's jagged digit against the trigger.

The front of his face exploded, and Jets Jersey dropped to the ground.

The other two men stared at Henry, wild-eyed and frozen. Henry wiped the blood from his eyes and smiled. An energy rose into him. A warming rush of power that filled him with grim satisfaction.

There was no more laughter, and Henry couldn't have heard it even if there was. All he could hear were the hundred million bees in his head, all commanding him to attack.

Jittering with adrenaline, Henry smashed his heels into the asphalt and launched himself from the wall.

He grabbed the last man in line with a hand bunched around a fistful of his red t-shirt. His momentum slammed them both into the van. Red Tee's sternum split from the impact, and blood spurted from his mouth.

Henry let go, and the man slid to the asphalt, leaving a bloody smear in the center of the huge metal crater. He turned to face the final thug.

Black Hoodie aimed his shaking gun at Henry's face. "Wh … what are you?"

Henry was confused by the question, but smiled again, enjoying the energy coursing through. His body perked for the pleasure of the third man.

Black Hoodie fired his gun empty, missing every shot.

"Wow! You are a shitty shot," Henry said, laughing and shaking his head.

The thug threw the gun, and Henry smacked it away.

Black Hoodie ran. Henry growled as he gave chase, leaping over him and landing on the other side, spinning to face him. Black Hoodie's eyes were wide enough to pop from his skull.

Henry looked him up and down. The man was the same height as Henry, but skinnier. With clothes at least three sizes too big for his wiry frame, Henry was looking at a perfect fit. He smiled. "Gimme your clothes."

"What?"

Henry roared, and the man jumped back, his hands fluttering up to pull the hoodie over his head. He stripped to his pinstriped blue boxers.

Henry had no idea what was happening. Why was he was feeling so powerful? How could he move so fast? Killing two men in the blink of an eye while jumping his fat ass over a kid half his age? It couldn't be real, but it had felt amazing, dream or not.

Once the punk dropped his clothes, Henry growled and sent the fucker running.

The thug fled, and Henry dressed with a smile.

Much better.

Now, to get home.

He pulled the hoodie over his head, and walked toward the van to see if they'd left the keys inside. He managed two steps before getting smacked on the back of the skull. Sharp déjà vu on his way to the ground.

Not again.

Chapter Five

HENRY WOKE up on what appeared to be an Eminem video set, or a meth house party gone wrong.

Naked again.

He sat up and blinked through the empty bottles of Jack a few feet away on a filthy coffee table, and more empty Pabst Blue Ribbon cans than he could count. A sea of pork rinds, chips, and two kinds of Oreos. Because shit sometimes wrote itself, the glass tabletop was also littered with an empty carton of American Spirits, a pack of Lee Press-Ons, and a can of Beanee Weenee casserole.

The garbage bag at the end of the stained couch sharpened into focus a second before the bodies on the floor behind it.

Henry spent a half minute blinking before he could believe what he saw. Thirty seconds for his mind and logic to concur. There were four corpses, three guys and a gal, all deader than Henry had been. Covered in blood, arms mangled, and bodies so crooked they looked like they'd been playing Twister with a serial killer.

What did I do?

Henry staggered to his feet, swaying as pain lanced through his temples.

I've gotta get out of here.

Henry went to the bathroom, turned on the faucet, and squinted against the harsh light above the mirror.

He closed his eyes and splashed cool water on his over-heated face, pressing his palms hard against his cheeks and lightly rubbing life and feeling back into them.

What did I do? How did I get here?

His headache dropped to a dull throb, a low pounding that rose and fell with his nausea. He reached back and felt a large lump on the back of his head. It was tender, but it probably should have hurt a lot more than it did.

Henry turned off the water and stared into his reflection, expecting to see his usual dark goatee covering his chubby pasty face. Ready to hate himself for a few minutes, like usual.

Instead, he screamed.

Henry was a monster. Twisted, gnarled, grotesque. His face was all wrong. His goatee was gone, as was his dark, thinning hair. Henry was worse than bald. He ran his hands over his smooth head, which seemed to have been stretched out to make room for a bigger brain or a tumor under his skull. His eyes were larger. Dark black instead of blue, with no white at all. His nose was swollen, pointed like a witch's.

"Jesus!" he cried as he ran his fingers over his face. The skin was soft, like his head, but hot to the touch.

And when he spoke the name of Jesus, he winced as his tongue moved inside his mouth.

The teeth!

Henry's teeth were now long and sharp.

Like a werewolf.

He shuddered and stepped back, and as he observed

his body, he saw that the changes hadn't just happened to his face. His entire body was hairless, and darker, a light brownish-red. Sun-burned and muscular.

No. No. This isn't me! This isn't my body!

Henry screamed at the ceiling. Wordless and helpless.

When did this happen? I was a man when I woke up in the morgue! I was normal. What the fuck is happening?

Henry screamed again, louder, then clapped his hand over his mouth.

He heard the laughter behind him, seeing Boothe's reflection in the mirror as the demon drew nearer.

"You're thorough, I'll give you that, Henry. But you make a big mess. I'd watch that if I were you."

Henry jerked away, spinning to confront him. "What the Hell did you do to me?"

"I did nothing to you. You've done this to *yourself*." He gestured toward Henry's reflection, rather than at the man himself. "I brought you back home. Exactly as asked."

"What the Hell are you talking about? How did I do *this* to myself?"

"How many times have you looked in the mirror and hated yourself, Henry? How many times have you broadcast that hatred for all the world to hear?" Boothe laughed, as if the reflection was humorous rather than horrible. "This is how you see yourself, and how you are now. Your old body is gone. You don't get it back in the condition it was taken, you get it back in the shape your brain spent a lifetime beating it into. *That's* not my fault."

Boothe slapped a gentle hand on Henry's back as if he owed congratulations. "As for all this?" He gestured out of the bathroom and toward the four corpses on the floor of White Trash Castle. "That's all you, too. I accept no responsibility for your rage. You must learn to control your emotions, because the same thing will happen again if you don't. Jekyll and Hyde? That's you now, Henry. Or the Phantom of the Opera if you're more of a romantic, which I suppose you're probably not. Lose your temper, and terrible things will follow. Embrace that part of yourself. Learn to channel it, and you'll do what you came back here to do."

"What do you mean what I *came back here to do?* I came back for my family, to protect them. How am I supposed to be with Samantha and Amélie looking like this? They'll never recognize me, and even if they do, they won't accept it."

"You're right," Boothe shrugged, as if his admission meant nothing. "Your wife will never recognize you. Then again, she's not supposed to. *That's* not why you're here, Henry. That's not why I brought you back. I brought you back for something *better*."

Boothe smiled again.

Henry wanted to rip the grin from his face. "We had a deal, Boothe. I came back to be with my family."

"You're no longer human. You're something else, so that won't work. You're not exactly like me, but you're also little like you were."

"You never told me you were gonna turn me into a freak show! This isn't what I expected."

"Your fault, not mine. How many times have you said that about someone at your show, that it's not your fault if they don't laugh when they're bringing their own problems into the routine?"

Henry growled. *How the hell does he know me?*

"Growling changes nothing. What I didn't tell you bore no relevance to our conversation. New facts wouldn't have altered your decision, they would have merely delayed the inevitable and cost you valuable time. Remember, Nowhere seconds are minutes here."

36

"Randall was right. You tricked me. I had no idea what I was getting into."

"Yes, you *did*, Henry. You knew *exactly* what you were getting into. You *chose* to return. That's what you wanted, more than anything else, and this was the only way. Your other option was to wait in the Forgotten for an agent of Heaven to escort you to Judgment, but *you* wanted something different. *You* wanted to know what happened to your family. Am I correct?"

"I didn't know I was choosing *this*. You didn't tell me what I was giving up. You never even gave me a chance."

"Really, Henry?" Boothe stared. "Would you have chosen differently? Would you rather I take you back and you can spend eternity not knowing what happened? I can do that. Say the word. We can return right now. You'll even get your old body, though I'd say this one's a slight improvement, at least in the looks department."

Boothe held his stare.

"No," Henry whispered. "I want to see my family."

"I'll take you to your family, the second you agree to the rules."

Rules? Now there are rules?

"What are the rules?" Henry said, his voice empty of his inner rage.

"First, get dressed. We must get moving. You've been here a few days already."

"Days!" Henry said as he went into the living room in search of his clothes. "How the Hell? Why didn't you come and get me?"

"I needed to make sure you could survive on your own. Build your strength. Like a mother bird and all."

Henry wasn't sure what that meant and didn't care. He wanted clothes on his body and his family by his side. He went to the hoodie and jeans crumpled on the floor beside the blood-spattered couch, examined the clothes to make sure they weren't too bloody, then quickly dressed.

Boothe smiled. "We must get you to a tailor. But first, the rules."

"Fine. What are the rules?"

"You'll be happy. They're impossibly simple. I'll take you to your family. You can expect to see them, but not for them to see you. Do you agree?"

Henry looked in the mirror at his monstrous body and nodded. "Agreed."

"Excellent. One more thing."

"What?" Henry said, hating the *one more thing* already.

"Take my hand, and don't let go, no matter what. Even after everything changes."

And a second later, everything did.

Chapter Six

HENRY STARED out at a sea of neatly-trimmed cemetery grass, with many waves of mourners rolling across the sprawling lawn. Some stood, but many were already seated in the hundred or so white foldout chairs alined in rows in front of the pastor, Blake Owen.

Beyond the chairs and mourners was an ocean of cameras. More than Henry had ever seen. Even more than the hundreds at the Red Carpet for *Sitting at the Back of the Bus,* a mockumentery with a Rotten Tomatoes Fresh Rating of 92 percent, and Henry's first script to reach the screen.

Is this my funeral?

"Where are we?"

Boothe laughed. "How about an addendum to the previous rule? From now on you don't ask me any stupid questions, and I'll do my best to answer your non-stupid queries without any *trickery.* Deal?"

Henry hated Boothe more by the second and squirmed under the discomfort of the demon's hand wrapped tightly around his.

"You know where we are. And stop trying to free yourself." Boothe squeezed Henry's hand. "Even if you managed to pull away, you'd be sorry. You must not let go, no matter what you see. Say you promise."

Henry said nothing.

Boothe squeezed harder. "Listen, Henry, I get that you're angry and feel a bit deceived. But if you don't play ball, you're going to miss all the best stuff. Your fault, not mine. Like your ugly face. Are you ready?"

Henry grumbled, "Yes."

Boothe pulled him across the lawn toward the place where Henry's casket must have been, though he'd yet to see it through the crowd.

"Are we invisible?" Henry felt stupid for asking.

"Not exactly, but something like that," Boothe whispered. "I'd love it if you could mind your volume. You're invisible, but that doesn't mean your voice is."

Henry fell silent, and for the first time noticed the surrounding chatter. As they drifted in the sea of black, slowly making their way toward his coffin, he gathered snippets of whispered conversation.

"See, this is the kinda shit that happens when you offend so many people."

"Great, like the world really needed a brand-new Elvis."

"There's no body. How can you have a funeral without a body?"

"I heard someone sold his body on eBay."

"To be taken so young, what a loss."

"What the Hell are they talking about?" Henry growled.

"Your body, of course. What did you think? You came back as a body, not as a ghost. Per your request, Henry. You got your body back, but they had to bury *something*, so they're dropping an empty coffin six feet down until you turn up. You can imagine the trouble that caused. Especially for poor Samantha."

"But *this* isn't my body."

"Yes, it is. Your frame has been twisted by your years of self-hate, but it's still *your* flesh and blood."

As they inched closer to where Henry's empty casket had to be, he felt a rising panic. Again, he tried pulling away from Boothe. The demon tightened his grip and yanked him back. "I said don't let go. Try that again only if you're prepared to regret it."

Boothe pulled Henry deeper into the crowd. His unease grew as they moved closer to the front. He felt others when they came too close, or when he bumped against them. Thankfully, there were so many people, no one seemed to notice the nudge from an invisible mourner.

Once they were near the front, seconds from when Henry would finally see his Samantha again, he asked, "How does this work? The invisibility, the teleportation, all of this Purgatory stuff?"

"I really prefer if we don't use the P-word." Boothe pinched the bridge of his nose. "I never cared all that much for the word to begin with and have grown to hate it quite a lot. Not your fault, and not too different from how you hate the word *dude*. Either way, Henry, all excellent questions."

Boothe squeezed his hand, probably to remind him of the dangers of letting go.

"It's simple, really. You're not truly invisible. You're simply vibrating on a different frequency from everyone else. They're here, same as you, but they can't see you since they're not looking and wouldn't know where to cast their eyes even if they could. Dogs hear dog whistles when you can't because of their pitch. This is no different. Same holds true for teleportation — all locations exist in a single space, you decide where in that space to vibrate. But teleportation isn't in your bag of tricks, I'm afraid. You're still a rookie."

Henry's face must have looked as confused as he felt.

"It's simpler than it seems." Boothe smiled. "Being invisible is as advantageous as you would imagine, but it requires tremendous energy. You've no idea how exhausted I am right now, with me doing this for the both of us. I'm not asking for a hero parade, but I'd love it if you quit trying to pull away. That makes my work so much harder."

They reached the front of the crowd, and Henry's world crumbled further.

The first coffin was hard enough to come to terms with. The second, half the size of the first, kicked him into an abyss of immediate, unbroken agony.

Amélie!

Henry wanted to cry, scream, collapse, fall to his knees, die again, but Boothe grabbed his other wrist and warned, "Stay quiet and don't let go, or everyone here will see you. Do you want to make this day even worse for your wife? This is your final warning. Understand?"

Henry said nothing.

Boothe squeezed harder until Henry nodded.

The demon dragged him around the crowd's front, then to the side of the rows of mourners. Only after raising his gaze did Henry realize he was standing directly across from a weeping Samantha, draped in black, eyes beneath her dark bangs as red as a Valentine's rose. Everything else, from her cheeks to her lips, was a ghostly white.

"Why here?" Henry tried to keep both rage and volume from his voice. "We can go anywhere. Tell me what in the fuck is happening, Boothe! Why are we standing right across from Samantha?"

"We are standing where we must stand for you to feel what you must feel. Question me no more."

A heavy finality coated Boothe's voice. Henry snapped his mouth shut.

"I've no reason not to tell you the truth. Understand, Henry, I've given you one hundred percent of what you wanted. It may not have happened exactly how you expected — or wanted — it to, but again, *your* fault. Not mine. I answered your request, now it's your job to listen and understand so you can get what was promised. If you're not happy, I'm not happy. Understand?"

Henry nodded. "I want to know what happened. Now."

Boothe whispered, "No more interruptions, unless you want everything to sour. I'm not sure how much longer I can hold my focus."

"I asked you to tell me what happened when we were back in *Purgatory*." Henry said 'Purgatory' like the word had extra syllables. "Tell me *now* or I'm letting go."

"Fair enough, if it shuts you up," Boothe said. "The men who broke into your house wasted no time with you. They put you down to silence your wife and daughter. It worked on Samantha, but poor Amélie was too small to understand. So the third gentleman, your unseen assailant, did what he was supposed to do without being told. He sent your lovely Amélie flying over the stairs and to the ground below. Dreadful, really." Boothe's face withered.

Henry dragged whistling air through his nose, barely controlling his breath.

"Inevitable, even. Your daughter would've been nothing but screams while the three men raped your wife."

"They *raped* my wife?"

"Yes, as she lay staring at both of your corpses," Boothe said, his sympathy loud.

"How did she get away?"

"Someone called the police, reported something happening at the house. When the police arrived, Samantha managed to get free before the men could kill her. She ran outside and into the arms of the police, while the men took off through the back of the house. Unfortunately, they all escaped."

Henry could no longer hold his rage inside. He screamed.

Commotion tore through the crowd, much of it settling on Sam's face. She knew Henry's voice better than anyone. People stared without seeing them as Henry tried to pull away, invisibility be damned.

Samantha spun in a circle, seeming to search the sea of people for her lost husband. Boothe's fingers clawed into Henry's as he tried to pull away. With a strength that didn't seem possible, he pulled Henry to him, then whispered, "You must calm yourself now, or *everything* is ruined. Now, we walk."

Henry followed Boothe, hating him for the suffering of seeing Sam and wishing he could snap the demon's neck.

As they moved away from the stirred crowd, Henry turned to Boothe. "Why did you bring me here? Why did you want me to see all this? Are you trying to torture me?"

"I'm not." Boothe looked at Henry, his eyes almost sad. "I'm trying to help. You said you wanted to know what happened to your family. It's not enough to *know*. You had to be here, to see for yourself. Stop considering the trick and start thinking about the solution. Randall has burrowed too far into your mind. You should be thinking of *him*."

"Randall?" Henry asked, confused.

"No," Boothe said, shaking his head. He lifted his

finger and aimed it at a man in the crowd, standing across from Samantha, staring at her with his tiny, beady eyes.

"Him," Boothe said, pointing at the man who'd held a gun to his wife's head. "I brought you back for revenge."

Chapter Seven

HENRY WANTED to tear the skin from the fucker's face.

He raged toward Tiny Eyes, one of the three murderers who had taken everything from him. Henry went nowhere, though, instead slamming into an invisible barrier. He struggled to pull free from Boothe, but the demon tightened his grip and yanked Henry back toward him, away from the murderer.

Henry stood beside the demon, furious and panting. Without any understanding of how he could throw so much thrust behind his movement and still go nowhere.

What is Boothe made of?

"Are we really going to do this?" Boothe whispered.

Henry answered with grunting, tugging harder against the wall of air around him. At first he went nowhere, then fell an inch forward as the figurative rubber stretched from the band. Henry kept pulling until it finally snapped, and he went flying.

Instead of soaring toward the murderer, Henry rotated through the air, sailing over something that wasn't grass.

He blinked through his tumble, rolling across a polished hardwood floor and landing with a sharp smack on the corner of a kitchen island.

Henry slowly stood, wiping blood from his forehead as he absorbed his surroundings. A sprawling apartment, with less furniture than support columns, and perhaps a hundred windows wrapping the flat to account for the deficit. Sparkling glass circled the place, displaying Burg City's concrete sprawl in a wide panorama.

Boothe was already on his way to Henry. Two feet away, the demon handed him a washcloth.

Henry examined the blood in his hand. Black and thick, like oil. He held up the cloth and raised his eyebrows. "It's white."

"I have plenty. Besides, you won't be needing it long."

Henry set the tiny towel to the wound on his forehead, which had already slowed to a trickle. He dabbed the gash for another several seconds until it stopped bleeding entirely.

"What in the actual fuck?" Henry looked down at the washcloth, then out the windows, working to determine their location. The harbor was on his far right, Twyker Island a dot on the left. "Where are we?"

"Safe," Boothe said. "I told you, you can't go around doing whatever you want, whenever you feel like it. That makes you a danger to me. You're also a danger to yourself, and to Samantha. Correct me if I'm wrong, Henry, but you didn't return from Nowhere to be of no use to anyone, did you?"

"Where are we?" Henry repeated, hating Boothe for how often he used his name, like a professor to his idiot students.

"My apartment in Martinsburg. I've not had it long, so

you'll find it a bit sparse for the moment. You will have every necessity, though, and are welcome to use the flat at your discretion. For now."

"You're a demon! Why do *you* need an apartment?"

"Don't say *demon* like that. You make the word sound so *ugly*. Besides, Henry, if I'm a demon, you're a demon too."

"Do all demons have such fancy apartments? How do you sign a lease? Does your landlord know you're a demon? Do you get a special demon checking account from Chase?"

Boothe smiled, probably at the hundred million secrets he knew that Henry didn't. "We have ways of operating wherever we need to. You'll learn each when appropriate. Money is plentiful, so yes, things are nice more often than not. I have many places, everywhere, from hovels to manors depending on who I'm hosting, but I appreciate your recent ascension to a certain standard of living. This place has all you need, including a massive bathtub, which you seem to love so much. Above all, the apartment will give you privacy."

Henry blanched, as though *privacy* were a dirty word.

"I suppose *privacy* isn't quite right. Humans require privacy. Demons require a darker sort of veil. The two needs are not the same and should never be confused. But your windows are tinted, so nobody can see in, at least not during the day. At night, I suggest you draw the blinds."

Henry looked past Boothe and out the window with a sudden longing to be among the many millions of people swarming through life on the other side of the glass.

As if reading his thoughts, Boothe said, "You're staring at a memory, Henry. That world is dead to you now. Demons live in secret, and your concealment can never be compromised. You must leash your instincts, at least until you learn to control them. You can't go around killing people willy-nilly like you're a star athlete or pampered kid sucking on the trust fund teat, especially not with witnesses. Every situation deserves care, caution, and well-reasoned execution. Understand?"

Boothe held Henry's eyes until he nodded.

"Learn to walk well so you're never forced to run. You are a hunter, Henry, and predators should never chase prey when they can stalk it instead. Start thinking as an assassin. You never see assassins coming, and nobody ever knows they were there until they're long gone. That's your world now, Henry. Forever."

Forever?

Henry decided not to argue the point or question it. Yet, he marinated in their mutual silence for several seconds. After those seconds turned into a minute, Boothe said, "If people see you as you truly are, they will run to their God, clutch their Bibles, and start converting faster than deathbed atheists. Don't worry, you'll get your chance for vengeance, and it will be grand. I've not brought you here for nothing. But you have to understand, things must be done in a certain way. Our universe has rules for everything."

"Fuck. I didn't know the Devil was a stickler for rules!"

"I said the *universe*, Henry. Learn to listen. We're all subject to rules. Rather than being the class clown, why don't you pay attention? Otherwise, I'm afraid I'll have to drop you back in Nowhere where you can wait in line for your Judgment Day like all the other suckers. Would you prefer that, Henry?"

Henry sulked. "No."

"Good lad. I'm not sure how well waiting for Judgment will work out for you after your little incident this morning at Hillbilly Flats. I can't imagine that won't somehow mar your permanent record, and I've no clue how much longer that little *oops* might keep you waiting for the Pearlies to open. Honestly, I don't think you possess the patience for Purgatory, Henry. You are stupid from too many years on this plane, vibrating at the same insipid frequency. You've no concept of time, or what Forever actually means."

Henry stewed, flexing his toes, clenching and unclenching his fists, and trying to rein in his anger. He was centimeters from snapping and worried he *would*. A decision to attack Boothe would likely be the last he ever made.

Once calm enough to speak, Henry said, "I had a chance to start making things right at the funeral. He was *right* there, and you stopped me! What if I never get another shot? What if that was it?"

"You are speaking as if you're defeated already, Henry. Why?"

Henry stared at Boothe, hating him. "I don't need a shrink."

"You need to stop seeing everything as some unsolvable problem and start realizing that there's always a solution. You spend so much time worrying, I don't see how you ever got anything done. Now, I'm going to be talking fast, so you'll need to keep up and not interrupt." Boothe crossed the kitchen to the refrigerator, pulled out a pitcher of cold water, then filled a pair of tall glasses drawn from a cabinet. He handed one to Henry. "Drink this. Your body is weak."

Henry gulped his water as Boothe continued speaking. "Why do you think that man was at your funeral, Henry? To pay his respects? No, of course not. He was there for something else. But you're seeing so much red that every other color seems black. Close your eyes and stare into the darkness, Henry. Now think. *Why* was he at the funeral?"

Stop saying my fucking name!

"Stop fretting about what I am or am not doing, *Henry*." Boothe doubled his volume on Henry's name. "Start worrying about getting the answers you're desperate to get. I promised to help you, not that your task would be easy."

Henry closed his eyes, then waited, inhaling and exhaling with measured sighs, until his anger slowly melted. And then he saw — and felt stupid for not having seen sooner.

"My God," Henry breathed. "He's not finished … he's stalking Samantha!"

"You're pretty smart for a guy who told dick jokes for a living."

"I've gotta get back to the funeral! I have to protect Samantha!"

Boothe laughed. "Look at yourself, Henry. You're so angry, you can't think straight. You need to stop *doing* so you can start *thinking*. Would you like to know why it took you twelve years to land your TV show instead of the two or three it might have taken a more practical comic?"

Henry looked up, wounded by the demon in a brand-new way. He was surprised Boothe knew about his TV deal, let alone how long it took to get. "I don't know how long you've been dead, Boothe, but nobody gets a deal in two or three years."

Boothe shook his head, as though he felt sorry for Henry. "Work harder, tour longer, write more material. You had enough by your third year to make the fourth your best ever. But you never believed in yourself, at least not enough. Saturated by the defeat you see inside, you willingly listen to anger and doubt. *Stop*. Listen to logic rather than fear. Logic says there's no benefit in striking at your funeral."

An odd sort of calm replaced Henry's rage. His tightened shoulders softened and the boulder on his back was gone.

"Samantha will be safe, even after the funeral," Boothe said. "Someone is watching her house right now. And at all times."

"What do you mean *someone?*"

"Well, I suppose it's not a someone, so much as a *something*. I put a goll at your house."

"A what?"

"A goll. I guess they're like goblins, but I find that particular term nearly as crude as *demon*. Golls are short, gray-skinned, and I suppose they sort of resemble children, except for their faces, which look like Satan's orphan bastards."

"You put a fucking demon at my house?"

"He's not a demon, Henry. He's a beastie from Purgatory, not all that different from you or I, really." Boothe laughed. "Ezra won't eat your wife. I'm sure he's still quite full from yesterday. He cleaned up your little mess, and white trash never agrees with him. Gives him the runs, every time. Believe me, that's nothing you want to see. Or smell."

Henry took a long swig of water as Boothe continued talking.

"You'll need to learn control yourself before anything else," he repeated. "I'll help you prepare. In the meantime, if Ezra sees something off, he knows what to do. If he can't handle the situation on his own — highly doubtful if you've ever seen Ezra in action — he'll tell me immediately. Samantha is perfectly safe."

"Are you sure?"

Boothe shook his head in annoyance, ignoring the question. "Now," he said, taking his empty water glass and setting it on the counter beside him. "I can't teach you to be a god, but I can come awfully close. So, pay attention."

Chapter Eight

Henry wasn't impressed.

"I need to get to my wife," he said.

"Why? So you can stare at her? Think, Henry. What could you do? Pine from the shadows? Wish with all your *woe-is-me* that things were different? They're not, and right now you're most suited for revenge. Fail to learn what you must, and risk impotency when you're needed." Boothe laughed. "I'm sure you know about that, don't you, Henry."

"Fuck you."

Boothe paced the apartment as he spoke with his hands. "I have things to show you, but if you don't pay attention, I'm going to leave you alone to figure it out for yourself. Understand?"

Henry growled and nodded.

"I would tell you to look in the mirror, but I'm not in the mood to hear your screaming. So why don't you rub a finger on that giant cut on your forehead, instead."

Henry took two fingers and softly rubbed his smooth forehead, but felt nothing. No torn skin, no wound.

"Miraculous, yes?" Boothe beamed. "Wait, it gets better."

Before Boothe finished his sentence, he was hovering an inch from Henry, brandishing a blade. Henry blinked twice in surprise. By the end of his second blink, Boothe had cut Henry with a long swipe across his left arm.

Henry screamed as blood gushed, then stopped when he realized there was no pain, only the idea of it. He went to the kitchen counter, grabbed another white washcloth, dabbed the gash until it disappeared, and turned to Boothe.

The demon smiled. "I told you. Not quite a god, but close. See how efficient we can be when running on my schedule? I've shown you three things at once. You heal almost immediately, you feel little to no physical pain, and I can move like a bullet. You can do that too, provided you have the energy for *any* of it."

Henry stood in the living room, breathing heavily, sucking more of this new, impossible reality into his mind and body.

"Ready?"

"No. But let's do it, anyway."

Boothe walked over to Henry, set one hand on his right forearm, and the other on the healed skin of his left. Henry instinctively closed his eyes, feeling his body growing quickly insignificant. The world vanished around them, replaced by a momentary flashing from light to dark to light again. After the flickering, and a momentary dizziness, Henry found himself standing beside Boothe on the rooftop of an old warehouse about a half mile from the docks. Charcoal smoke plumed above the harbor.

"Where are we?"

"I thought we had an agreement, Henry. You weren't

going to ask me questions you already know the answers to."

"We're at the docks," Henry said. "But where? That's a fair question."

Boothe smiled. "Yes, we're at the docks, in an old part of the warehouse district where few ever go. We're safe here."

"Safe to do what? The deluxe apartment in the sky seemed safe enough."

"You heal quickly, Henry, as do I. My apartment, however, does not." Boothe smiled, condescendingly, as though Henry was an infant who might someday understand. "You need to learn, and this rooftop allows us the space to do that well. You must know yourself better, and much of that … *insight*, shall we say, has to come from me. We'll keep our training light, and I promise, I'm a second from Samantha, always. Ezra, your goll, might be afraid of interrupting us, but he is far more afraid of failing *me*. Do you believe me that Samantha is safe?"

Henry wasn't sure what to say. No, he didn't believe Boothe. At least not completely. But he didn't want to anger the demon, either. Henry nodded.

"Brilliant." Boothe beamed. "Let's get started."

Boothe blurred into motion, leaving a black trail behind him that had barely faded by the time he stood on the opposite end of the roof, looking at Henry with a calm smile, his hands behind his back. He beckoned Henry over with a tip of his head.

Henry took a deep breath and pushed off to follow. Launching across the roof with the wind roaring past his ears, He reveled in the speed. His surroundings compressing and stretching. He skidded to a halt in front of Boothe, chest heaving as he fought for breath.

Boothe inclined his head in salute. "That is not the worst I have ever seen, but you are limiting yourself."

"How the fuck am I limiting myself? That's faster than I've ever done *anything.*"

"Yes, but you see …"

Boothe was gone. Henry saw him in his periphery, moving from standing to full speed without transition. He spun to follow him, but Boothe was already on the other side of the roof.

Henry launched into a sprint, pushing as hard as he could, but his speed was no better than his last attempt.

Boothe shook his head. "It's not about your body, Henry, but about your *mind.*"

Henry bent over his knees, gasping for breath. "Well, my *mind* certainly says that was fast."

"And it was, certainly. But your mind must learn that it can see things beyond what you have already defined."

Henry stood up straight with his hands on his hips. "I don't care what you say. I did pretty good just now."

Boothe sighed. "Why are you out of breath?"

"I just sprinted my big ass across twenty yards of hot rooftop."

"Then why am I not?"

Henry shrugged. "You're in better shape than me."

"It's because you remember what it was like before you died. The knowledge of your new form is there, Henry. You must reach for it and accept it."

Henry thought of how it had felt to smash the guy into the side of the van. Thought about doing the same to the animals that had raped his wife. Killed his baby girl. He didn't want to hear another word of Boothe's bullshit. "You're saying my body knows what to do, even if my mind doesn't?"

Boothe face twisted in annoyance. "Not exactly."

"Then, what exactly?"

"Your brain works far faster now. Unlike aging as a human, the longer you're a demon, the sharper you get."

Boothe took him to the rooftop's far corner and put his strength on display by lifting a length of heavy steel, bracing over his head with one hand, then hurling it to the opposite end of the roof.

That thing had to weigh two or three hundred pounds.

Henry was almost giddy as he took his turn.

Hulk smash!

He picked up the first length of steel. He remembered being nine, playing at Heritage Park and pretending he had super strength, flinging branches through the air, imagining that they were uprooted trees.

Henry let the steel fly … and a searing pain ripped through his body. Starting at his shoulder, tearing through the muscles in his arm, it rattled across his chest. He dropped to his knees as the steel clanged several feet of his target. He clutched at the ripping agony.

I'm having a fucking heart attack.

"The pain isn't really there, Henry. It's in your head. You must allow your mind to accept your new form, and agree with what it actually sees and feels."

Henry answered by picking up another section of steel, his anger powering it over his head. He hurled the thick metal bar across the roof with a bellow of rage. The second throw hurt less than the first, and by the third, it was little more than a tickle. Henry grinned at Boothe as he fought to catch his breath again. Boothe answered with a slight smile that only lifted one side of his mouth. A few days before, five minutes on the treadmill would've drenched him in sweat. Now he lifted heavy beams like toothpicks. At least, until Henry came to the last one.

This can't be real.

The final piece of scrap, not quite as large as the others, held the weight of a planet. It ripped from his grip and smashed his foot between the metal and concrete. Because a lifetime of experience swore anything else was impossible, pain exploded from his foot, shooting up his leg. He swallowed his anger and took the punishment, closing his eyes and telling his brain it wasn't there. After several seconds of concentration, the pain faded from a searing heat to a dull throb. To nothing. He opened his eyes and turned to glare at Boothe.

"What the fuck?" He reached down, yanked the steel off his foot, and tossed it aside with a heavy thud.

Boothe chuckled, as though amused by Henry's failure.

"Why did that happen?" He limped toward the demon with his hands in fists at his side.

Boothe didn't budge. He held Henry's eyes with his own as he spoke into his heavy breath. "It might be any number of reasons, but my best guess says doubt. Or maybe that's only me psychoanalyzing you. Your focus has waned from exhaustion? Perhaps it's that. Every action requires focus. This is true of any normal body, and more so for you. Your body does more, and thus requires more to operate. Whipping through the air like wind or taking punishment like a rock takes a tremendous amount of physical strength. Your body refuels itself automatically, but still requires time to regenerate."

Boothe smiled, more like a friend and less like a snake. "You ready to go back? You're going to need a nap soon." He held out his hand.

"Not yet. I wanna know more. What about the other stuff? Like turning invisible and teleporting. How do I do that?"

"Those abilities will come, if they are within your skill set, but there's no sense in watching paint dry. You may eventually be able to do the things I can, assuming you pay attention. Remember the time when magic still held so much wonder, before you were old enough to understand the mechanics serving illusion? Magic is the practice of altering natural laws, or at least seeming to. Science is the practice of harnessing natural law to get what you want or need. My science may one day become your magic. Soon, Henry."

"Where do you live?" Henry kept ignoring the hand. "If you're in Pur... Nowhere, aren't you supposed to stay stuck?"

"Only *people* get trapped in Nowhere. I've not been a person in a long time. What you think of as angels and demons do as they wish. Many choose to stay on this plane, because we have no power in Nowhere. Only words. Randall is stronger than me here. But there," Boothe laughed with a dramatic shrug, "he doesn't stand a chance."

Henry asked, "So Randall is an angel?"

"A fallen one, yes. He can't get into Heaven any more than I can get into Hell."

"What do you mean?"

"While you think of me as a demon, I'm not from the depths of Hell as popular culture would have you believe. I was a dead man in Nowhere, same as you, many years ago. But there are other demons, monstrous, evil beasts, who would more properly be called Hell Demons. They can't enter this plane. But they *can* go into Purgatory to enlist others to join them and do their bidding in this world."

"So you volunteered to be a demon? Why?"

"Why's not important, Henry. Just be glad you're dealing with me and not a Hell Demon. You've no idea how lucky you are."

"So what is it they have you doing? Is that why you're

helping me? To meet some kind of evil quota? Are you like fucking Amway?"

"The why's not important for you to know. But I've yet to lie to you, Henry. And I'm not lying now when I promise our interests are the same. I seek revenge, same as you. Now, is that it with the Twenty Questions?"

Henry's suspicion tasted sour in the back of his throat. Arguing with Boothe would serve no purpose. He'd play ball until he figured out exactly what was going on.

"So, what else can I do, *Boothe?*" Henry tried to make the demon's name sound as deliberate as his sounded when Boothe said, *Henry.* It didn't quite work.

"A few big things, and many small ones. You can leap as if you are flying. Not exactly tall buildings in a single bound, but you can hop to the roof of a bus by barely trying. That's better than your muffin top could've managed last week. You can also become one with the shadows, using the dark to your advantage, molding it around your body so you can hide inside, as if the shadows were a second skin. And you can travel fast from one shadow into another, almost like gliding from thought to thought." Boothe lowered his voice. "All of this expends energy, though, which is what you're experiencing now. I didn't force you to drain yourself, but I did allow it to happen. I wanted you to *feel* your fatigue because you must know how awful it can be."

Henry wasn't sure if it was merely the power of suggestion. He felt like his body was turning inside-out. His hands found his midsection as his body swayed with exhaustion.

"You're like a car, Henry. Run your tank to nothing, and you'll break down. Never waste your body's fuel on turning invisible if you can turn shadows into friends. People don't want to see you, Henry. *Ever.* You'll horrify them. Fortunately, their terror makes it easier for you to gel with the shadows. Less concentration to start and minimum focus to control. Once you're rested, we'll try invisibility. Then, when you're drained, I'll show you how even one breath in your body is enough to help you sink into shadow."

"It's been a while since I've sunk into shadow. I usually prefer a bath."

Boothe narrowed his eyes on his apprentice. "More questions, Henry?"

"Why don't you just help me? You *could* show me where all three men are, teleport us to them, and BAM! Asshole sausage."

"I don't know how much clearer I can make things for you. As I've said, there are rules, for this and for everything. I'm not all-knowing or all-seeing. In order to appear somewhere, I must have been there before. Or be with someone who has. I can't just blink you right in the middle of the *bad guy* secret headquarters."

"Okay, I get that. But it still seems like we're going the long way around. I'm not so fragile, at least not after what you've shown me. Unless I'm missing something, I've a total of three guys to kill. I did that before lunch back at the White Trash Castle, and I'm saying that without even trying to be a dick."

"You've answered your own question. *You* have three men to kill. Not me. Revenge isn't *my* job. My job was to get you here. That's finished. Now I'm doing more than required by making sure you don't get too much blood on my white linen. Every death has a cost, even for a demon. Taking someone before their time, and yes, there *is* a time, always alters the balance. The universe may seem chaotic to you, Henry. It's not. You see but a pixel in its picture.

Upset equilibrium, and you upset those who pull the strings."

"Who pulls the strings?"

"I'm tired, Henry. I brought you to somewhere from Nowhere, and am running close to empty myself. I don't have long before I fade. Might we discuss this later?"

There was something so sad and honest in how the demon asked. He seemed hollow and exhausted. Henry nodded. "Okay."

But he knew Boothe was showing him only what he wanted him to see, and in his calculated order.

Chapter Nine

BOOTHE STOOD OVER HENRY, who lay on the couch with his eyes already closed. "Promise you'll sleep."

Henry nodded and curled his body tighter.

"I mean it. You're vapor-empty. If you leave this apartment in the next few hours, you will likely die, ridiculed on your way to Hell. Understand?"

Henry nodded again. He wanted to ask what Boothe meant about him going to Hell but was too exhausted.

"If it's day when you wake, wait until dark. The night harbors millions of shadows, one reason you expel less energy after hours. Going out after dark is always better, as the daytime can be quite dangerous for our kind. Do so only if you must and never when drained. Too many things can go wrong. Promise?"

Henry nodded again, then Boothe was gone.

So was Henry.

In the dream, he was up in his office. Not the new one downstairs. There he had a cinema screen and projector, an endless wall of his favorite books, a treadmill-mounted desk — a contraption that helped him hate himself while writing his routines — three monitors to fulfill his ADD's every need, with his newest iMac in the middle. Any routine, song, book, movie, or TV show he wanted to inspire him only a click or two away. Plus, the new office held the small safe where Henry kept his weed. And yet, for all its awesomeness, it wasn't his office of choice.

He sat in his attic office, instead. His favorite room in the house. The place where he preferred to work on new material, especially the untested stuff. He couldn't think in the fancy office, where too much other shit battled for his attention. Upstairs was sparse and dark, the perfect nest to nurture creativity.

They had built his new office after moving in. Samantha wanted the construction done early, so Henry's workspace was ready along with the rest of the home. Construction took longer than planned — a wall needed to be removed, and Henry grew impatient and made a temporary office in the attic instead. No wall-sized screen or any devices larger than his laptop. But the lack of distractions was more conducive to writing, anyway. That, and the weed. Henry realized he preferred the tiny space. When people came over, which they were doing more all the time, they always went to his downstairs office. For his *private place,* it was awfully public, and that stripped much of its magic. But not even Samantha went in the attic. Only Amélie, who would sometimes sneak inside when he was working, giggling the entire time since she knew she wasn't supposed to be there.

Dreaming, Henry sat at his attic desk, working on the most important comedy routine of his life. In both dream and memory, he'd been trying to nail it for a week. His first Tonight Show gig was days away, and the act wouldn't write itself. He had to ace the beats. One shot and a few minutes to get everything right.

As the perfect closing bit entered his head, Amélie burst into the room, laughing.

She was five at the time, still at an age when she didn't understand why Daddy needed to be alone for his work. If he was home all day, then of course he would want to play before dinner. She ran through the attic like her butt was on fire. Henry spun from his chair, ready to scream at her as he had in the memory from five years ago, but she waved her jazz hands, palms to her audience of one, fingers splayed so proudly it was impossible for Henry not to laugh.

"Hey, Daddy, I invented a new word. Wanna hear it?"

He couldn't be mad at Amélie for being the kid he always wanted, the one he never had a chance to be.

"Yes, honey, of course I do. What is it?"

"It's called *reintarnation*. It means when you come back from the dead, you live in Texas."

Henry slapped his knee, surprising himself with a genuine laugh, rather than the manufactured one he expected. *Reintarnation* had been Amélie's first made-up word, though she followed with plenty in the years that followed. Six months before the blow to the head that sent Henry to Nowhere, Amélie had asked, "What's an *ignoranus*?"

"A person who's both an idiot and an asshole?"

"Bingo, Dad. Use it in your act."

Henry had never been prouder.

At only five, Amélie stared up into her daddy's eyes, waiting for approval. "*Reintarnation*. Do you like it? Do you think it's funny?"

"I do! Could be a comedy classic. Think I should add it to my set?"

"Yes! Do you promise you will?"

"No, I can't promise that. But I can promise to try.

Funny's less funny when you stuff stuff inside it. Comedy has to be natural. But I promise if I can ever find a way to fit *reintarnation* into my set, and I almost totally probably can, I will. Cool?"

"Yes!"

"That it?" he asked, wondering if that was her reason for interruption. And even though Henry had used his mouth and not his fist, Amélie looked beaten all the same.

"I'm sorry, sweetie. I didn't mean it like that." Henry eased himself from chair to floor, walking toward Amélie and taking her hand as she started to cry. He bent to his knee. "I didn't mean anything, Ami. I just have a ton to do. I have a big show coming up, and there's going to be a fancy-pants guy watching. Since he wears fancy pants, he gets to make fancy decisions. Those fancy decisions turn into suggestions for fancier people in even fancier pants. Once the super-fancy people hear the fancy ideas, they decide whether those ideas are worth doing something extra super fancy with. And guess what?"

Amélie smiled.

"Say it …"

She shook her head, giggling.

"Say it!"

Amélie laughed, and said, "Then super-fancy things can happen to us?"

"That's right." Henry sat back in his chair, turned back to his desk, and pulled Amélie up on his lap. "Would you like to hear a story?"

"Is peanut butter nuts?" Amélie said, trying to make a pun, and coming closer than she ever had, even if the wording didn't quite work.

"Sometimes."

Amélie nuzzled into her father's chest as he told the tale of Wordslinger Wendy, the space cowgirl who could never be destroyed since her words busted down every door, even if they were triple reinforced with titanium and coated with rubber and glue that made everything bounce off the door and stick to the courageous cowgirl.

Henry had made up the character one night at bedtime, by accident, and bit by bit had added to the story many bedtimes since.

Though Henry faced the desk, with his daughter on his lap and his back to the attic entrance, he could feel Samantha watching as he recited the story. Amélie had fallen asleep with the heat of her back warming his chest, and he had carried her to bed, tucking her in with a soft kiss on her forehead.

After he left Amélie, Samantha met him in their bedroom.

"Thank you," she whispered, kissing him on the mouth, then his nipple, and then of course the only place that mattered.

Henry woke up alone, sadness and hate roiling in his thoughts.

It was as dark outside the apartment as it was inside of him.

He couldn't stay.

Henry had no idea how long he had slept, but he felt energized and strong. Boothe had either exaggerated his need for a nap or he'd been sleeping far longer than he thought. Either way, Henry wasn't staying in the apartment a minute longer. He had to see Samantha.

Henry threw on his hoodie and jeans, then headed for the door. His hand hit the handle as he realized his stupidity. A monster like him didn't roam the halls or take elevators. Monsters weren't even welcome on stairs. Henry had surprisingly little information on how to get around.

But he knew what felt right.

He went to the window, opened it, and with barely a thought, leapt out of the apartment and onto the fire escape. After clinging to the metal railing for a second, Henry launched himself several feet, grabbing an iron rain gutter running up the building's side. He relaxed his grip and slid to the bottom. A sharp current shocked his body from toe to earlobe as Henry's heels hit the concrete.

The hard landing energized rather than hurt him.

Henry fell into the first shadow as if he'd been doing it all his life, then slipped into the second as smooth as if he were sliding on ice, except he didn't collapse on his ass like he had the few times he had attempted to ice skate. He crossed the street and turned back, looking up at Boothe's building. The Mason Lofts, fourteen floors of high-end apartments layered above four floors of offices, having once been a department store owned by the Mason family in the early 1900s before the Burg had become the bustling city it was now. While the building's interior, at least on his floor, looked to feature the latest in architectural aesthetics, the exterior still looked a century old.

Soon Henry was at the corner of Kress and Walker, two-and-a-half miles from his *real home*.

Slipping from shadow to shadow made for immediate travel. Henry reached his house. Even not living there, it was impossible to think of it as anything else. The goll, who'd been sitting on the roof, saw Henry first. An excellent indication of Samantha's quality protection.

The goll leapt to the ground, landing a few feet in front of Henry, and greeting him before he'd finished his first bounce. It was as ugly as Boothe had said it was, surprising Henry with its odd appearance. Of course, Henry wasn't one to talk about odd appearances these days.

The creature spoke. "Master Henry, how are you tonight?"

"I'm sorry. I'm not your master. Just Henry, please."

"Sorry, Master Henry. But that's your name, at least for me. Every goll has a master. You're mine, until Master Boothe says otherwise."

The beast's voice was deep, a bit on the slow side, but formal and polite. And yet there wasn't a single thing Henry liked, or even appreciated, about being loaned a goll.

Except that at least Samantha was safe.

"Thank you for protecting her, my wife, I mean. I appreciate it. Who am I thanking?"

"My name is Ezra," said the goll. "I'm one hundred and three."

"Impressive," Henry said, finding it curious that the creature introduced itself like a child, stating its age. The only thing missing from the scene was the goll holding up its fingers ten times, followed by three fingers once. "Do you normally tell people your age on the first date?"

"It's custom."

Henry stared at Ezra, not knowing if the goll was joking or even capable of humor. His smile seemed simple and sincere, even if the teeth Henry glimpsed were incredible in number and sharpness.

"Did you come to say thank you, Master Henry? Surely your time is more valuable."

"I'm here to check on my wife."

"But that's what I'm here to do!"

"If I thought a hobbit could do the job, I wouldn't be here."

Ezra looked down, either ashamed or unwilling to fight. "You're not going to let her see you, are you, Master Henry?"

He hadn't spent enough time around golls to know if

they were easily scared, but the creature was trembling. "No. Why, what happens if I do?"

"You cannot let her see you," Ezra breathed, like fire from his throat. "Trust me."

"Why?"

"Just. Trust. Me."

"Okay. I think I have the invisible-thing down. How's this?"

Henry *flared* himself, sending his body into a different vibration, still with no true understanding of what he was doing or how. The ability came to him, like instinct, as if he'd learned it in his sleep. His eyes hummed under their lids as he blinked, certain of his invisibility.

"I can still see you," Ezra said as Henry opened his eyes. "But don't worry," he added, waving off Henry's frown, "there's no problem. You did everything right. Golls see more things than most creatures, especially humans."

Henry said nothing, staring past the goll and at his house.

"Promise you'll be careful?" Ezra seemed genuinely terrified. "Master Boothe will be angry if you're not."

Henry never had a chance to tell Ezra not to worry, because the goll was screeching almost as soon as he ended his sentence, hopping frantically on the sidewalk while pointing madly at a white van behind him. "He's here, he's here, he's *here*! I can smell the death on him!"

Henry turned toward the van and instantly recognized the driver. The man with the tiny eyes who had held a gun to Samantha's head.

Chapter Ten

HENRY REACHED the van as its door started to open. He pulled it the remainder of the way, grabbed the guy's left hand, yanked it toward the opening, then pulled him by the wrist, slamming the door so it raked across the top of the bastard's knuckles.

Blood splattered the white paint in a fan of red.

The murderer screamed, then surprised Henry by throwing the van door back open, and kicking him in his gnarled nose. Henry reeled back as the door slammed shut.

The fucker gunned the engine and peeled into the street.

Henry primed his body to race after the van, but the van stopped a block away. Then it turned around, engine racing, and rocketed back at Henry.

He stood, snarling.

The van got two inches from Henry before he *flared*, leaping ten feet into the air. Three away from getting crushed by the grill. He misjudged his landing by an inch, maybe two, and flew to the pavement, ass first. He growled, bounced as if made of rubber, then roared toward the van.

It accelerated, going faster than Henry, but only because his new demon body was already exhausted. He gave the chase everything he had, and more, reaching the van's back and grabbing onto the bumper.

He clung to the metal, dragging himself toward the van as his knees scraped along the asphalt., skin dragging and leaving a black trail of blood.

Pain is only thought.

Henry's right hand found the back-door handle, frustrated to find it was the kind that lifted, with nothing to pull, and nowhere to gain purchase. Still growling, he clutched the bumper with his left hand and reached up with his right, pressing his fingers into the metal. Black claws bloomed from his fingertips, puncturing the door and pulling Henry to it like a magnet.

He ripped the back door from its hinges and released it into the air, where the white painted metal stayed for a half second before falling back and bouncing off the road with a horrible screeching. Henry pulled himself into the van's back as the murderer drowned the whipping wind with his terrified screams. His bald head gleamed with the reflected glow of streetlamps.

The van swerved wildly, as if the murderer at the wheel was more frightened by the thing that had ripped his door off than he was by any danger of dying in a crash. The vehicle slammed to a stop and the man moved for his door as Henry flew forward, unable to halt his momentum.

Henry grabbed the murderer by his jacket collar as he was about to jump out of the van, then flung him over to the passenger side. The killer's nose smashed against the window, crunching cartilage and spattering blood on the glass. The coward lay crumpled in the corner of the passenger side, crying.

He growled, climbed into the driver's seat, and slammed his foot on the gas, tearing back into the street and through a pair of stop signs. He raced along the road as the murderer turned the van floor into a one-man show of despair and pleading. Henry wasn't sure where he was headed, but he made it three blocks before the emptiness claimed him.

Henry turned to Tiny Eyes. "What's wrong? Scared?"

He stepped on the gas and pushed the van harder. Far too fast for a residential street, but he was blinded by the moment's rage. "How about now?" The van swerved out of control and he slammed into a parked car pointed the wrong way on the street. The van came to a crashing stop.

Two air bags went off, preventing him and Tiny Eyes from flying through the window, though the impact surely hurt the man to his right. Henry tore the bag from the steering wheel, tossed it aside, then turned to Tiny Eyes, ready to finish him off.

Lights appeared, one after another, dotting the darkness.

An orchestra of dogs started barking in the surrounding yards and houses.

If Henry didn't flee, he was dead. Just as Boothe warned.

Henry crawled from the driver's side, slamming his left heel into the murderer's chest. Tiny Eyes whimpered.

He spied a duffel bag behind them, half-wedged under the driver's seat, then jumped over the seat back and hunched over the bag. Picking it up and unzipping it, Henry growled at the tape, rope, and hammer. The bundle of assorted knives.

He dropped the bag to the floor, then clambered back to the front. "What in the fuck were you planning to do with all that, huh? A few late-night repairs?"

The murderer stared at Henry in horror, homicidal eyes bugging from his face. Eyes, the last time Henry had seen them, that had been tiny and fierce.

Henry wondered what he looked like to Tiny Eyes. How much could the man see beneath the hoodie? Enough to know he was dealing with a monster, not a man?

Sudden activity outside the vehicle. Neighbors approaching with whispers and shouts. Henry would have to cut things short, and he realized Boothe was right.

He should have waited.

Henry grabbed Tiny Eyes by the throat, then yanked him from the passenger side and into the back of the van with one clenched fist. He picked him up and slammed his body against the metal floor. The murderer lay there, broken. Bleeding inside by now, for sure. Henry straddled the man, pinning him down. In his best gravelly Batman voice, he roared, "Why were you outside of my house? What do you want with my family? Live and die by your answer!" He leaned in close, splattering the man's face with spit as he repeated, "One chance. Why were you outside of my house?"

"Your … your house?"

The murderer barely made words as he whimpered. Tiny Eyes had no idea who he was.

"Samantha Black! Why were you outside her house?" Henry roared so loud, the coward would have to be an *ignoranus* to not see he was a wrong answer away from not breathing.

"I came to f-f-finish the job."

Henry squeezed his fingers into the killer's throat.

"Keep going," he growled, letting loose enough for the man to confess his sins.

"Lady got lucky first time, got away when the cops came, and we couldn't catch her. She disappeared. Didn't show up until two days later. We were supposed to come back and finish her off. It was my job to do it."

"Who sent you?"

The roar made no difference. Tiny Eyes said, "Fuck you!"

Too many lights and barking dogs made it time for Henry to go.

He was about to send Tiny Eyes to Hell when the tattoo on the asshole's forearm stopped him cold. An *F* and a *C* inside of a circle. And it looked damned familiar, though Henry couldn't place it.

The tattoo filled him with rage, though he had no idea why.

Henry had only seconds.

He shoved the tattoo from his mind, turned his attention back to Tiny Eyes, and squeezed his fingers into the asshole's Adam's apple.

The man tried to scream, but couldn't. Instead, his arms and feet thrashed as Henry choked him.

Henry let go of the man's throat, pulled the hoodie back from his head, and forced his true self through the shadows, revealing the monstrosity that was about to end Tiny Eyes's life. The man gasped for air as he tried to push Henry off and squirm away. His fear felt like a rush of adrenaline through Henry, fueling him in a sudden powerful surge, gathering inside him, waiting to explode upon the murderer.

Tiny Eyes screamed, louder and more horribly than anything Henry had ever heard, frantic to get away.

"Shut up," Henry snarled. He grabbed the man's right

wrist and planted his foot on his shoulder. He heaved, and he tore the arm from the murderer's body — the one he had used to threaten Samantha.

Tiny Eyes screamed, his eyes bulging wide. The man was about to either die or pass out.

There were people outside the front of the van. Maybe three. A few dogs.

He leaned into Tiny Eyes, holding his murdering limb like a trophy. "Is this the hand you used to touch my wife?" He was close enough to bite the man's face from his skull.

"I didn't touch the bitch," Tiny Eyes whimpered.

Henry thundered, "Fuck *you!*"

There were definitely three people outside the van. Two men and one woman. The moment Tiny Eyes screamed at the loss of his arm, they backed away. Still, they were too close, and Henry couldn't be sure how much they could see through the windows. Henry felt their fear as if it were his own, flowing into his nostrils with every fresh breath.

From a Hell inside him, Henry bellowed, "I'll find the others!"

Claws sprang out, and he thrust his hand through the man's chest, like a stake through a vampire's heart. Fingers splayed inside Tiny Eyes's torso, giving Henry the leverage he needed to lift the murderer's body and hurl him out the back of the van to shrieks and screams.

Energy flowed up through his arms. The scent of fear replaced with a sweetness on his palate. Time slowed, and he felt every heartbeat as the passing of an hour. The scraping footsteps outside. The hushed voices. Light and sound rising into his senses like the taste of the kill.

Henry heard a gun cock. The number of dogs barking had climbed to a half dozen.

He pulled the hood over his head, made himself one with the shadows, and raced out of the van and into the night. A blur.

It was time to see Sam.

Chapter Eleven

"DID IT FEEL GOOD?"

Henry looked at Ezra. "Is it supposed to?"

"It depends on the man doing the killing."

Henry wasn't sure what to make of that, so he ignored it. "What time is it?"

"Forgive me, Master Henry, but why does it matter? I mean now, after everything ..." Ezra looked down, as if Henry's eyes might burn his.

"I know Samantha's routine. Knowing the time gives me an idea of what I'm walking into."

"But her routine is different, Master Henry. Nothing is the same."

"What's the time, Goll?"

"One in the morning, Master Henry."

"Thank you."

"Maybe you should hold off on going inside. You're still very energized from the kill, and less likely to control your emotions." Ezra pointed to the top of the guest house on the far side of the pool. "Come up to the roof, stay with me. We can keep watch together."

"No, thanks. There's nothing to watch right now. The thug they sent tonight is a baby mountain of broken bones. No reason to worry about *him*. As far as my emotions are concerned, we're good, and I'm going in."

"How do you expect to get inside the house without this?"

Ezra handed Henry a key, fat and wide on one end, instead of long and skinny like the old one. Copper rather than silver. He ran his thumb across the top. Something about a new key to his house made him feel even more like an outsider. An intruder.

"Thanks. I guess I'm not supposed to ask you where the key came from, right?"

"It came from a locksmith, Master Henry. No magic. Samantha had her locks changed. That's a copy of the new key."

He had a hard time looking at the goll. The poor creature was too ugly. Henry winced. The same thing was true about himself.

Henry told Ezra not to worry, waited for the goll to go about his business, then turned the key in the lock, trying to keep his movement at a whisper. He opened the front door, stepped inside the house, and closed it quietly behind him. He stepped into the foyer, making five strides in six seconds before the alarm started screaming.

Shit!

Henry froze, too surprised to find the focus to turn himself invisible. He leapt to the corner and ducked under the winding stairs. No time to try any of the dozen kill codes he imagined Sam using to silence the alarm. He slipped into the shadows as if they were a second skin and pressed his body hard against the wall.

Samantha's feet thundered down the stairs.

"Is anyone there?" she yelled, her voice stronger than

he would've imagined, though he knew his wife well enough to hear the truth behind her facade. "I can hear you! I have a gun!"

Does she really have a gun?

She had been anti-gun, both before and after Amélie was born. She even had a T-shirt with a rifle in the center of a red circle and a line through it. Not that she ever wore it. Henry wanted to buy a gun back when they had lived on the corner of Chaumers and Dixon. The ghetto thugs seemed always a wrong look from putting a cap in his ass. But Samantha had said no.

After the TV deal, Henry was convinced they were an easy target, but she thought he was being paranoid and told him so whenever the subject surfaced. But getting raped after your family is murdered in front of you would probably turn most people into a card-carrying member of the NRA.

Samantha hit the bottom stair and moved slowly through the foyer, pistol in front of her body. Henry knew approximately dick about pistols, but the one in her hand looked like she'd swiped it from the set of *Minority Report*. Henry wondered how in the hell she'd managed to get a gun so soon.

Isn't there a waiting period? How long have I been sleeping?

With her gun held in a straight line in front of her chest, Samantha made slow steps back toward the door and the shrieking alarm. Once there, she switched the weapon from her right hand to her left and moved to the control panel.

She entered the code one button at a time, taking peeks back into the darkness between digits, still aiming her gun in front. Right at Henry's chest. He stared out from the shadows, knowing he was being paranoid. Of course she couldn't see the whites of his open eyes, even though it seemed as if she was staring inside them.

Samantha silenced the alarm, then crept through the foyer, pausing by the door for a full minute as she drew an invisible line across the room, moving from left to right with the barrel, several times in each direction. Her breathing was shockingly calm. Henry figured she was telling herself that the new alarm was acting quirky. She turned her back to the stairs and took them slowly, one at a time, gun still in front, marching as if to a drumbeat.

Henry waited in the shadows, longing to charge from his hiding spot, upstairs and into Samantha's arms. When she reached the top, he followed.

Samantha crossed the long hall to their old bedroom, leaving the door open and making it easy for Henry to slip in behind her. She went straight to their bed, collapsed on the mattress, and started to sob.

Samantha cried for an hour while Henry watched. She finished, but only long enough to make a call to someone he couldn't identify. Something told him it was a man. She thanked *him*, said she'd see him in the morning, then killed the connection, tossing the phone to the foot of the bed, falling back into her tears.

Eventually she stopped crying, but since she was the sort of woman who liked to stare at her wounds while waiting for them to heal, she left their room, crossed the hall, then went to Amélie's room.

Henry followed as she drifted through their daughter's bedroom, fondling many of her more tangible memories, one at a time and in no particular order. She started with a Percy Jackson book, picking up one before adding another and making a stack, running her fingers over their worn spines. Rick Riordan books were the only ones Amélie didn't read on her e-reader, even though she had them all and preferred reading on the device for everything else. His books were special, the first she had ever read as a *big girl*.

Samantha finished with Percy, then moved to Amélie's endless collection of stuffed animals before going to her art folder, then finally to the computer, where she sat, turned it on, and slowly sifted through Amélie's photos and videos, sobbing through every one.

Henry sorted through a million thoughts of his own as Samantha looked through their daughter's belongings. He wondered what she was thinking, and whether she had gone through this routine each night since the impossible had demolished her.

Samantha looked out the window, staring at the large pool for a tiny forever, until she finally turned from the glass, seemingly haunted and spent from the horror of what her life had become. She stood mostly still, slightly swaying. Again, he wanted to go to her, to hold her tight, and let her know he was there. That he'd never let anything bad happen to her ever again.

But he couldn't.

Henry wondered what Sam would do if he were to step forward. Would she be relieved or terrified? He clung tighter to the shadows, slowly losing his grip, afraid he'd suddenly flicker from the swaddling dark and into the dim light of his dead daughter's bedroom.

Samantha stood by the doorway, three feet from Henry, not moving.

If he lost his shadows, Samantha would see his ruined body.

She finally found her momentum and made it another step toward the door where she stopped short, turned around, then went back to Amélie's bed and crawled under the covers.

She clutched Amélie's pillow, pulled its squish into her

chest, buried her face deep into its faux down, and inhaled. Samantha sobbed so hard into the pillow that when she finally pulled it away, Henry could see the soaking wet circle darkening its center.

He trembled in the corner, his heart in pieces.

Samantha started, sitting up in the bed.

Did she feel me?

She dropped Amélie's newest favorite stuffed animal, Doggy the Rabbit, onto the bed, then darted her eyes through the room.

Henry would give anything to let her know everything was okay. Amélie was gone, but something else waited. A place where they could one day be together, and he had seen it with his own eyes.

But Henry could barely breathe, let alone move.

Eventually, she lay back in the bed, closing her eyes. He trembled in the shadows, upset and aching, ashamed for being a coward, terrified his wife would find him shivering in the dark. He couldn't let her see him like this. He couldn't risk what Boothe might do if he revealed himself to her.

Henry waited for Samantha to start snoring, which never took long when she was horizontal with her eyes shut. He slipped from one shadow into the next, outside of Amélie's bedroom, then out into the hall.

Henry crossed to the more modest side of his house, the wing where he was most comfortable. When her parents had come to visit the previous spring for three weeks before finally going back home, Henry had been embarrassed by every room to the left of the foyer. The house to the right still felt like *him*, even if the left was nicer and newer and an awful lot larger.

Henry reached the hallway's end, then climbed into the

attic. Moonlight illuminated the room through a large square window leading out to the roof.

He went to his old laptop and opened the lid, but several days of being left unplugged had murdered the battery. His attic computer was used only to write and had nothing installed but a copy of Scrivener and a connection to his DropBox.

Henry sat at his desk, looking through a notebook at the last jokes he'd ever written, jokes he'd never share with an audience.

Sitting at his desk, with Samantha sleeping downstairs, Henry felt his first bit of normalcy since his world had gone to Hell.

He hoped he wouldn't have to return to Boothe's apartment and wondered if the demon could force him. As nice and as private as it might be, the apartment held nothing for him. He was already in a place where he had everything he wanted, all that had been taken, and all he was driven to protect.

If Henry thought it was a good idea, Boothe would likely hate it and tear into him like a little bitch once Ezra went tattling. So Henry figured he would soak in the moment and enjoy his slice of home until Boothe's inevitable reprimand came, tomorrow or whenever.

After reading through the last of his final musings, Henry rose from his chair and hobbled to the couch at the back of the attic, so exhausted that once he lay down, he thought he might never wake again.

But Henry was wrong.

He opened his eyes, startled by a noise blinking into the darkness, straining to unblur the hazy golden light circling the small girl standing by the attic entrance. Right where she had always stood while trying to grab his attention.

"Daddy?" Amélie said, staring at Henry, her eyes wide.

Chapter Twelve

HENRY HAD SEEN a funhouse full of impossible shit since his death. But nothing shook his insides so much as seeing Amélie's ghostly image flickering at the entrance to his attic office. She was in a white robe, like Randall had worn.

"Amélie … Is that you?" Henry inched toward the flicker, stepping through his disbelief, slowly at first, then faster, until he stood an inch from an Amélie who couldn't be there.

She flickered again, her image more insistent, as if screaming for solidity.

She repeated, "Daddy? Is that you?"

Henry crouched, level with Amélie. For a moment she was almost there. His fingers twitched, as if they knew he should reach out and touch her. The second lasted as long as its name before Amélie was merely a gold-colored shadow. Another passed, and she was gone.

"Amélie?"

Henry waited, but saw only darkness around him.

"Amélie?" he screamed his whisper, waiting through more of the horrible silence.

Amélie was gone for good, and the black she left behind felt somehow worse than the black in her coffin. Losing her for the second time made him feel even more helpless, even more confused.

His body grew hot, and he felt his anger building, as if he were going to *flare*. He breathed. In and out and in and out. Enough times to be sure his rage wouldn't bloom. He stood still, knowing that the only thing keeping him from rampaging through the house was a focus on the emptiness inside him.

Stay calm.

He turned to the couch. "Daddy! Daddy! Are you there? Daddy!"

He spun, flailing his arms for balance. "I'm here." Henry's hands flew in front of his body, swatting the air in search of his daughter. "I'm here," he whispered again, as loud as he dared without waking Samantha and drawing her to the attic. He was too weak to hide if she came up to see what was going on.

"Daddy!" Amélie's shape grew brighter. Her body more corporeal and her voice a bit louder.

"I'm here, baby girl. I can see you! Can you see me?" Henry said, grateful for the hoodie and the attic's dark.

Amélie nodded. "Only a little."

He blinked, trying to make the tears move backward. "Where are you?"

"I don't know, Daddy. I've never been here. How do I know where a place is if I've never been there? Do you think you'll be able to tell, if I describe it?"

"I can try." Henry wasn't sure he wanted to recognize wherever she was.

"It's so cold here." Amélie's scant image shivered. Then all of her blurred.

She fell silent, her mouth moving but muted, lips forming rapid words he couldn't read.

Does she realize how fast she's talking? Or know I can't hear her?

A million questions fell atop the first two. Henry felt the sudden, tangible possibility that he was dreaming the encounter. Or that maybe he'd lost his mind.

He was torn. Dreaming meant she'd vanish along with the day. Reality meant danger had found his daughter. The thought chilled his body, Was he somehow communicating with his daughter's ghost? If so, was she as lost as he was?

He had to help Amélie with whatever she faced, talk her through it as best he could. He'd failed her once, and that had ended her life. He couldn't fail her again.

"Look around you, honey. What do you see?"

There was a long pause, as if Amélie was using every possible resource to absorb her surroundings and consider her words.

"Are you there, sweetie?"

"Yes, Daddy. I'm looking around. There's lots and lots of shadows. And a lot of space. It's everywhere. Some of it white, the rest is less than that. Sometimes there's color, but never for long. Everything is broken, and old. It looks like buildings used to be here, but they're all crumbly now."

Oh, God, no.

Henry wanted to scream for his daughter, but he had to be strong.

She doesn't deserve this.

Amélie is better than Nowhere.

Doesn't a child deserve to pass GO and advance straight on to Heaven?

He asked, "Have you seen a Tree?"

"A tree?"

"Yes, baby girl. A giant Tree."

"No." The image flickered with her shaking head.

"There's nothing alive here. I think I see blue sky behind me."

"Okay, sweetie. Turn around and start heading toward that blue sky behind you."

"Okay, Daddy."

"Are you walking?" It looked like she was moving, but Amélie still faced Henry, as though some nonexistent camera had spun around.

"Yes, I'm walking. When do I know to stop walking?"

"I don't know."

"Okay, Daddy." Henry's heart warmed at his daughter's steady march, as if the only fuel she needed was a little girl's faith in her father.

"Everything is still broken. Everywhere, Daddy. How long do I keep walking?"

"I'm not sure, but I think I might know how to make everything closer."

"Okay, Daddy."

"You're going to see a Tree soon. Do you believe me?"

"Yes. What will the tree look like?"

"It might change from time to time. But I think it will be big. The biggest thing you've ever seen, and once you see it, you can't doubt it. Like believing in Santa."

Henry wasn't sure why he was suddenly certain about the Tree and how it thrived on belief, but it felt right, Again, like understanding that seeped inside him while sleeping, perhaps collective knowledge shared by all who'd been in Nowhere. He hoped to God he wasn't steering Amélie the wrong way or giving her bad advice.

"Okay, Daddy." She walked faster, her face more determined.

After a minute, Henry said, "See anything?"

"No." Amélie looked at the ground as she walked, as if

feeling guilty for her disappointing answer. A minute later she squealed, "I think I see a Tree, Daddy!"

Henry felt a smile flush his cheeks. He wondered if it looked as twisted as the rest of his face.

Amélie gasped. "It's so pretty, Daddy. But cool, too. Like a tree from the *Alice in Wonderland* by the *Nightmare Before Christmas* guy."

"How big is it?"

"The biggest thing I've ever seen." Amélie was almost too awestruck to whisper. Her eyes went wide and her arms shot into the air. She started to run, racing toward the Tree as if answering a call.

"You'll get there soon," Henry said. "When you do, you'll find a garden. If you're in the right place, you'll see a long stone table. Look for the old man wearing all white and playing chess. His name is Randall. He'll help you until I can get there. I will find you, Ami. Whatever you do, don't say anything to the man in black if you see him. And don't listen if he says anything to you. Only the man in white. Okay?"

Amélie's mouth moved without sound, like before. She flickered several times before disappearing. Henry's heart pounded while waiting for her return. Then she finally came back, but only long enough to say, "I'm so scared, Daddy," her voice full of static.

Henry reached out to hug his baby girl, pull her closer to him. Maybe he could turn their two nightmares into one, then find a way to end it together.

But Amélie was gone.

Henry sobbed, trying to outrun an insistent thought. *Life after death was a curse.*

He had wanted to return and protect his family, but ended up barely better than worthless. He wasn't needed in his old attic. He was needed by his daughter, who was stuck in Nowhere and crying for him to save her.

"Boothe!" Henry yelled in a whisper, pacing the attic, nervous over the noise but unable to curb his rising frustration. "Boothe!"

The demon was Henry's only hope of returning to Nowhere and rescuing Amélie from whatever had her so frightened. He had to find him.

After minutes of pacing and failed cries to bring Boothe to his attic, Henry figured he'd go to the demon directly. Ezra could lead him to Boothe.

Henry went to the attic window, then lifted the sash and started to climb out onto the roof. Halfway out he realized he was halfway too far.

Henry's tank was empty.

He fell back through the window, hard against the wood, and passed out.

Chapter Thirteen

HENRY COULD'VE SWORN someone tapped him on the shoulder.

His body lurched from the couch, launched with a jolt that shot to his fingertips. His head slammed against the sloping attic ceiling, cranking his neck to his shoulder and scraping the side of his already fucked-up face. He landed on the floor with a crash and an aftershock. He rubbed his temples, more annoyed by the sound of his landing and the blur of slowly waking than the ringing between his ears.

He stood, trying to remember his dream. Something long, horrible, and ... he was quite sure, immediately important. But Henry remembered nothing and could barely recall sneaking up into the attic before plummeting into sleep.

He closed his eyes and rocked his head back and forth, trying to remember. With a sudden horror, Henry's mental projector went live with the memory of Amélie standing at the entrance to his attic office.

That wasn't real, was it?

What *was* real? A starving and famished Henry. His bones felt like they belonged in a graveyard. He headed for the stairs and the kitchen but paused at the first step, thinking back to Sam's mysterious phone call the night before.

He turned back and went to the window, peering through the glass and looking outside toward the pool, where Sam liked to sit and stare at the water while sipping her coffee.

She was nowhere in sight. Something inside Henry insisted she was at the carport.

He tore from the attic, dropping to the second floor and running to the far window. Samantha was outside, climbing inside her pearl-white Porsche Cayenne. He didn't feel energized enough to chase her, but he had to know who she'd been talking to last night.

FUCK!

Henry *flared*, and surprised himself by blinking to the carport, right beside his own nondescript Lexus as Sam pulled out of their driveway. Dizziness rocked him on his feet, and his vision narrowed to a compressed dot of gray. He shook his head, leaning on the car for support until it cleared.

Henry opened the door and climbed inside. He opened the glovebox and scrabbled his hands through the papers and old gum. He slid the key out and fired up the Lexus. Like all of Henry's cars, it had tinted windows just a hair above the legal limit. Grateful for the masking, he tore from the carport and raced down the drive, pulling out into the street in time to see Samantha hang a right. He followed for three miles, until Sam pulled into the parking lot of the Burg Spires Church of Hope.

Samantha opened her door, but then immediately shut it and leaned her head against the steering wheel, sobbing for several minutes. He could barely see her, but Henry could somehow *feel* her crying. The shock of her emotions lit his mind with surprised pain. It was almost as though he were seeing the hues of her true color.

A thin black cloud darkened and swirled around her. After a few moments, it dimmed and parted, tendrils still clinging to Samantha's hair as it faded. She dried her eyes and climbed from the Cayenne, then she crossed the parking lot and stepped through the side entrance of the beautiful old church.

Henry shot from the interior of his Lexus to the shadow of a Camry. Three patches of shade after that found him wrapped in the shadows of the church's entrance.

She was being greeted by Pastor Owen, their regular man of the cloth, spiritual adviser, and occasional marriage counselor — all three jobs designated by Sam. Henry would be fine having nothing to do with any of it. Though raised Catholic, he had never bought into any of the pious bullshit while living.

Now dead and consorting with demons, he could finally start to believe. And being a demon himself, Henry supposed the last laugh was on him. Sam was right. There was a God. And a Devil, apparently. But he still didn't think the church had their shit together and was damn sure most organized religion was clay. Shaping itself around man's attempts to exert his will unto others. And of course, to exploit fear while getting rich in the process.

Henry figured God was too mysterious for an animal as dumb as man to truly understand Him. Still, he never transferred that lack of faith to his family. He occasionally went to church, and to the counseling sessions, out of respect for Sam. Sometimes he felt like a sucker for playing along, feeling he should stand his ground and refuse to participate in something he didn't believe in. Instead, he defended his honor in the one way he knew how. Humor.

Henry was a comic, not a pretender, so he would unleash the occasional joke, such as referring to the pastor as Samantha's "Patty-cake Pastor Owen." He didn't play patty-cake, at least not that Henry knew of, but because he was clergy, Samantha found Henry's joke disrespectful. She didn't forbid it, but the one about the dead priest and his magic rabbit?

Now, though, Henry's absence made him grateful she had someone of faith to console her. He was maybe thirty yards away, in a building designed to carry the voice to the seats in the back. He could hear perfectly as the pastor pulled her into an embrace.

"How are you?"

"A disaster. Sorry I called you so late last night."

Pastor Owen held her for five seconds, and another five after she didn't pull away. "It's okay. Everything will be good again, Samantha. And it's good to grieve. Grieving is the *right* thing to do." He smiled and held out his hand. Sam's fingers fell inside the pastor's palm as he led her through the nave and down a short hallway toward his office.

Henry followed, cloaked in shadows, gliding along the walls and ceiling, spreading into the gnarls of darkness among the hand-hewn beams. His movement felt almost dreamlike in his ability to float and propel himself from one surface to another and cling to the walls. Or at least the shadows. It was as if his weight had been reduced to almost nothing inside them.

The pastor guided her along the wall under the stained glass windows. "You know you can tell me anything, right? You don't have to go through this alone."

Samantha nodded. "Yes. Of course, Pastor Owen."

"I promise He has a way of making all the wrong things right when you let Him."

"I'm happy to let Him. I just need to know how. Right now, I can't believe what I'm feeling."

"And what's that, Samantha?"

"Guilt."

"Guilt?" The pastor stopped at his office door.

"Yes, guilt. And it's horrible. I feel like I'm dancing on Henry's grave."

"I'm sure you're doing nothing of the sort." He opened the door and smiled gently. "And don't worry, there's no such thing as a wrong thought. We can't help how we feel about something, but we can control what we *do*. That's what counts."

"That doesn't sound like the Bible to me." She stepped into his office and sat. "The Good Book seems pretty clear on right and wrong thoughts."

Henry slipped by Pastor Owen, sliding from one bundle of darkness in the hallway to another in the corner of the high ceiling. The pastor stepped into the room and sat at his desk, letting the door close behind him. They sat across from one another at the pastor's desk, seemingly oblivious to Henry clinging just a few feet above them like a fly on the wall.

"Not all churches are the same, Samantha. You should know that by now. Evil only exists beside good. Everything has two sides, each always needing the other. Sometimes your worst thoughts are there to surface the best. Whatever you're feeling, there's a reason. Would you like me to help you find that reason?"

Samantha nodded, clearly trying not to cry.

"Tell me why you're feeling guilty."

"I don't know … It's like I want to scream at Henry." She laughed. It sounded accidental.

Pastor Owen smiled. "You want to scream at Henry for what? For leaving you?"

"No, not that." She shook her head as though unsure of her next words.

"You often wanted to yell at Henry. Surely you don't think that's abnormal? I'm certain you and your husband have unfinished business, like every other married couple."

Samantha laughed again, covering her mouth with her hand.

"You know this tragedy couldn't have been avoided, yet a part of you is angry with Henry for leaving you alone. After all, his success invited those murderers into your home in search of easy opportunity. Those murderers took your husband, daughter, and life. Amélie's dead. It's either *your* fault or *Henry's*. At least according to how you're probably thinking. Best for your sanity if you let Henry take the rap, for now."

"All of that's true. But it's not what I mean."

"Oh?"

"Yes, I'm angry with Henry. But it has nothing to do with … what happened. I'm pissed at him for a million other things, stuff we never got to hash out, mad he never took our sessions with you seriously. Counseling was always a joke or an obligation to sit through. Like being on a talk show he didn't want to do, where he had to smile and say all the right things. He even had a routine about coming here, but I hated all three minutes, and told him that if he took our therapy on stage again, that was it."

"Unfinished business," the pastor said. "Perfectly normal."

Samantha ignored him. "Remember the W.A.A. joke I told you about?"

"Of course."

"I don't think I ever forgave him, even though I

promised him I had." Sam waited through half a minute, gathering her thoughts. "I understand Henry had to be funny, and that our future was born from that humor. I got it then, I get it now. It was always part of the deal. But, Pastor, that man has *no* filter. Or *had* no filter. There are basic boundaries of everyday decency that apply to offstage life that should be carried onstage, too. Life's not lived with a microphone in your hand."

Samantha's speech grew fast, almost high pitched, like it always did when she told the *Waa! Story*. "I was the charity director for Women Against Abuse, and that bastard called it *Waa!*, like the women were all crying over spilt milk. He had no right to ruin that for me. When that video hit YouTube, I had to resign from something I cared about, something I believed in. Something I was great at and did good for. He *knew* that joke wasn't okay. And if he didn't, that's *worse*. Almost. Nothing's worse than it seeming like he didn't even care. Acting like it wasn't even a big deal that I quit and saying it wasn't like the job was making us rich!"

The pastor nodded, just like he had every time the story was told in one of their counseling sessions.

Watching Sam sob was horrible. Worse was choking on his laughter after remembering the joke's rhythm and reciting it in his head. He cared that she lost her job, but Henry was also pissed that the organization would get so bent about a joke that was *clearly* ironic. He wasn't making fun of battered women, ever. He was making fun of the idiot misogynists who made stupid jokes like the *Waa! Story*.

How the fuck can you tell jokes when you have to be so politically correct, forever afraid to offend someone somewhere. Of course you're gonna offend someone. If not, no one's laughing.

Sensitive cunts.

Still, watching Sam cry, Henry felt no different from those loutish men.

Samantha sobbed for several minutes until the pastor finally rose from his seat and walked over to her side of the desk, dragging his chair behind him. He sat beside her, stroking her long black hair. Henry felt worse with every stroke.

Once Samantha stopped crying she fell into a laugh, a real one, the kind that made Henry fall so hard for her in the first place. "I don't know, I just felt like he loved his career more than me, sometimes. I know it's crazy, and I should appreciate the struggle he went through to get where he got, but still, I think making it was more about him than providing for us. That he cared more about what strangers thought of him than about his own family."

Pastor Owen smiled. "I'm sure he loved you very much."

I did! I DO love you, Sam.

But even as he thought that, Henry saw the painful truth in what she was saying. And he had no defense. She was right. He had cared way too much about what strangers thought of him, and hadn't realized how much it had come at the expense of Sam.

His stomach churned. Her voice half-cracked through her next pair of sentences.

"I know you can never prepare for this sort of thing, but I didn't realize I'd feel so empty. So unfinished. He's gone, but it's way worse that *she's* gone forever, too."

Samantha cried again. Not as hard as the first time, but deeper. Henry knew the tone. She'd be finishing her cry alone.

She stood from her chair and the pastor stood from his. He pulled her hands into his and drew her into a light hug.

"The church has an ear for you, Samantha. *Please* don't be afraid to bend it."

She nodded. "Of course."

Samantha thanked Pastor Owen again, then turned and left his office.

Henry aimed for a cluster of shadows outside the doorway. A second from launch, the pastor looked up. "It's okay, Henry. You can stay."

Chapter Fourteen

How can he see me?

Henry allowed the shadows to fade into wisps as he fell to the ground and revealed himself to the pastor.

Grateful for the hoodie still shrouding his face, Henry avoided the man's eyes. "How did you know I was there?"

Pastor Owen smiled at Henry, his lips looking as genuine as they would on any normal Sunday morning. "I wish I had a better answer, Henry. Something to ease your mind. Unfortunately, my response is sure to disappoint. I didn't expect to see you, and didn't know I would until you were there. Once I did, it all seemed like part of a plan. For that is how He works."

"But *how* can you see me?"

"Because I show God everything, while never holding back, the Good Lord keeps little from me."

"How can you be sure what God does or doesn't want you to know?" Henry took another step forward, this time lifting his hands to his hoodie and drawing it back from his head.

"Did he show you this?"

105

Henry recoiled at his own mangled face, cast in the reflection from the mirror between two full bookcases. Twisted and tormented, hair sprouting on his scalp in dark patches. Points of skin rising above his temples.

Is that fucking horns?

He expected Pastor Owen to fall back in horror, but while clearly surprised, the pastor didn't flinch. He seemed more fascinated than anything else.

Except perhaps sympathetic.

"I am so, so sorry, Henry." He placed his open palm to Henry's face, as though he held gauze and dabbed at blood.

At his touch, Henry was struck by a sudden, soothing calm.

"Would you like to sit?" Owen gestured toward the chair that still held the shape of Sam's ass in its fabric.

Henry pulled the hood back up over his head, then sat across from the pastor, who had dragged his chair back behind the desk.

What, you don't want to stroke my hair?

Henry worried about Samantha going home alone and wondered what might happen if she returned to the carport and discovered the missing Lexus. Yet even the weight from that pair of worries couldn't pull him from a man who saw through his shadows and asked him to stay.

"Would you like to tell me why you faked your death?"

"I didn't fake my death, Pastor. I died."

Pastor Owen raised his eyebrows. "Well, this sounds like quite the tale."

"Where do I start?" Henry was really asking. He had no idea.

"How about at the beginning? What happened during the break-in?"

"I've no idea what Samantha said, or the media, but it

wasn't a break-in so much as three murderers forcing their way into our home. I was reading to Amélie when I heard something downstairs. I made it halfway down when some asshole with a gun started waving the barrel at my face. I was running through these different scenarios in my head, to either get them out of the house, or maybe even get one of their guns away. Guess I've seen *Die Hard* too many fucking times."

Pastor Owen winced at Henry's language but said nothing.

"Before I had a chance to do anything, though, one of the bastards shot me. That was the last I can remember until I woke up dead. And this is where you may think I'm at least one sandwich short of a picnic, but I woke up in Purgatory."

"And how long were you in Purgatory?"

Henry had no idea whether the pastor's question was serious or if he was merely placating him, but Henry felt his disturbing new appearance was all the proof he needed to show the pastor that something odd was happening in The Burg. "Just long enough to make a deal with a demon so I could return to save my family."

"A deal? With a *demon?*"

"Yes. The demon said he could bring me back. I didn't know what happened after I was killed, but I had to find out. I had to see if I could come back and do something."

"I see."

"Turns out, the demon tricked me, since I have no family left to save. At least not like I thought I would. I would tell you more, but it's all just too fucked up."

"And you anticipate my disbelief? I've listened to everything you've said to me so far."

With assurances that he believed, and would continue believing, the pastor urged him to continue. Henry finished his story about his time in Nowhere, then told him about the different frequencies Boothe had shown him, as well as what each did. He admitted to being at his own funeral and described Boothe's apartment and everything else bobbing on the surface of his memory. As promised, the pastor took in every word without a hint of skepticism. He wouldn't have blamed the man for giving him the same *oh yeah right* attitude that Henry had always brought to Sunday sermons.

Pastor Owen stayed quiet, his eyes thoughtful as if measuring his options. After Henry finished, the pastor sighed. "I'll be able to help you, but only if you put your faith in me. You must trust me, more than anything or anyone else. Can you do that?"

"Of course, Pastor," Henry nodded. He didn't believe himself, but the nod felt right. "What can I do?"

"For starters, tell me *everything*." The pastor smiled through a long pause. "What is it you're still not saying?"

"I *told* you everything."

"No, Henry." The pastor shook his head. "You *haven't*. You've told me *many* things, nearly everything except for one *final* thing. *That's* what I'd like to know. The thing I need most to help you, right now."

Henry remembered his dream.

The dream that might have been real.

How could I forget about that? And how could he know I was holding something back I couldn't even remember? Is God showing him shit again?

I have to find Boothe and tell him I need help getting to Nowhere!

"Last night I might have dreamt of Amélie. At least I hope it was a dream. I was too faded to be sure. If it wasn't a dream, then I saw Amélie was crying for help, screaming for me from Purgatory. I couldn't do anything, though. I just had to stare at her flicker like a dying TV."

Surprise surfaced on the pastor's face for the first time, followed by a ghostly pallor. "Have you told the demon that you saw your daughter?"

"No." Henry shook his head. "Of course not. This happened last night, either right before or after I fell asleep. I was on my way here five minutes after I woke up, following Sam. Why?"

"The demon cannot know. Not under any circumstances."

"Why?"

"I'm not sure, at least not exactly. But I know God, and have learned to listen when the Lord tells me something isn't right. If you're here to protect Samantha and Amélie, then you must not allow the demon to know that your daughter is able to speak with you. She will be used against you. Rules are different in places that are not Here."

"But I have to find her. I have to return to Purgatory!"

"No." The pastor shook his head with authority. "Amélie is safe in Purgatory. If she is somehow coming Here, you must keep it from the demon."

Pastor Owen continued speaking, but his words were suddenly thick and scrambled, like someone slowing a record. Henry wasn't able to decode a single sentence.

Something was wrong, and it was burning Henry's insides.

There was Hell inside him.

What's happening?

Henry fell from his chair to the floor, writhing and moaning.

"Are you okay?" Pastor Owen cried, his worried words cutting through Henry's pain.

Henry groaned, waving the pastor away and trying to focus while working to stand. The pastor tried helping Henry to his feet.

"Oh, my," he whispered, touching Henry. "You're burning up."

Henry squeezed his eyes shut, shaking his head until he realized the fire was coming from outside the church. He pushed the pastor from his path and raced from the office. Down a short hallway before erupting from the side door and into the parking lot.

Something pushed him to get away from the church. Like a ball from a cannon, Henry flew across the lot and headed to his Lexus. He'd be safe once inside. He knew it.

But he froze thirty feet from the Lexus, his eyes rolling up to a woman hovering in the air, high in the sky. She seemed to Henry at least ten feet tall, maybe even twenty. She descended, with long, flowing hair of white fire. A flaming sword in her hand, fashioned from a star's worth of hard light. She was bathed in flowing robes covered in golden armor. The heavy light that had made her seem so large were wings pointed above her head as she fell. Pure white and covered with soft feathers, she spread them wide to slow her descent. She drove them down a single time, and the dust from the parking lot kicked up into twin spirals that shot behind her like exhaust. Then she slowly floated toward him.

As she moved closer, her voice filled the air around him. And his mind. A lullaby that pulled Henry toward her light. He stared as if doing so could somehow allow him to take in all of her majesty. Captured by her beauty for what felt like minutes, Henry was unable to turn away. He needed to see more. He *had* to hear the song.

Until it turned into a scream, and her sword dropped with its point at the center of his chest.

Her shriek sent Henry to his knees. They smashed into the concrete. His jaw followed. He was on the ground, twitching and blinking between Pastor Owen coming across the parking lot and the strobing light above him. She drifted closer, until she hovered only a few feet above Henry. Her voice was so loud. It pierced his body with true pain, not something in his head that he could somehow ignore.

A second light joined the first. Another voice driving the song into Henry's soul. The glow doubled as a man in the same robes and armor slipped from behind the woman pointing the sword at Henry's heart. His wings closed as his feet touched the ground, and he pulled a net made of sparkling light over his shoulder. The net unfurled, settling over Henry like a parachute. Wherever the light touched him, it burned and sizzled against his skin.

The heat and agony tore through him, until suddenly, the pain disappeared. Henry felt nothing … and then he was warm. Impossibly, wonderfully, thoroughly warm. He smiled, waiting for the sword, certain that the moment it touched him, his world and everything in it would be flooded with light.

He would feel whole for the first time ever.

Surrender to the light.

The voice boomed in his mind. Commanding. Soothing.

Close your eyes, child.

Boothe appeared in the cracker-thin space between Henry's aura and that of the descending brightness. Black shadows and white light collided, crashing with each other into an ugly gray mud. Boothe stood with his back to Henry, thrusting his palms in front of his body. He sent a blast of ink-black smoke swirling through the air in an angry spiral. Darkness coiled around the light, slipping like snakes around their brilliant bodies and through the feathers on their wings, extinguishing luminescence as it slithered around their necks.

The man and woman screeched at a pitch deafening enough to shatter his body. He would explode like frozen glass. The bright light pushed Boothe to the ground, on his knees beside Henry's head.

A brilliant ball of white fire gathered in the center of the woman's chest. She screamed a battle cry, throwing her arms wide. The ball unraveled, flying from her body in a thousand tiny strings.

Henry had died once. He wondered how different the second time might be.

Chapter Fifteen

BOOTHE SPUN AND SPREAD OUT, smothering Henry with his body.

The world folded away, more painfully than before, as if the encounter with the light had left shrapnel inside him.

Henry and Boothe blinked away from the chaos.

Back in Boothe's apartment, Henry's head swam. His mind and face felt burned and melted. A sorrow welled up, like he almost missed the nightmare's brilliant beauty as he looked around Boothe's apartment.

Then the memory of the net burning in his head sent him screaming.

"Stop screaming, Henry. You sound like an infant." Boothe tapped his foot.

Henry hitched a breath, like a child gearing up for another fit. "What *the fuck* were those things?"

"One of the many reasons you shouldn't leave the apartment during daylight. And a prime example of the potential consequences of ignoring me."

"That's not an answer," Henry gasped through gritted teeth.

"Those *things* were Trackers."

"Oh, Trackers, well, why didn't you just say so?" Henry glared at Boothe. "You wanna tell me what the hell a Tracker is?"

"Remember how I said there are rules? Some angels take these rules *very* seriously, and seem to believe it's their purpose to go around killing our kind on Earth. They track demons and trap them in those nets."

"Then what? Do they send us to Hell?"

"Worse. They destroy your soul. Erase you like you never existed."

Henry shivered as Boothe finished his sentence.

"So, you're telling me I can't let people see me as I really am, and I also have to watch out for glowing fucking angels who might *erase* me in broad daylight? I think you could've maybe mentioned something about them before now."

"No need to shout, Henry. I can hear you fine. If you don't keep it down, the Trackers will hear you, too. This time there will be more, and we both will die."

Henry trembled.

"Not really." Boothe laughed. "I just wanted to see your face. They can't hear you now. You're perfectly safe. But they *do* know you're in the city, and that's not good. They will hunt you until you're found. It's their job to cleanse this plane of demons."

"Why in the Hell didn't you tell me about them? I had a right to know."

"Of course you did, Henry. Fair argument. But I never denied you the information. And if you rewind to our prior conversations, you'll recall that I warned you. I told you not to leave during daylight. To rest, regain your strength. Strike when smart. You ignored me. This is what happened. But hey, I saved you, right?" Boothe went to the fridge, grabbed the pitcher of water, and poured it into the two glasses they'd left on the kitchen island from before.

"Barely," Henry said, almost sulking as he took the water and gulped.

"Look at it this way. Now you know they're out there and what to look for. Stay away from the daylight, where they hold advantage. They will try to get you, day or night, but they're much easier to see at night. And to avoid. Promise me one thing. You must," Boothe elongated the word, "absolutely *must* not look directly at them or you'll be swept by their beauty and hypnotized as they close in for the kill. If you see them, run. Or teleport away if you can. Otherwise, you'll wish you were back in Nowhere."

"I felt like I was being hypnotized. And there was this weird music, almost, that was…"

"Beautiful?" Boothe asked, as if fondly remembering the song.

"Yes! Have you ever looked directly at one?"

"Once." Boothe fell silent. Before Henry could ask about the incident, Boothe cut him off. "The only way to keep yourself safe from getting pulled into their light is to burrow so deep inside the darkest parts of your mind that you can find enough black to swallow their white. It works, though it soils something inside you, and that something stays ruined forever."

Henry couldn't imagine things being *more* ruined than they already were. But then he thought of his daughter's uncertain situation. Yes, things could get worse.

Much worse.

"Sorry for being a dick. I should've listened."

Boothe laughed. "Well, Henry, that's quite enlightened. Thank you. Would you really like to make it up to me?"

"Sure."

"Go to sleep, Henry. The minute I leave, if not this second. No hyperbole. If you don't, you will die."

Henry blanched. He swallowed the acid flooding his mouth.

"You exhausted your body before the Tracker. And she has depleted you further. You've nothing left. No fight. Rebel against that reality, and it will be easy for Death to find you."

"I thought I was already dead?"

"You are. Or were. You came back, but like *this*." Boothe waved his hand across Henry's body in a shaky Z. "Die again, go straight to Hell. Unless the Trackers get you, of course. Then you just stop being."

Henry could feel the exhaustion, but he had enough in reserve to assuage his curiosity by asking, "So, what's wrong with going to Hell? If that's where I'm eventually going, why not get it over with?"

"No," Boothe said, "you want to stay here, or in Nowhere, as long as you can. Trust me."

"So why are you helping me? Surely it's not from the goodness of your icy black heart." Henry twisted his mouth in a sarcastic smile.

Boothe smirked before his face soured. "Go to sleep, Henry. I don't care to discuss this. The universe hasn't revolved around you for trillions of years, and it's not about to start now."

Henry wouldn't let it go. "Why are you helping me?"

"As I said, Henry. We have shared interests. That's all. It isn't *personal*. No destiny. No fate. Just business." Boothe put a hand on Henry's shoulder. "Can you do as I've asked?"

"You mean take a nap?" He shrugged. "Sure, I'll take a nap."

"Don't be flip, Henry. Rest, and rest well. When you wake, go to sleep again. Don't leave, no matter what. Understand?"

"Yes."

"When awake and finally fully rested, use your instincts. Your mind has already absorbed more than you realize. You have a plan, and your body will respond when needed. Be smart, always. That means not being stupid, like going to Samantha's. That's not the place for you right now. Ezra is there. Let the goll do his job."

Henry looked away but something about Boothe's presence demanded his eyes. "I mean it, Henry. Don't go back. You should not be in that house. You can upset things."

"What do you mean, *upset things?*"

Boothe sighed, not answering.

Henry shook his head. "How did you know I was back home?"

"Are you joking? I thought we had an agreement about not polluting the air with drivel you already know."

Henry wasn't sure if Boothe planned to leave at that moment, or if he had disgusted him into an early departure. Either way, the demon was gone.

Thankfully, Boothe never mentioned or questioned Henry's proximity to the church. Henry didn't want to explain why he had been there, or what he'd said to the pastor — assuming Boothe didn't already know every detail of his visit.

Henry padded into the bedroom, crawled into the giant bed, and sank into the mattress as if it were a pool. He pulled the covers over his body, then immediately threw them back and climbed out. He pulled off his pants and hoodie, then crawled back under the cool sheets and let them kiss his skin.

The monster closed its eyes and dreamed a monster's dream.

Again, he saw Amélie. They were only in his attic a moment, just long enough for Henry to draw a hopscotch court on the hardwood floor and for Amélie to take two times hopping across it.

"No," Henry said when it was his turn. "I'm too fat."

The office disappeared in a fog, and they were waiting in line for Pirates of the Caribbean at Disneyland with Mommy. Henry was sweating as much as Samantha was complaining. Staring between them, clenching seven years of fury in each of her fists, was Amélie, eyes wide with betrayal. They'd *promised* not to fight this time.

Disneyland dissolved, shoving Henry into a later memory, where he was parachuting a blanket onto their brand-new living room floor. As big as their old house and entirely empty except for the TV and smartly assembled picnic.

In real life, it had been the three of them. In the dream, it was Henry and Amélie. He saw the Tree behind the TV, but ignored it, knowing too much reality would shatter the dream. Instead, it went on for a wonderful forever. Henry and Amélie watched every movie they'd ever seen together, just to relive it, then every flick he would've wanted to share when she was older, but couldn't because his daughter was dead.

They ended with *Amélie*, the movie he and Sam had named her after.

Henry ignored the Tree until they had watched so many movies there was nothing left to see. They started writing jokes, and did that until Amélie started to scream.

It sounded like someone was bashing her face in.

Chapter Sixteen

THE CRIES WERE DEAFENING. And horrible.

The screams are real.

Henry leapt from his dream and onto the floor. He had no idea how much time was missing, but he was a new beast, still naked.

Now that he was up, Henry wasn't sure if the scream had been in his dream. He squeezed his eyes tight, hoping that might help him drown the ringing in his ears, heavy enough to send the man back to his knees. He pulled on his pants, moving through the painful scream inside his head, not entirely sure why he was getting dressed, but following his instincts because it was better than standing still while listening to the bellows in his head. Maybe his instincts would help him discover why the screams were there.

Pain is only thought.

Bullshit, this is real!

The screaming stopped.

He threw on his hoodie and headed toward the door.

His legs went to rubber halfway there when the screaming started again.

The sound faded, echoing in his ears like an infant crying. The screaming didn't belong to his daughter, as it had in the dream. Instead, it was someone else. He could almost feel its owner. A woman in pain. Somewhere close.

Henry wasn't exactly shocked to find himself feeling another's pain. The surprise came when he smiled at the bittersweet taste filling his mouth. Rolling up into his nose.

The scream tore through the apartment again, burning into Henry's guts and driving him to action. This was what a demon was supposed to do, what Boothe meant when he told Henry to *follow his instincts*. Werewolves craved moonlight, and vampires blood. Whatever Henry was, he feasted on sorrow. He hungered for pain.

He opened the window like before and leapt to the fire escape outside. Rather than racing down, he took a chance, hurling his body across the alley and landing on another fire escape on the opposite side.

Driven by the cry, Henry leaped from building to building, up six blocks toward the source of the anguish running through his mind. He scampered up the weathered fire escape of a five-story building, stopping at the fourth floor, where he hung from the rusty grate before flinging himself through the open window.

As Henry landed on the cheap carpet, he lowered the hoodie to reveal his hideous face.

"What the fuck?" An asshole stood in front of an unfortunate blonde flower, wilting beneath the heat of his still-raised hand. He lowered his open palm, made a fist, and took a step toward Henry. "The fuck you doing in my house, bitch?"

This should be good.

Henry ran toward the asshole.

The asshole was expecting him, and tried to dodge the attack. He just wasn't fast enough. Henry tackled him and sent him crashing to the filthy carpet. Most of him wanted to tear the asshole to pieces and feast on his skin. That part craved the kill and wanted to savor it. Another part of him wanted to flee. Hide from his need to cause pain.

Henry could smell misery wafting from the asshole, mixed with the musk of his body spray. Torment spread like seeds in a meadow. Weeping women and casualties of cruelty, careless and as frequent as breath. Henry no longer wanted to hide.

The asshole deserved to die. Henry deserved to enjoy the slaughter.

The blonde screamed from behind, as if she thought Henry might be doing something bad or not in her best interests. He turned to her, snarling without meaning to. "It's okay, I won't hurt you."

He turned back to the asshole and punched him in the face.

The asshole screamed in pain, blood running into his hair from a split in his eyebrow. He blinked his eyes into focus on Henry's looming face. "Who the fuck are you?"

"Right now, I'm the monster that's going to figure out the most painful bones to break. Tomorrow, I'm a story she'll tell that no one will believe." Henry nodded toward the blonde with the red face and winked.

"Who *are* you?" the asshole spat. "Isn't it sort of a waste if you don't say? Someone sent you here to get to me, right? Don't you got a message? Ain't I supposed to know *why* I'm getting killed?"

Henry laughed, though it wasn't quite like any sound he'd ever made. A low rumble, thick with cruelty. He was cynical, not unkind. At least he didn't used to be. Now, looking at the vermin, Henry felt nothing. Indifferent.

Wanting the asshole to choke on his final breath and in a hurry to make that happen.

"You're going to die for making her cry." Henry nodded toward the blonde again.

He grabbed the asshole's left arm, dropping a knee on the guy's heaving chest. Henry held him by the wrist and rolled his short sleeve up near the shoulder, ready to shatter it at the elbow. A tattoo emerged from the folded fabric, and Henry nearly dropped the limb in surprise.

The asshole's tattoo was exactly like the one Tiny Eyes had sported. More ornate, an intricate twisted vine as a circle with a similar vine shaped as an *F* and *C inside* the circle. The design had jagged roots at the bottom, an explosion of chaos erupting from the top, and two neat bands with tiny *X*s inside them on either side. Henry turned his eyes from the asshole's arm, and all the brambles and branches drawn upon it. They were made from tiny words, and Henry was certain those tiny words would make him crazy if he forced his eyes to read them.

He snarled, squeezing the asshole by his forearm. His claws sprang out, driving into the skin and muscle, and rivulets of blood flowed as the asshole hissed in pain. Henry thrust his face toward the man's wide eyes. "What is this tattoo? Where did you get it?"

The asshole smiled, happy that Henry finally wanted to play.

"Fuck you."

"Really? That's how you're gonna talk to the man who holds your life in his hands? You've either got balls of steel or a brain of rust. You've got one chance to live. What does this fucking tattoo mean, and where did it come from?"

"I had it inked when I went to Fuck You Island.

Remember? About two years back, after your mom held a fleet week special?"

"That was your chance," Henry growled, jumping to his feet and slinging the asshole over his shoulder like a sleeping bag.

He ran toward the window, swinging the asshole from his shoulder like a batter trying for a home run.

The asshole crashed into the drywall, rattling the glass in the window when he slid down the wall and landed in a curled puddle. Henry grabbed him by the ankle and ducked out the window to the fire escape. He scampered up the building, dragging the asshole behind him. At the top, he threw him on the roof before jumping the final few feet and landing in a crouch in the shadows.

"One last chance!" Henry thundered.

The asshole skittered across the rooftop, backward on his palms. Henry took the retreat as rejection. He charged as the asshole turned to crawl on all fours.

Henry grabbed the man again by the shoulders, pulling him into his chest and snaking his arm under the asshole's chin. He laced his fingers through the greasy mop on the asshole's head, and carried him to the edge of the roof.

Henry didn't know if the asshole's hair would hold, but he sure as fuck was gonna try. "Last chance," he repeated. "Where did you get the tattoo?"

Henry was shocked by the asshole's laughter. "Go ahead and drop me, dicktip. I ain't saying shit."

Henry dug his chin into the guy's neck, pressing his lips to the asshole's ear. "Where'd you get the tattoo?"

The man laughed like he didn't care that he was seconds from death. "The world is nothing without chaos," he cackled. "Chaos is oxygen to progress. Go ahead and kill me. If you have the balls."

The man's cackling ate into his heart. The memory of

him standing over the woman, raising his hand for another blow. Henry's anger rose to fill his vision with red. He tried to resist, but couldn't. The anger pitched into rage.

"Fuck it," Henry said.

He loosened his fist and let the asshole go, down five stories and into a splat. Henry leapt down from the rooftop after the man's broken body, and landed a few feet away. "It was a simple question," he said, as the impact from the landing shot through his body, sending a jolt through his spine that he saw as a flare of red light in his skull. He kneeled, checking to make sure the asshole was dead.

From that high up, the asshole hadn't stood a chance. Henry touched the fallen body from top to bottom, marveling at how it seemed softer inside. Like a bag of pudding. He stared until the fourth-floor scream turned his eyes to the asshole's girlfriend. Maybe it was his wife. Henry shrugged as she leaned out the window, holding her cell phone. She took a picture of Henry standing over her ex's corpse.

The blonde could live, but her phone was his.

He leapt to the side of the neighboring building, and hurled himself across the alley onto the fire escape across the way. He started to climb, then saw the light swirling in the sky.

So beautiful.

Henry stopped climbing and turned, staring into the light.

Don't look! Turn away!

He couldn't. It was too much. The angel spread its wings and descended from the blanket of stars.

The light filled him with the glee. Like a hit of acid. An opiate's euphoria.

Oh, God. So much bliss.

Henry lifted his hands in acceptance and stepped

toward the light. His foot hit air, and he tipped forward, falling from the fire escape.

Wind whistled in his ears as he fell. With the light behind him, he could focus on the alley's shadows. The darkness that held his salvation. He plunged into the black and flew through the city, hiding from the light, running without thought, never realizing he was aiming for the most dangerous place in any world for him to go.

Chapter Seventeen

HENRY DIDN'T REALIZE where he was running until he was there, staring at the front of his six-million-dollar mansion, wondering for the thousandth time if there was a reason everything in his life had gone to shit.

He stood for a minute before spotting Ezra in the shadows beneath one of the large trees in his front yard.

Henry was surprised to see his Lexus in the carport and wondered how it had come back. Boothe must've been responsible, covering Henry's fuck-up before the Lexus wound up on a police report. Idiot. Should have thought about the problems the missing Lexus might have caused if he hadn't returned before Sam. Next time, he'd have to find another way to keep up.

Ezra stepped toward Henry.

"How long have you been there?"

The goll said, "Since about three seconds before you."

Henry looked at Ezra with a sort of reluctant gratitude. "Good job."

"You're not supposed to be here."

"Yeah, about that. Tough shit. I'll be back here a lot,

and that's non-negotiable as a cover charge. So, any way you can see to keeping that from your Master Boothe? Or is this destined to be a problem between us?"

"Sorry, Master Henry, but you aren't supposed to be here."

"That's not really a yes or a no, hobbit. Whether Boothe likes it or not, I'm asking you if we can keep it between us."

"You should not be so insulting when begging for favors, Master Henry." Ezra lowered his head, then stopped like he'd reached the end of his thought. In a mumble he added, "Master Boothe knows what he must know without me."

"Good then, we're on the same page. At least it won't be coming from *you*."

The goll agreed to no such thing, but Henry still hoped he'd bought some silence. He wondered how Boothe knew as much as he did, and if the demon became aware of events only after they happened or as they were unfolding.

Was it possible to see ahead of time?

Does Boothe have any idea what I'm about to do?

Henry hoped to God not. Otherwise, he'd show up and stop him before he could do it. No way would Boothe be happy with what Henry was planning.

"Any clue about the alarm code?" Henry pulled the oversized key from his hoodie's side pocket.

Ezra sighed, looking down at his clawed feet. "Seven-Two-Three-Three."

Maybe *he* sensed what Henry was about to do. "Thanks. Would've been cool if you'd let me know the last time. Would have saved me a heap of trouble."

"You're not supposed to be here," Ezra repeated like a child trying to enforce an absent parent's rule on a sibling.

Henry ignored the goll, let himself inside the house,

killed the alarm, then crept from shadow to shadow in search of Samantha. He finally found her sitting alone in the movie room, drowning in many shades of misery.

A stack of Blu-rays was piled beside her. Each disc a movie she and Henry had seen together. None of his favorites. *Or* hers. The tiny mountain was made from only movies they loved in tandem. *Kill Bill (One and Two)*. *The Matrix*. The first one. The only one that mattered. *The Sixth Sense*, *Fight Club*, *The Incredibles*, and maybe twenty others. None was in the player. Sam was spinning heartache instead.

On the screen, as wide as the wall, was the haunting evidence of the life Henry's family once lived. She was streaming from iTunes, so Henry was clueless to what scene would appear next, but Samantha had no shortage of torment. The clips came at random, since the one where Amélie was pirouetting across the stage during her second grade dance recital was finishing just as Henry entered the movie room, and now they were a minute into the *Daddy Flying to Las Angeles* video, which made Henry want to cry every time he saw it. The only thing worse than Sam's face in that clip was Amélie's.

"When are you coming back home, Daddy?" she asked.

"Soon, baby, I swear. As soon as I can."

"What happens if you get lost?"

Henry wasn't sure where the fear had come from, but just before that trip, his baby girl became obsessed with knowing where he and Sam were at all times. She was so afraid that they'd either get lost or lose her.

"I won't get lost," he said. "And if I ever do, I'll always be able to find you."

"How do you know?"

"Because I love you so very much, and that love is like

an arrow. It will always lead me back to you." Henry felt corny at the time, and downright prescient in reflection while watching from the shadows.

Samantha clicked *Stop* and cried out, grabbing a wad of tissues beside her on the couch and blowing her nose.

Beside the pile of Blu-rays stood an empty bottle of wine. Cheap shit from Trader Joe's, not the good stuff she'd been buying since Henry had landed the deal. Not a good sign. Sam loved good wine, but part, if not most, of her still felt guilty when spending large sums of money. Especially on something like wine, which she referred to as her recipe for expensive piss. Cheap shit meant she planned to drink by the gallon.

Which was even more worrisome with the bottle of OxyContin beside it.

Henry stared at Samantha from his shadows, helpless as she picked up the bottle, shaking who-knew-how-many pills into her palm, then slapping them past her lips and into her mouth.

Henry wondered how long she'd been crying. Her face was so red and splotchy, and her eyes were bleached of their twinkle.

He couldn't stand seeing her suffer, couldn't allow it to happen. Not a few feet away, where he could end her torment with a sentence or a touch. He stood in the shadows for another minute, pushing his arms through the dark, almost daring Samantha to see him, most of him hoping she would see him and draw him from the shadows to comfort her.

Would she see him for who he once was? The man who loved her back even when she was broken? Or would she see the monster he had become?

Go to her. Let her know you're here.

Fuck Boothe. Let him do his worst!

He can't steal this moment.

It wasn't fair to leave her in anguish, not when he could soothe her pain. She didn't have to be alone. Henry stepped toward Samantha, shedding shadows like dead skin.

I'm here. Look up.

Please, just look up, Sam.

Then she did, her eyes opening wide in surprise.

Their eyes locked, and fear, joy, and a hundred other feelings swelled in Henry's heart as he approached her.

He would've told her everything, but before he managed another step, or said a single word, he was gone.

Henry's body hummed, vibrating with a screaming frequency that ripped him from one spot in the universe and dropped him into another. He blinked, back in the shitty apartment where he'd ended the asshole an hour before.

Boothe stood over the asshole's girlfriend. The blonde who had taken the photo. He stood with one foot on either side of her dead, crumpled body. Henry screamed, not at the dead girl beneath Boothe, but at being taken away from Sam just seconds from contact.

"Why?" Henry yelled, though he quickly realized Boothe might not know where he'd been, and he should aim his anger at the present scene to perhaps conceal what would surely piss the demon off. He shook off his usual blur and disorientation. "What the fuck, Boothe?"

"Like so many things since we met, this is your fault, not mine."

Henry wasn't sure if he was getting scolded for going home, for stepping from the shadows to speak with Samantha, or, somehow, for the dead body lying cold between the demon's feet.

"Wanna give me a fucking hint? I'm way better at taking my spanking when I know what it's for."

"You let her take a picture of you, Henry. I told you, explicitly, that you are never, ever to be seen. I've cleaned your messes a few times now, but I might not be there next time. Believe me, you'll learn far more from the experience if I'm not, but then I won't get my part from our little arrangement. That doesn't seem fair to me. Does it to you?"

Something about how Boothe carelessly stepped over the blonde's body sent a flush of anger through Henry. He flashed back to her terrified face as the asshole's hand hovered above her, ready to strike. Her eyes had gone from surprise to horror to gratitude as Henry destroyed him.

He turned on Boothe and screamed. "How could you kill her? She was innocent and didn't deserve to die! I thought we weren't supposed to take innocent lives!"

Henry wanted to scream louder, to beat at the demon's chest and break him to nothing, like he had broken the asshole. Instead, he only muttered, "She was innocent," over and over.

"You're right, Henry. She *was* innocent, but I didn't do this. *You're* responsible."

"No! *You* killed her!" Henry roared.

"Maybe you shouldn't have been in such a hurry to get home to your wife. I told you not to return, and yet, what did you do the second I turned my back? You went running to Samantha like some lovesick puppy."

"She's my *wife!* Do you expect me to suddenly forget our life together and sit back and pretend like I can't see her? She's a wreck, Boothe. She's on the verge of self-destruction, and I'll be damned if I'm gonna sit back and do nothing!"

"I told you not to go," Boothe said, calmly.

Henry exploded. "My *wife!* Maybe if you ever cared about anyone other than yourself and your stupid fucking *rules,* you might understand. Maybe I'm not human anymore, but I'm not dead inside like you."

Something flashed across Boothe's face, an expression Henry had yet to see in their short time together, and one he definitely didn't understand. It was almost as if the demon's face displayed a new emotion. Something between rage, anger, and a resigned breed of defeat.

He didn't ponder it long, because before he knew it Boothe grabbed Henry by the throat and snarled, "Never speak to me that way again, Henry, or you will spend an eternity in Hell getting raped by Hellounds with no sun to ever set on your torment. Do you understand me?"

The demon's hands bent into claws, digging deep into his throat. He fought for the air to answer. Suddenly, the discomfort of vibrating into a different plane folded through Henry's body. He found himself able to scream as he opened his eyes back in Purgatory.

Boothe wasn't there.

"Hello!" Henry cried into the silence.

Broken city and ashen sky were everywhere, their colors all missing.

Henry screamed until he thought of Amélie, and remembered Nowhere was exactly where he had wanted to go.

He headed down the broken road in search of his daughter, hoping to God Boothe didn't find her first.

Chapter Eighteen

HENRY STUMBLED THROUGH NOWHERE, walking in circles while cursing Heaven above, hating Boothe for dropping him back into the soul-twisting vacuum. He had to find Amélie, but the world around him was a dark haze.

Amélie had probably gone toward the garden, since that's what Henry told her to do. He couldn't find it, though he looked everywhere, trying to think of anything besides Amélie crying, lost and searching for safety.

He spun, frantically looking around as his eyes begged for color. Green, blue, lavender like he'd seen growing in long rows around the table. Anything other than the fog of nothing.

Thunder rumbled above, bringing a cool breeze which threatened rain. The thought of even drizzle in Nowhere frightened Henry, though he wasn't sure why.

He pressed on into the darkness, chasing instinct rather than memory. Eventually, the haze dimmed, giving way to light in the distance, gradually growing brighter until Henry blinked in disbelief at the giant Tree's glowing outline. He ran until reaching the garden, ignoring its majesty as he raced forward, unwilling to allow its beauty to awe or overwhelm him.

"Amélie!"

The Tree was different. Taller and wider. Blacker somehow, despite its glowing leaves. The long table was still suited for one hundred, but held none.

He screamed "Amélie!" until his throat was raw, turning in a full circle, eyes scanning the thick mist darkening the garden for any sign of movement. Something behind him hissed. The rustle of fabric. Henry turned as a shape formed in the mist.

Randall, not Amélie, stared at him as though he'd been watching for a while. A small smile lifting the corner of his lips. His pewter hair and white robe swayed in a breeze that seemed to follow at his back.

"Good to see you again, Henry Black."

Something about Randall angered Henry. He had no idea what. Maybe because he should have done more to stop him from accepting Boothe's offer. It could've also been his smug judgment, or simply the white of his robes.

"Have you seen my daughter, Amélie? She was here, calling, begging me to find her."

"Yes." Randall nodded. "I've seen her. I tried to help, but she was too frightened to listen. I told her it was okay, and that her father would want her to trust me. She didn't believe me, and ran back toward The Forgotten."

"The Forgotten?"

"Yes, the Forgotten. Lost souls are stuck, often for centuries, many losing their minds until what used to be human is putty."

Henry swallowed. "The place with the crumbling buildings and people in windows? Looks like a bomb exploded a thousand years ago and all the road crews are on strike?"

"Yes."

"Oh, God. I've gotta find her!"

"No!" Randall's hands flew to Henry's shoulders. "If you go inside, you'll never leave."

"I'm not abandoning my daughter in that broken pile of Hell. Besides, I've already been there once and found my way back. I'll do it again." He turned from Randall, even though he had no idea how to reach the Forgotten. There was nothing but darkness around them.

"You are not an innocent, Henry. Only the mind of an innocent is safe from being haunted by their sins inside the Forgotten. She's a child, so she'll be safe for a while. And far less likely to get lost."

"But *I've* already made it through," Henry repeated. "And I have to find her."

"That was before your transformation. Enter now, and you'll be lost within a day. Even if you find Amélie, you'll be of no use. And might be a danger."

Henry refused to listen. "Is there a *chance* she could get stuck? A chance she could lose her mind?"

"Of course." Randall nodded. "Nothing exists without chance."

"Then you've gotta show me where it is."

"I will tell you how to reach the Forgotten ... if you tell me what Boothe has you doing on Earth."

"What?" Henry was reminded of every night club manager he'd ever dealt with.

You do this if you want that.

"What business is Boothe having you tend to?"

Henry shifted, uncertain what he should, or even *could*, say. Boothe wouldn't want him talking to Randall. Yet, if the man in black was bad, odds and common sense agreed — the man in white was good.

"Can you tell me where the Forgotten is first?"

"Yes, but I won't. I prefer a show of faith from you, Henry." He smiled. "Not an unreasonable request."

"Boothe is helping me find the men who murdered my daughter."

"And murdered *you*, Henry," Randall reminded gently.

"Yeah, and me. And raped my wife," he said, tasting the hate on his tongue.

Randall winced as if Henry had used the C-word to his grandma, in church.

"I'm going to kill all three of them."

Randall stared at Henry, saying nothing. His eyes broadcast a bottomless sorrow into Henry's soul. Not at him, but *for* him. Henry felt rage rather than comfort.

Who are you to judge me, you condescending cocksucker?

"Are you sure you're using the right word? There is a difference between *help* and coercion."

"Thanks, professor, but I don't see it," Henry sneered. "No such thing as coercion when the coerced is locked, loaded, and ready to pay these fuckers back."

"You're weaving a rope, Henry, thread by thread, tying your future to a fate you're blind to. Consequence is bred by your *choices*. Tie yourself to what's *right* … or to an anchor around your ankle, dragging you to Hell. How do you want to spend your eternity?"

"Last I heard, free will didn't cover *shit happens*. I'll link the fucking chain as long as I need to, until it gets me where I need to go. Boothe's done more for me and my family than *you* have."

"You can't trust him. Boothe, like all demons, will wrap your neck in silk so you're half asleep before seeing the leash. His insides are twisted, and he twists yours further with every lie. He will say whatever he needs if it will get someone to help him, and he will *omit* that which does not serve his cause."

"Get someone to help him do what?"

Randall was quiet. Then, in barely a whisper, "I cannot say."

"Can't or *won't?*" Henry glared at him.

"Both." He held Henry's stare. "There are rules around what each of us can and should know."

Henry wanted to find whoever made these so-called *rules* and wear his skin as a dress. "Again with the fucking rules?" he barked, somewhere between a laugh and a yell. "What's with you people and your rules and all the secret-decoder-ring bullshit? Can't you ever speak clearly?"

"That isn't how it works here." Randall moved his eyes to the sky. "Or up there. Some things are a matter of faith. You must trust me so you can turn from the darkness. I can help you more than any demon, and will, *if* you allow it."

Randall's smile was an invitation, but Henry ignored it.

"Sorry, Mr. Man-in-White, I've never done well with the 'I'll gladly pay you Tuesday for a hamburger today' bullshit. I'm not trying to be a dick, but your God didn't do much to encourage my faith. It'd be a *lot* fucking easier to devote myself to something with fewer contradictions, evil assholes, and slick salesmen acting on His behalf. Even people who *want* to believe can't ask legitimate questions without getting slapped on the hand and being told to *have faith.* People aren't wired like that, Randall. Shit has to make sense. We need *answers,* not *faith.*"

"Answers are there, if you're willing to look."

Henry suppressed a laugh. "Great, more mystical mumbo-jumbo. You want people to believe in God, tell Him to get His ass to Times Square and use one of those giant light-up billboards so everyone catches a glimpse of Him."

"You think God should light a room with a star?"

"I'm not saying I don't believe in God. I'm saying He

has a PR problem. Even if I could cross my heart and hope to die right here, it'd be ridiculous for me to deny His existence after all that's happened, especially since I was nearly murdered by your *angels.*"

Randall seemed surprised for the first time since Henry had met him. "You were almost killed? By angels?"

"Yeah." Henry shrugged. "These fucking glowing assholes in the sky, right outside the church. They had massive wings, and swords and nets."

"And they saw you?" Randall's eyes appeared to measure Henry's words.

"Saw me? They were *hunting* me!"

"You must stay here in Nowhere, Henry," Randall said, his voice uncharacteristically firm. "Do *not* return to Earth."

"That an order?"

"No." Randall shook his head. "Of course not. I can't order you to do anything. But I care what happens, and your return to Earth won't be good."

"Boothe already warned me about the angels. Said they were called Trackers, and that they hunt demons on Earth."

"Did he also tell you that once they see you, they'll never stop trying to find you?"

"Sure did. But so what? If I'm not afraid of a demon, I sure as shit won't be scared off by an angel."

"You weren't frightened?"

"Okay, yeah, I might've been a *little* scared, but that won't keep me from doing what needs to be done. I'm certainly not in Purgatory because I *ran.* I'm here because I'm stuck. Boothe was pissed, so he put me on timeout like I'm a fucking toddler."

Randall winced at Henry's language.

The F-word that broke the angel's back.

"Sorry," Henry said, almost meaning it. "Look, I've answered all of your questions, and I need to find Amélie. Are you going to help me, or not?"

Randall grabbed Henry's shoulders again, gently. "Please, when Boothe returns you to Earth, which he certainly will since he needs you to finish what's already started … you *must* tell him you refuse."

"But I don't," Henry said. Curious, though, he asked, "Can I really do that? Let's say I tell Boothe I refuse. Will he really let me go, or will he send me back here? What happens after I say *sayonara?*"

"Boothe will send you back here. But here is better than *there*, Henry. Refuse him now. You can't afford to wait."

"Why?"

"Because you can't refuse Boothe once you've finished his task."

"I've already killed *one* of the men. Does that matter?"

"There are three men, correct?"

Henry nodded, unsure whether he'd told Randall, or if both he and Boothe knew the details of his death.

"I don't know. But I suggest you stop. Before you are swallowed by the dark and it's too late to turn back."

Henry paused, considering Randall's words, wondering if the man in white was steering him in the best direction or telling him things to foster confusion. "Boothe's a stuck-up asshole, sure, but he's hardly the personification of evil."

"That's the horrible truth, Henry." Randall's smile was thin. "Evil isn't always obvious, and it's often attractive enough to turn even the strong into an eager accomplice."

Henry hated himself for asking, and Randall for making him doubt, but he couldn't throttle his follow-up question. "How do I stand up to Boothe then, assuming I wanted to? I have no leverage."

Randall's smile finally thickened. "Yes, leverage. You do need that. I can't tell you what Boothe wants most, but you *can* ask him yourself."

"No dice. I tried, but Boothe was vague as always."

"He was vague because *you* were. Ask him about Maria."

"Maria?" Henry echoed, fighting his smile. It felt like Randall had handed him a sword.

"Yes, Maria. Now, go to your daughter. Follow the sound of her voice."

The wind whistled with Amélie's cry. "Daddy?"

But Henry had already turned toward the sound of his daughter's voice and the broken city surfacing through the lingering mist.

Henry ran, leaving Randall behind.

Chapter Nineteen

GOING ANYWHERE in Nowhere seemed to take forever, but Henry managed to reach the broken city in less than an eternity.

On the outskirts of the crumbled ruins, crawling from a shattered window on the bottom floor, spilled an ancient man in a tattered blue uniform — old, faded, and with a few tarnished brass buttons.

From the little Henry knew of Civil War history, the soldier's coat cast him as Union Infantry. A deep chill frosted his insides as he looked at the man's ancient uniform. An icy reminder of Nowhere's spongy time.

How can something look old in a place where time doesn't move?

Henry approached the old man. Up close he wasn't ancient, but only slightly older than Henry. He took a step toward the soldier. "Hello?"

The man started, and turned to Henry, eyes wide with surprise and laced in a different fear than anything Henry had ever seen on Earth.

"You coming or going?" Henry gestured at the miles of rubble.

The soldier followed Henry's gaze. "Just leaving."

Henry held out his hand. "Name's Henry, Henry Black."

The soldier stared at Henry's empty palm for several seconds, then added his own. "Duffy. Jason Duffy." His voice sounded old but unused.

"Good to meet you, Duffy. Even here." Henry let silence settle between them, for longer than was smart with Amélie in earshot. "Can I ask for your help?"

"Of course," Duffy said, almost eager. "Though I don't know how much help I'll be. Been ages since I was a help to anyone."

"I'm looking for my daughter."

Amélie's cry cut through their conversation. "Daddy!" Henry called back, and Amélie screamed louder, "Daddy!"

"Where are you?" Henry shouted but heard nothing back. "Amélie!"

Still nothing.

Duffy brightened and started to speak, pulling Henry's attention. "Sure, I saw a girl. She was running right into Nowhere, not even slowing to look at the lurkers."

"The lurkers?"

"That's what I call 'em. Lurkers." Duffy pointed up toward the haunted eyes staring from the countless broken windows in the row of decrepit buildings facing them, reminding Henry of the horror waiting in the city.

"When?"

Duffy scratched his head.

"When did you see her?" Henry urged.

"Didn't seem like too long ago, though I'm not sure how much my time can be trusted."

"Did you see where she went?"

Duffy nodded, pointing toward what was likely once a

neat row of five buildings but which now seemed to be growing crooked and sideways, sprouting from the rubble like stray teeth in need of dental care. "She went there."

"Do you know which one?"

Duffy opened his mouth to answer, but then shook his head. He stared at the middle building, the shortest of the five with only two stories. Once his eyes locked on the ruins, he couldn't free his gaze. He mumbled broken syllables, speaking in tongues of lunacy before collapsing into a manic sort of laugh. Drool glistened in the scraggle of hair on his chin.

Henry tried getting the man to say more, anything that might move him closer to finding Amélie, but Duffy offered him nothing. He threw his arms out in frustration and stood, covering his eyes with his hands. He turned to stumble toward the twisted city, and the soldier reached out and grabbed him by the shoulder.

Duffy's laughter seized with a snarl. "Where's my Annabel?"

Henry stared, unsure what to say, or what to think about the wild fire now lighting Duffy's eyes.

"You did it! *You* took my Annabel!"

The soldier leapt on Henry, beating at his chest with hard-clenched fists as he screamed a string of nonsense and curses, showering his face with spit. The only intelligible word was *Annabel*. Over and over.

He tried to push Duffy away, working not to hurt him, but he finally accepted reality and drove a fist into Duffy's stomach. The soldier doubled over with a surprised *WHOOF*. Henry followed it with left to the temple. Duffy dropped straight down onto a pile of broken rubble, wheezing in shock and pain, every breath sending a puff of dust into the air.

Henry stood from the fallen soldier and looked back

toward the middle building. A flicker of white, fluffy like Amélie's favorite jacket. She had called it her *cloud*. A swirling flash across a doorway.

"I'm coming, Amélie!" He screamed, running toward the building and making it a dozen steps before the city folded in on itself. Boothe's vibrating current hummed through his body, and he was abruptly ripped from Nowhere again.

Chapter Twenty

"BOOTHE!" Henry cried as he flickered from one plane to the other, blinking to find himself back in the demon's apartment. Still running, Henry slammed into the kitchen island and crashed to the floor. He leapt back to his feet, a growl rumbling from his chest. "Why in the Hell did you do that?"

"What?" Boothe raised his eyebrows. "Send you there or bring you back?"

"Both," Henry snarled.

"I need you to drop the petulant child routine, Henry. Save it for your revenge. I'm certainly not in the mood." A deep line formed between Boothe's eyebrows. His shoulders rose with a deep breath. He looked at the ceiling then dropped his eyes back down to Henry. Blue had turned black. "You disobeyed me, Henry. I tolerate what I must, but never that. Between the two of us, *I* am in charge. That isn't up for debate and never will be. Listen to me and enjoy your revenge, or I'll return you to Nowhere."

"No, you won't," Henry said, standing straighter.

Boothe rocked back, tilting his head and raising an eyebrow.

Henry stood his ground. "You need me to murder more than I need to kill."

Boothe smiled, but for the first time the expression seemed uncomfortable on his face. Like he was testing the fit.

"I said our goals were aligned, not that you're the only person who can help me score mine. Sorry if I'm souring the time you've poured into Project Self-Esteem, Henry, but you are *not* unique. The need for revenge is a base human emotion. I can spit and find a thousand souls more bitter than you who would not only love to kill, but would beg for the same opportunity I'm handing to you. I thought you'd *appreciate* the chance to avenge what happened to your wife and daughter."

Henry stepped toward Boothe, emboldened by his conversation with Randall.

"Then why didn't you spit and find someone else? You don't hear me begging, do you?" He took another step, as if daring the demon. "No, it's *me* you need. Something about me specifically helps you get what you want, either better or faster."

Boothe stayed silent, smiling and saying nothing, his hooded eyes unfazed. Henry wondered if he should mention Maria, but bit his tongue.

No, not yet. Don't play that card until needed. Piss him off and he could kill you, or throw you in Purgatory, Hell, or God knows where.

Just.

Shut.

Up.

"I like you, Henry. Despite everything, I truly do. And you're absolutely right, there *is* something special about you, something unique. But as much as I love unique, I never confuse it with irreplaceable. Neither should you." He smiled. "There is nothing in you so rare that it couldn't be replaced or improved. As much as you may refuse to believe it, I'm quite loyal. I chose you and am invested enough to help you finish the job. We can part ways then, and you'll never have to look at me ever again. Do as you wish. Stay here and keep the apartment, or go home and wallow in invisible misery with a wife who will never love you again. I care not at all."

Henry thought of Amélie and Nowhere, then Heaven and Samantha.

As if to make Henry wonder once more whether his thoughts could be read by a demon, Boothe added, "Or return to Nowhere and see if Randall can get you into Heaven with your daughter, so the two of you can wait for Mommy together. Again, I won't care … *after* we finish what we started."

He held out his hand, waiting for Henry.

If Randall was telling the truth, then Boothe was a liar.

I kill the three men, I don't get into Heaven. And you know it!

Yet Henry said nothing, preferring Boothe remain clueless about what was nested in his heart and mind. He took the demon's hand and they vigorously shook. Boothe's smile thinned to a pressing line, and he held his grip, squeezing the moment into uncomfortable silence. Henry's skin felt coated in slime, until he finally broke free of his grip.

Boothe said, "Good, we're agreed. There will be no next time. Violate the rules and I take you to Nowhere. Next time, you'll stay longer."

"Longer than what?"

Boothe laughed. "Longer than the three weeks you spent *this* time."

"Three weeks?" Henry shook his head, blinking in confusion

"Yes." Boothe smiled. "Time flies when you're going Nowhere."

Though Boothe tried to bait him, Henry strangled his rage, pushing it down into the pit of his stomach where the bile roiled and the acid rose into his throat. He swallowed then drew a deep breath. "How's Samantha?"

"She's fine. As promised, Ezra is still looking after her. I won't break my commitment to you, Henry. Not unless you give me a reason."

Henry hated the fucking demon. The smooth voice that filled him with helplessness. The unrelenting drip of his will against Henry's resolve. Eroding him away like sand.

"Get some rest, Henry. That's one thing you're clearly not doing enough of. When you wake, follow the sorrow like a wolf to your prey."

Boothe disappeared from the apartment, and Henry went to the California king then collapsed on the mattress.

He hoped to God Randall was right and Amélie was safe. He could do nothing to help her unless he told Boothe what happened and begged to go back. But Randall and Pastor Owen had warned him against trusting Boothe.

Even if he *could* trust the demon, the last thing Henry wanted to give him was another weakness to exploit.

More sand to wash away.

More …

And then he was snoring.

Chapter Twenty-One

Henry rose in torment.

Pain is only a thought.

The same something was wrong with his body as when he woke to the asshole's girlfriend screaming. Like then, Henry was starving for sorrow.

His throat was Gobi dry. He went to the kitchen, grabbed a glass, and set it under the ice-maker, wincing as the ice clinked into the bottom. Henry filled it to the top with water, gulping it empty in seconds.

He swallowed a refill, draining the glass a second time before slamming it on the counter with more force than he intended and accidentally shattering the glass into shards. He lifted his right hand, staring at the blood, black and sticky between his gnarled fingers. Knobs of bone for knuckles. Shining black nails, thickening into points.

Henry ran his hand under the water, then wiped himself dry on his pants. He growled and ran to the window, then lifted the sash, climbed through the opening, leapt to the fire escape and across to the pipe on the other side. He slid to the concrete, hitting it with a now-familiar jolt through his body.

He pricked his ears and heard the colors of a metropolitan sorrow. Felt the brushes of pain painting the night.

Henry ran into the darkness, racing four blocks before he found the loudest of all the cries — an old man with his hands raised, standing a few feet from a young mugger, both beside a reeking open dumpster.

In Henry's eyes, the mugger was a thief and a monster, delighting in the old man's fear. Worthy of Hell.

Henry burst out of the shadow, suddenly standing six inches in front of the mugger. "Whatcha doin'?" He grinned and spread his hands.

The thug cried out and bobbled the gun, barely managing to hang on to it. He lifted the shaking barrel to aim at Henry's face.

Henry laughed. "And what are you gonna do with that?"

The mugger did exactly what Henry expected and pulled the trigger.

But he wasn't fast enough.

The instant Henry saw the mugger twitch, his arm shot out and slapped the gun into the air. The mugger cried out, his whimper similar to the old man's. He fell back a few steps before losing his balance and crashing into a filthy puddle.

"D-d-don't hurt me," the mugger stuttered.

Henry laughed again, enjoying every molecule of the moment. "Begging *already?*"

The old man retreated into the shadows behind Henry. He lowered his arms when his back hit the wall, then stared with narrowed eyes, as if curious to see what might happen to his attacker. Henry met the old man's eyes.

He reminded Henry of his grandfather. A proud Irishman who fought in the war and took shit from no one. He stayed that way until his pride had been devastated by age, body and soul. Twisting him into a decrepit skeleton, with paper-thin skin stretched across his face, linked to machines that turned a slow death into lingering agony.

Henry remembered his grandfather's anguish, his feeble fingers shaking as they lifted to touch what was only in his memory. It had made Henry see the world's inequity, for punishing a hero with unending Hell and indignity.

No man should have to face such horrors.

And no man should be mugged by some punk fuck in a filthy alley.

Henry smiled at the old man, even though his mouth was masked by the shadow of his hood.

Don't worry. I got this.

He reached down, grabbed the mugger by his collar, and slammed him against the dumpster.

"You like scaring people?"

The mugger added a shaking head to his whimper. "No!"

"That's not gonna keep you alive, asshole!" Spittle flew from Henry's mouth into the mugger's eye. "Lie to me again, and I'll ask the guy behind me what he thinks I should do with you. Do you like making people afraid?"

"Yes, yes, yes," the mugger sobbed, hitching his breath and sniffing like a child. He was almost too pathetic to kill.

"Are you afraid of *me* right now?" Henry bellowed from the bottom of his gut.

The mugger froze, staring at Henry's mouth in horror.

Henry threw back his hood and thrust his face toward the mugger's eyes with a growl.

The mugger screamed in Henry's face. His breath carried the sweet taste of his terror.

The old man's answer must've been the same as the mugger's. He found a sudden burst of energy, turned on his heel and launched himself back through the alley.

No witnesses!

Henry didn't care. The man was old and didn't have a camera phone. Who cared if he told some people about the guy in jeans and a hoodie. The old man had only seen the back of his head, and a demon's voice was hard to identify.

Henry's hand tightened around the mugger's neck, his fingers pressing deeper into the man's flesh as he lifted him up and slammed him into the brick. The man shrieked in pain, and a surge of energy coursed through Henry, a hundred times better than the best of his drugs. Flavors exploding across his palate. Aromas rising into his nostrils.

"Ah, that's grrreat!" Henry yelled. Like Tony the fucking Tiger. He roared, pulling the mugger back like his body was an empty sack. He launched his cargo forward, smashing the mugger flat against the wall, driving a fist into his chest.

Something broke under his knuckles, squishing past his fingers as his hand made contact with the wall. Henry pulled his hand out of the mugger's broken body, and the stinking heap slid to the ground. Henry bent and grabbed the mugger's ankle. He took a breath filled with the power of his kill then hurled the body into the open dumpster.

Power coursed through him, begging for use. He spun and sped into the night, swimming through the shadows like a shark. He ran blind until instinct became an arrow directing him from one of The Burg's points of pain to the next.

The night's second mugger also attacked the elderly, this time a woman. That alone would've sent Henry into a rage. He warned her before turning his attention to the mugger. "Run as fast and as far as you can. Even if you hear him screaming".

She nodded, thanking Henry while trying not to cry, taking several steps back before finally turning and racing away.

Unlike the first mugger, the second showed no fear. Probably too high to think straight or too stupid to recognize a demon and his inevitable death. Henry barreled into him, and the mugger sailed through the air to land on his back. Henry rushed across the alley to plant a foot on his chest, but the man only stared with a derisive smile.

He took the mugger's indifference personally, as though someone were sitting in the front row of one of his shows refusing to laugh. The man's silence seemed especially bold since he had no leverage, lying flat on his back with Henry's heel pressing into his sternum.

The mugger growled and spit, even though the spittle only managed an inch from his lips before splatting back on his cheek. He finally yelled, "Who do you think you are, motherfucker?"

Henry wanted the second mugger to see what he was too stupid to fear, so he lowered his hood and showed him a nightmare with a face.

The mugger laughed.

Henry had no choice but to assume something was wrong with the asshole's eyes, so he mashed his thumbs into the mugger's sockets and turned them into two tiny bowls of pink jelly.

Finally the man screamed, arms and legs kicking out. Thrashing as if controlled by electricity.

Henry grinned. "Oh, didn't like that last one, buddy? That's a shame. *That* one usually kills. Get it? *Kills?*"

The mugger bucked under Henry's foot. Henry felt a rush of the man's fear. The excitement of the kill.

"Damn." Henry shook his head. "Some people just don't get sophisticated humor."

He snapped the man's neck and waited until he stopped moving.

The first encounters came close to each other, but Henry had to growl through another couple of hours while waiting for the next one. A guy setting up shop and selling crack on the corner.

Before the dealer, Henry ran into a pair of taggers defacing a building with crude slogans. Graffiti was a blight in any neighborhood, but not worthy of a death sentence. Now, staring from the shadows twenty minutes after letting the taggers go, waiting to catch the dealer in the act, Henry thought back to the graffiti. A red circle with the *F* and *C*. Matching the tattoos of Tiny Eyes and the domestic abuser.

That's why he recognized them now. Henry had seen the tags spray painted on walls around The Burg, many times throughout the last year or so. He figured they were some sort of gang signs or pop culture reference someone his age, or living in a six-million-dollar mansion, wouldn't understand.

If Henry's enemies were part of a gang, that meant numbers. How many more were out there? And why target *him*?

He waited in the shadows until the buyer left. He had no quarrel with *him*. Drugs were an addiction Henry understood all too well. Vermin like the asshole on the corner, siphoning misery to profit, deserved to die.

Unlike the two muggers, Henry snapped the dealer's neck without ceremony and realized what most of him had ignored before. He was feeding from the murders, but a part of him was also thriving from the emotional pain and fear of the victims he was trying to save. Not having a witness to the dealer's murder, and the old lady running off before, had lessened Henry's *high*.

Worse yet, a part of him was tempted to go back and kill the victims he'd saved. He imagined the joy of sparing them, only to murder them in the heat of their gratitude. Leaving them alive felt like something left undone, an emptiness in need of filling.

A sudden and overpowering hunger gnawed at his gut, followed by a shame deep enough to keep him from chasing the buyer. He rocked back on his heels, pulling the shadows in tighter around his shoulders.

Why do I want to kill them?

Am I not being led to victims to help, but rather to turn their pain to certainty?

Henry tried shedding the notion, but nothing else made sense. He was a lightning rod for the misery that fed him. And it wasn't long before Henry found his way back to the trough.

He ended his evening catching a rapist, red-cocked. He had his pants down with his victim, a thirty-something redhead, pressed up against the wall. The man was panting and ready. Rapists were almost the lowest form of animal in any kingdom, exactly one layer of scum above anyone willing to harm a child.

Henry tore the rapist's cock from his body, shoved it deep into the bastard's mouth, driving to cover the rapist's fleeing scream with a fist that broke teeth and tore the skin from his lips. He pinched the rapist's nose until he finally choked to death on his own dick.

The woman sobbed, fumbling with her torn skirt. She stumbled a few feet away before stopping to hold her ruined clothes against her, turning back to stare at him like an accident on the wrong side of traffic.

"You okay?" Henry asked, though the hunger to kill

her swelled inside him. He closed his eyes, trying to drown out the thoughts.

Let her go. She's been through enough, you monster!

She said nothing. She turned to run, and Henry felt the woman swallow her scream. He sighed as she vanished around the corner. Out of sight, but only *slightly* out of mind.

I'm going to be the worst demon ever.

It was Henry's recurring thought as he returned to the apartment. Once inside, he crashed on his mattress and slept like the dead.

Chapter Twenty-Two

HENRY WOKE up to the news, hearing the broadcast before his gummy eyes opened to the TV's blue glow lighting his dark bedroom. On his third blink, Henry saw Boothe standing in front of the televison.

How long had the demon been in the apartment? Did he come to rub his nose in the reports of his exploits? Henry worked up enough bitter saliva to swallow, sitting up and scooting back to lean against the headboard and watch the report.

"Oops," he said.

The coverage was brutal.

The anchor, a black woman in a red sweater, said, "While police have yet to confirm if the murders are related, sources within the department tell us that witness descriptions all mentioned a man wearing a black hoodie, blue jeans, and black boots. Residents here are saying they've been blessed by a vigilante they're calling the Hooded Angel."

"*Hooded Angel*, Henry?"

Henry shrugged, spreading his hands and laughing. "What?"

"This amuses you, does it?"

"Hey, I did exactly as you said. I followed my instincts. Was I supposed to do something different? Did I misunderstand? I followed the sorrow like a wolf to prey. Just like you said, *Boothey.*"

Ha, Boothey, I'll have to call him that more often.

The demon stared, and for a moment Henry thought he might explode, grab him by the neck, and drag him back to Nowhere. Fine by Henry. He could return to Amélie.

Boothe never boiled. Instead, he looked at Henry as if he were the village idiot.

"I can't understand why you feel such an incessant need to insult me with shaded honesty, Henry. We both know a lie when we hear it, white or black. You know what you're saying and why. If you *were* following your instincts, you wouldn't have left witnesses. You do realize the number one source for witnesses are people whose hearts are still beating, correct?"

"Well, sorry to disappoint you, but I'm not that kind of demon."

"You think I'm complaining." Boothe smiled, approached the California king, sat at its edge, retrieved the remote from the bedside, and aimed it at the TV. "I'm not. Your little hero streak might've given us some excellent leads. Let's peek at the story." He nodded at the screen and cranked the volume from fourteen to forty-four as a pair of familiar faces flashed across the screen. The asshole and his girlfriend from a few weeks before. *HOODED ANGEL'S FIRST VICTIMS* scrolled by in bold underneath.

Another witness, an old Hispanic woman said, "Yeah,

he was just beating the -beep- outta the man, right there on the street! He musta' seen that *pendejo* kill that poor lady."

"Not quite how shit happened." Henry was more amused than anything. "I never beat the guy to death. I threw him, or actually, dropped the fucker from the roof of his building. Then I jumped down after him. I guess it's a good thing she didn't see *that*, huh?"

Looking at the TV rather than Henry, Boothe said, "You're still linked to the crime.

The anchor continued, "Police are asking for anyone with information on this, or any of these crimes, to call the anonymous tip line for a possible five-thousand-dollar reward."

"Would you happen to have any tips for the boys in blue, Henry?"

For the thousandth time, Henry wished he could kill him. Boothe paused the broadcast.

"Wipe that look from your face, Henry. You can't kill me, and you should stop thinking about it. Remember, we're in this *together*. I'm on your side. Not Randall nor anyone else. Not Samantha or Amélie. No one. I can do more for you right now than anyone else in this universe can, and I'm sick of arguing. Perhaps you'll learn to appreciate me once I disappear and leave you alone to fend for yourself."

Boothe pointed the remote back at the TV, rewound the DVR about twenty seconds, and turned the volume even louder. "Pay attention. This part is important."

The news anchor reported that police had linked the dead couple to another crime, the murder of one Kurt Hammond, whom Henry knew as Tiny Eyes. All three had worked at a bar called the Raven's Club.

"Well, well," Boothe said. "Seems Sherlock uncovered a clue."

Henry smiled, hating Boothe a little less. "Think the others might hang out there?"

"You floor me with your powers of deduction. Yes, that's a reasonable assumption. If not, I'm sure someone might be able to help you find them." Boothe laughed. "Whether they want to be found or not."

"So what the Hell am I supposed to do? Stroll into the bar and start asking anyone who'll listen, 'Hey, have you seen the people who killed me?'"

Boothe clucked his tongue. "Henry, Henry, Henry, you're too linear. Old ways are dead, and new ones have been born. Use your ample *gifts*. Stick to shadows, listen, gather information. Perhaps you'll get lucky. If not, at least you're further than you were before. Just make sure the cops don't see you, not with that sketch on every channel. It is an uncanny resemblance, don't you think?"

The TV showed an artist's pencil sketch of Henry in his hoodie. They'd gotten part of his transformed face right. Enough that someone might recognize him, though they'd missed the worst atrocities of his bald, swollen skull.

"Should I wear something else?" Henry asked.

"No, it suits you. And you don't want to worry about anything so silly as what to wear. What matters most is that you stay unseen. And for the love of God, Henry, don't get your photo taken. Agreed?"

"A little more instructions might have been nice." Henry looked down at the sheet covering his lap.

"If only you would listen. Create your own reality, Henry. The mind wills, and the body follows."

"Okay," Henry nodded, planning his next move. It didn't involve the Raven's Club.

He had to find out what had happened since he last saw Sam. Their eyes, and maybe their *souls*, had touched the night Boothe dragged him back into Nowhere. He wondered how much of him she'd seen. Was it mostly shadows she could easily pass off as fevered imagination or stone-cold certainty she'd seen a ghost? Or monster?

Henry's plans must've been all over his face, since Boothe was looking at him with a knowing frown.

"I suggest not leaving the loft until early evening, though I'm quite sure you'll do as you wish anyway."

"You know me so well."

Boothe disappeared and Henry leaned his head back with a sigh, rubbing the heels of his hands into his gritty eyelids.

He got dressed and ate some of everything in the fridge while pacing with impatience. Then, finished eating, Henry went to the rooftop for practice. Sinking into the slim line of shadows at the base of the ledge that wrapped the building's roof in two feet of safety behind the roof access door, he tried blinking himself back down into the apartment. But every time, the folds in space straightened out until he stood panting under a darkening sky. The sun finally grew tired enough to trade places with the moon, and Henry exchanged preparation for action.

He leapt into the night, across the asphalt chasm below, to the building on the other side, marring the white moon with a smudge of his darkness along the way.

Henry ran, not to Samantha, but to the Burg Spires Church of Hope.

He felt like a bitch not going home. And the only thing worse than feeling like a bitch was feeling like a demon's bitch. He'd had to die to find that one out, but it didn't matter. He had to talk to the pastor.

Still, Sam needed him, and on the way, he couldn't stop thinking about her. She had seen him, and he knew it, even if she didn't recognize him right away. He longed to be face-to-face with her again. To touch her. To stroke the side of her face. They could take turns leaning on one another's shoulder.

A few blocks from the church, Henry realized with a creeping confusion that he never thought of Sam sexually. Not anymore. Not since he'd died. Before, the thought was almost constant. Everything from a light breeze to *Two Girls One Cup* made Henry think about fucking Samantha. Or *making love* on Valentine's Day, and like nine other nights a year. The shock of his discovery slowed Henry's progress to a crawl.

Sam was hotter than a branding iron and liked it fast and nasty. In all their years, there wasn't once when they'd had sex when Henry hadn't wrestled the thought that he was a lucky sonofabitch who didn't deserve someone as hot as Sam. Now, especially in his hideous form, sex was the last thing on his mind. Instead, he wanted to hold her in his arms and never let her go. Just feel her against him, hear her voice in his ear.

Henry reached the church and hovered in the shadows of the entry, shrouded in darkness and watching Pastor Owen. He had hoped to catch him alone, but the many flyers festooning the doors said it was the Thanksgiving Play night, which explained the pastor sitting beside Mrs. Brennan on a long wooden bench, and the two dozen children in a semicircle at their feet. A few parents sat in the audience, while most of the others had likely dropped their kids off until returning for the performance later tonight.

Play nights at the church were one of Samantha's favorite things, even when Amélie wasn't starring. She loved hearing the children sing. Thought it the sweetest thing in the world.

"Yes, Mrs. Brennan," two dozen kids said in chorus.

"Okay, everyone together!" Mrs. Brennan stood, beaming at Pastor Owen. She turned to the children. A boy in front, with a face made by Pillsbury and cheeks as red as his shirt, stood first. The rest of the children followed in a wave behind him.

Pillsbury started to sing, making Henry want to forget.

Memories fell on top of him anyway, too fast to prevent, mostly from when Amélie had performed in the Burg Spires Thanksgiving play the year before. Cuter than a stuffed animal as second lead turkey, singing as though her voice wasn't cracking and well off-key.

He wiped his eyes. The church had a great group of kids. Henry knew half by sight but only a few of their names.

Pastor Owen smiled at the children. He turned to Mrs. Brennan, leaning in to whisper in her ear. She nodded, laughed, and lifted her eyes back to the children.

A tall, skinny girl that looked the same age as Amélie marched across the stage to stand in front of a kid that Henry always called Toby. Samantha had frowned at the name, but Henry had sworn that the kid would grow up to look exactly like Toby from *The Office* and the name had stuck in his mind. He was dressed as the king, and the girl demanded he give her family their land back.

Ten minutes into dress rehearsal, and Henry had moved from tears to a surprising half-smile. Then he turned and caught the pastor looking directly at him. He whispered to Mrs. Brennan again, then stood and walked over toward Henry, still shrouded in shadows at the back of the church.

He wondered if the pastor could see him. Unlike the time before, they weren't sharing proximity. He figured he *was* being paranoid, like Sam always said he was, until the pastor stood a few feet away, still holding his stare.

Smiling, he whispered, "I was wondering if you'd return."

Henry was silent, afraid to say anything.

"Would you like some fresh air?" Without waiting for an answer, the pastor broke their gaze, walked the aisle to the exit, then left the church without looking back. Henry flew to a cross-shaped shadow draping over the door and bled into the night.

The second he was outside, Henry asked, "Have you seen Sam?"

"Yes, of course. I am her *pastor*."

"What did she say?" Henry kept himself from sounding frantic. "Anything about *me?*"

"Are you asking if Samantha saw you?" the pastor asked, patient as always. "It would perhaps be helpful, and certainly faster, if you said what you meant. Remember last time how we discussed trust?"

"Sorry," Henry said, looking down. "So, did she?"

"Yes, Samantha saw you. Or *something*. She had no idea what and didn't believe her own eyes. She assumed she was drunk. Or losing her mind. Maybe having a nightmare. It's not as though you look like yourself."

Henry swallowed. "Did she see my face?"

"As I said, Samantha's not even sure *what* she saw."

"What did she say?"

"She said it was like looking into your eyes, then suddenly not. Like you were there, then weren't. She was freezing, but the feeling disappeared and then she was so warm she had to turn on the AC. She started crying harder than she already was. On her third hour of being drunk, Samantha opened another bottle."

"That's quite the confession."

"You know Samantha. Better than I do."

"Was she mad?"

"Mad? No." Pastor Owen shook his head. "Not angry. But quite upset. This is hard for her, Henry. I suggest you stay away, at least for now. No good can come from your visits. You will only hurt her further."

"What would you say if I said you sound like a demon I know?"

"I would say you should mind what you say, or that perhaps all thoughts aren't worth your breath." The pastor's mouth set, thin as a splinter. "The angels, outside the church, Henry. Did I see that?"

"Yeah, seems they're God's dogcatchers or something, coming along to collect demons. My good friend Satan's Little Helper appeared to beat up the bad guys and whisk me into the sunset."

"You mean the *good* guys."

"Whatever."

"So I did see what I thought?" The pastor swallowed, but not in awe, exactly. "There *were* angels outside my church?"

"Not exactly angels," Henry corrected. "The demon said they were Trackers."

"Trackers?"

"Yeah, a sort of angel who comes to this plane, to Earth, to track and kill my kind." Henry wondered if a monster could look as uncomfortable as he felt. "I'm not the expert on any of this, Pastor. I don't even believe the words leaving my mouth. I would've thought this was bullsh ... er ... whatever, a week ago, or however long it's been since ... *you* know."

Like always, the pastor cut to the meat of what Henry was trying to say. "What are you hoping for, Henry? Why don't you move on? Why are you here? Does the presence of angels tell you *nothing?*"

Henry squirmed while the pastor patiently waited for an answer. Then finally he said, "I'm going to kill the men involved with Amélie's murder. Everyone who ruined my life."

Pastor Owen spoke slowly, each word paving a path to his quiet accusation. "You're killing more than just the men responsible, though, aren't you Henry? Or is another *Hooded Angel* guarding Burg City's dark alleys?"

Henry wasn't surprised. If anything, it was the question he had come to Burg Spires to answer.

"Yes," he nodded. "That's me."

Henry waited for Pastor Owen's judgment, but the man said nothing.

"It's terrible," Henry said, unable to meet the pastor's eyes. "I have this horrible need to kill bad people. *More* than kill them. Destroy their bodies and feed from their... life force. Dark energy, I don't know. It feels like I'm even supposed to kill *innocents*. But I can't do it."

"You must stop, Henry. *All of it*. What you are doing will get you killed and send you to Hell, or back into Purgatory where Heaven's gates will stay closed to you forever."

"Aren't they already?"

The pastor turned. "That's not for us to decide. Only *God* can say. Let Him do His work. Have faith in Him, and you will one day join your family, including Samantha, in His Kingdom. You can't save the world, Henry. You'll kill yourself trying."

"God's asleep at the wheel," Henry said. "So I'm pitching in. A curse doesn't make me incapable of goodness."

As if he didn't want to argue, the pastor changed the subject.

"Are you any closer to finding these killers?"

"I'm following a lead tonight." Henry raised his eyes to the pastor. "But I wanted to come here first."

"Let it go, Henry. Go back to Purgatory before you do something you can't undo."

Henry settled deeper into the darkness. "I gotta go. The things I can't undo aren't getting done by themselves."

Pastor Owen opened his mouth, but before he could say anything Henry slipped to a faraway shadow.

"I'm going," Henry said as he fled.

"Where?" Pastor Owen called out.

"To do God's work," Henry said with the closest thing to a smile that he could manage.

As Henry hit the sidewalk, Samantha's Cayenne pulled into the parking lot.

Is she here to help with rehearsals or is she early to watch the play?

It was a monument to misery, her being a part of or watching a play without Amélie in it. Henry imagined Sam leaving the church after the final bow, driving home in tears, then crawling into bed alone, thinking of the full stage that was so horribly empty without her daughter.

His heart stopped in his chest as he stood, wrapped in shadow, tempted to go back and see her. He remembered the pastor's words.

No good can come from your visits. You will only hurt her further.

Henry disappeared before she left the Porsche.

He had to get far away, before he lost the strength to stay silent.

Chapter Twenty-Three

HENRY RAGED ALL the way to the Raven's Club. Seething. Boiling beneath his skin and wondering what he would do once he got there. Revenge was sweet, and he could practically taste it.

Henry had never heard of the Raven's Club before the broadcast, though that wasn't surprising. He made The Burg home back when he was a chubby college dropout, lasting roughly halfway through his freshman year before moving to the big city and bigger dreams. Though plenty familiar with filthy clubs with sticky floors and restrooms out of *Trainspotting*, his places always had a stage. A club without one, to Henry, was just goddamned depressing.

For some odd reason, and almost exactly as Boothe promised, Henry didn't have to check the phonebook, or do anything beyond following the musky scent of personal murder leading him straight to Raven's.

The place looked so filthy, Henry thought it should've had a sewer grate for a front door. Two bouncers stood on either side of the entrance as Henry stood across the street staring from behind his hoodie's shadows.

Both bouncers were massive, guarding the grimy front. A short line of what looked like hookers and johns waited to enter. Henry would bet his ticket to Heaven that admission wasn't worth the wait.

Still, he wanted in. He eyed the entrance, the bouncers, and the narrow margin between them. Too small for a thought, let alone large enough for Henry to squeeze through.

He waited for several minutes, growing too impatient to wait through another. He slipped to a shadow hanging over three painted women near the front of the line, standing beside a guy who looked like he had full custody of all three. In front of the trio stood what had to be the sleaziest couple Henry had ever seen. Drawing the shadows around him, rendering him almost invisible, Henry slipped behind the skank and yanked her skirt to the floor. Narrow cut thong panties over a tattoo creeping from the sides of her underwear. Pubic hair stubble sparkling in the neon lights.

Holy fuck. I've seen a lot of shit, but never a pussy tattoo!

Henry didn't have time to figure out the design. Maybe a butterfly, or more appropriately, a moth. The woman screamed, reeled around, and slapped the guy standing in the middle of the three girls across the face.

He reeled back, hanging onto his ladies to keep from falling over. "The fuck you think you're doing, bitch?"

"*Me?*" the skank screamed. "What the fuck are *you* doing, you pig?"

One of the other women joined the fight, her thick thighs jiggling with the force of stomping forward. Screaming and shoving, everyone turning to eye the commotion. Henry flew one shadow closer to the door.

As expected, one of the two bouncers took action.

With a heavy sigh, he waded into the line, leaving only one man guarding. Henry slipped inside, wondering what sort of trashy club doing shit business on the dingiest end of Burg City would need two mastodons guarding the door.

Inside, Henry's mouth watered at the reek of misery and sorrow wafting from the crowd like freshly baked pie. He lurked in the shadows, staring out at the writhing sea of potential victims and hearing Boothe's voice.

Follow your instincts, Henry.

Boothe in his ear made it easy for Henry to lie to himself. There were a hundred and one reasons why it would be okay, and maybe *wonderful*, to take life like candy from a jar. Henry inhaled the aroma, his eyes fluttering closed, and for the first time, thought he might not have the willpower to stop himself from sating his hunger.

Surely, the alcohol-and-sweat-soaked cesspool harbored untold opportunity.

Henry had come to find the men who murdered his daughter, but as he drifted from one shadow to another, he found himself wanting to sample the menu. So many people brimming with anger, hate, and self-loathing. All you can eat at the Suffering Buffet.

As Henry was wondering if he'd be able to stay on task, he saw what he'd come looking for. Not just a clue, but one of the goddamned men he'd hoped to find.

Bulldog, one of the three thugs that had destroyed his life. He sat on the other side of the writhing dance floor, hitting on a tiny black-haired girl with itty bitty tits and a half-pound of metal in her face.

Found you.

Henry watched Bulldog work. For the first few minutes, the chick put him off. Finally, she accepted whatever sleazy offer he'd whispered in her ear with a grin, the point of a

173

black-painted nail in her teeth. Then they started grinding next to the table. Lost in a sea of sweating dancers, mashing uglies for two songs before disappearing into the bathroom. The sign over the door designated neither male nor female. Just a crooked plaque of fading letters. *SHIT-TER*. Henry had no interest in seeing whatever was happening behind the closed door, but four minutes later Bulldog came out smiling.

He went up to the bar and whispered something to the bartender, who handed him a drink without waiting for anything back. Bulldog downed it with a smile then left, weaving through the crowd to a side door that opened onto a small parking lot.

Henry followed.

Outside, he was less certain. Most of Henry wanted to peel the skin from the murderer's bones. Pull back his hoodie just to hear the depths of the man's terror. But he shook his head.

Be patient. No rush in killing him. Wait until it's safe so you can question him and find the third man.

The one you didn't see.

No van for Bulldog. He climbed into an old Dodge Charger parked in the back, facing the street. He gunned the engine like an asshole and tore into a gap in traffic.

Henry dropped deeper into the shadows, stretching through the darkness to keep pace.

Bulldog drove for a mile or so, with Henry immediately behind, struggling to maintain his speed while staying cloaked in shadows, even as cars passed by. As Bulldog hung a left, aiming his Charger for the riverfront, Henry wanted to scream. He was hungry and pushing himself to stay in shadow form while chasing a car at breakneck speed. His mind scorched fatigue. Dizziness brought vomit into his mouth, and his path veered from the street.

He stood on the sidewalk, holding his stomach. He gasped and swallowed, fear and anger breaking his hold on the shadows.

He thought he might lose Bulldog but aimed his rage toward his own fucking uselessness. Samantha's scream echoed in his mind. Amélie's wide eyes stared in accusation. A second wind rose from the heat of Henry's shame, and he shot after the Charger, running fast enough to catch Bulldog as he made a right from Aberdeen onto Riverfront.

Bulldog turned and opened up, rocketing down the empty street. Henry pushed harder, slinging from one shadow to the next, gaining speed with every fresh dive into darkness.

Bulldog's driving went from aggressive, to erratic, to downright manic. He had left Raven's like an asshole. Now he was driving flat-out crazy. Henry would have thought Bulldog drunk, except the Charger never actually seemed to be out of control. At least, not until Henry nearly lost him.

He had a hard time keeping up with the vehicle's speed, but also because Bulldog was swerving so much. Henry had to make sure he didn't zigzag into the wrong side of Bulldog's turns. He could take a tremendous amount of punishment and healed like magic, but there was a limit to everything, and he wasn't sure if getting slammed by several tons of metal at nearly one hundred miles per hour would be his.

After several blocks, Henry realized Bulldog was joyriding, racing down the riverbank, fishtailing for fun. But something about it, maybe even *everything*, seemed intentional.

He knows he has a tail.

The fucker wasn't going to toy with him. There was *one*

cat and *one* mouse. After another minute of running, Henry was done allowing the asshole in front of him to mistake who was who.

The Charger slewed around a corner. Bulldog floored it. The ass end of the car swung around, tires squealing with missing traction. Henry smiled. Raced to the side street as Bulldog pulled out of the skid.

Henry was two blocks ahead, certain the bastard would keep racing forward. He leapt to the side of a warehouse and pivoted back toward a light post on the corner, where he scampered to its top to perch like a gargoyle. The Charger straightened out below him, and Henry dove onto the hood, creasing the metal and shattering the windshield.

His weight drove the front bumper into the street. Rubber screeched against asphalt. A crush of metal, deafening as the Charger made a trio of somersaults, tumbling over Henry's head before landing upright about a half block away.

Bulldog screamed in the cabin, but to Henry's agitated surprise, the murdering asshole didn't sound scared. He sounded angry.

Henry was at the driver's side in two seconds. He launched his fist through the window, showering Bulldog's laughing face with glass. He didn't even seem to mind when Henry unbuckled him, yanking him out through the broken window and dropping him onto the asphalt.

Still, the killer laughed.

A hard enough hit can silence the loudest fucker in the chorus, but when Henry launched his foot in between the murderer's legs with a demon's strength, Bulldog kept right on laughing. A maniacal shriek grew into a howl. Tears poured from both of his eyes.

Henry looked up and down the empty street, grateful the dickhead had chosen the long straightaway beside the river. He grabbed a handful of Bulldog's hair and dragged him to the edge of the street. He dropped him over the side. Bulldog sprawled on the concrete pier in a crunching spread that only stopped his laughter for seconds. A choked cough. A gasping breath, and the fucker started right back up.

Henry landed with a foot on either side of Bulldog's hips. He grabbed him by the front of his shirt and slung toward the water. He slid his fingers around the man's throat and lifted his upper body over the river. He put his knee on Bulldog's lap and drove his head underwater, bending him back until his ribs creaked. Henry shared in Bulldog's lunacy, grinning as he held the man under until the final second when he remembered the murderer might still be of use. He yanked Bulldog back, pulled off his own hood, and said, "I'm Henry Black. Remember me?"

Recognition flickered in the man's watery red eyes.

"Satan sent me back to find you, fucker. Tell me where to find the third man with you that night."

Bulldog found his sense of humor again and grinned like a lunatic, water squeezing between his teeth.

"Tell me who he is, or you're dead!" Henry dunked his head and watched the bubbles.

Bulldog still laughed even as he choked on water and gasped for air.

Henry didn't know what to do in the face of such insane indifference.

What is it about these fuckers in this gang that they laugh as I beat the shit out of them? Are they all crazy fucks?

He was tempted to kill the man, then return to Raven's and wait for another lead. But then he saw the tattoo. The circle, with the *F* and *C* inside. It didn't entirely surprise him. He'd figured the men shared a gang. Still, this was as good a chance as he would likely get to find out more about the tat.

He pulled Bulldog out again and held his outstretched arm by the wrist. "What the fuck is this?"

He coughed up water, curling into his heaving abdomen. The coughing trailed into laughing, so Henry snapped the fucker's arm, right at the tattoo, popping the bone from the murderer's skin. Bulldog's shriek finally brought the laughter to a halt. Henry snarled and waited for him to speak.

Bulldog panted with his eyes squeezed shut, but as soon as he caught his breath, instead of talking, he laughed.

Henry almost dropped him into the river out of frustration. He growled, "Why are you laughing?"

"Because," Bulldog said, haunting Henry with his smile. "You're too late."

"Too late for what?"

"To stop us. We knew you were coming, Henry. But that's okay, because although we may not be many, we are *prepared*."

"What the fuck are you talking about?"

"Your wife's at the church now, right?"

Henry's heart froze in his chest.

Why the hell is he asking about Sam?

How does he know where she is?

"What?"

"Yeah, I thought so. You're too late, Punchline." His smile died, and he looked up at the sparkling sky.

Henry was digging through the murderer's words when Bulldog reached behind his back. Henry heard the hiss of a blade as Bulldog grabbed a knife from an unseen sheath. Before Henry could stop him, or even wonder if he should, the knife made a fresh smile across Bulldog's neck, spilling blood from its grin.

Henry screamed and dropped the body in the water. He reeled back, rose to his feet, and spun in a panicked circle, his mind refusing to order him around. He jumped back to the street and ran past the wreckage, sinking into the shadows and shooting his body like a bullet back toward the Burg Spires Church of Hope.

Chapter Twenty-Four

HENRY REACHED the church just as a cop car scraped the curb, joining countless others, plus more ambulances than he could count.

Chaos.

What the hell is happening?

Where is Sam?

There were too many emotions for Henry to sift through, each with its own horrible color, surrounding him in a hazy fog.

Henry felt misery and hungered for more while fighting the desire at the same time.

He wanted to get closer but couldn't. Not with so many flashing lights. Cops and paramedics. People flooding in and out. Many crying or in a state of shock, all with racing hearts. Most with whispered prayers.

Henry dove into a hive of human bees.

Pain was everywhere, mostly delicious, and it sickened him.

Henry worked to ignore his urge, focusing on the other thing making him frantic. Finding his missing Samantha.

He shot himself into a thicket of shadows a few feet from a woman standing in the lights of a news van. She smacked her lips twice, staring into the monitor behind the cameraman. "Let's roll."

The cameraman aimed at her face as she stared into the lens, smoothing her features into practiced sympathy.

"This is Connie Collins, Channel 7 News, reporting live from a tragic scene at the Burg Spires Church of Hope, where police say masked men stormed inside and opened fire, killing more than twenty people, including several children, during a Thanksgiving play."

No.

God, no.

He scanned the madness, searching for any sign of Samantha, certain he was on his way to Hell, one way or another.

Chapter Twenty-Five

HENRY STARED at the chaos in disbelief.

Flashing lights draped the onlookers in a garish canvas of trauma. Wide-eyed and blinking, bathed in red, blue, and shadows. The shock of atrocity soured the air as Henry braced himself for more tragedy, edging nearer to the church, one shadow at a time.

He had to know if Death had come to finish the job.

Police poured in and out of the church, attempting to make sense of the madness and gather the survivors. The sheer number of people, coupled with their escalated sorrow and pain, made it hard for Henry to concentrate. He slipped into his shadow form instead of turning invisible, hoping he could keep it intact as he moved to within twenty yards of the church's main entrance. Right to the edge of the lights.

The closer he got to the church, the more intense the misery. The sweeter the accompanying euphoria. It begged him to come inside and bask in the sorrow, and to his disgust, it wanted him to *add* to the sorrow by murdering others.

He buried the urges deep inside himself, trying to focus on finding Sam. Her Porsche was still parked in the lot, so she had to be somewhere nearby. Hopefully alive.

Burg Spires was a beehive, and Henry was too nervous about losing his focus to chance going through the front doors. Instead, he sprinted across several patches of shadow, scampering up the side of the church and onto the roof, racing to the peak, the Spire's highest point. He stopped at the skylights, staring down where the chaos and sorrow were worst. No less than a hundred people moved in a sea below. Paramedics and survivors. Cops, in uniforms and suits. Their auras — black, red, and orange, — swirled around them in a flotsam of frenetic confusion.

Henry's eyes followed the movement, then stopped on the corpses lying bloody on the pulpit. Nearly a dozen dead children, none older than twelve. Another dozen or so dead, children and adults alike, lay sprawled in the nave.

So much death.

People he knew. Children who'd been friends with his daughter.

While the demon inside him lingered on the dead, the human within him wanted to turn away and un-see what he knew he never could. Dead eyes stared up at a God who hadn't saved them despite their devotion. And now they were staring at *him*, the fucking demon, instead.

He strained to see if Sam was among the fallen, but too many people shuffled below, blocking his view.

Henry would have to go down for a better look. Into the heart of darkness.

Staring at the bodies and thinking of his daughter, Henry wondered if Amélie would've died anyway, even if she had survived the home invasion. In this place that *should have* provided sanctuary.

The world wept beneath the skylight. Some parents cried so loud, Henry could hear them on the roof, like screams in his ear. Anguish hung heavy, its weight on the shoulders of police and paramedics below. But he didn't care about all that now. Henry had only had one thought.

I have to find Sam.

After searching the crowd of living and dead, Henry still couldn't spot Samantha. Or Pastor Owen. If they were still alive, he would unearth them together.

Find one, find the pair.

Henry turned from the skylight, about to cross the roof and drop back to the sidewalk to see if the rear of the church was unlocked so he could sneak inside from the other, less clustered end. He stopped short when the familiar burn in his flesh demanded attention.

He couldn't see them, but Henry felt the Trackers nearby. The burn wasn't as bad as before, but there was no mistaking it. They were close. And if he was going find Sam, he had to do it quick.

At least it's not daylight. Maybe I'll see them before they get too close.

He looked to the sky, spinning slowly, searching for the Trackers, or at least a clue that might tell him where to run. After seeing nothing, he crept to the edge and dropped into a pool of shadows. Still finding nothing after another glance at the sky, Henry turned his gaze through the large windows on the side of the church, the beautiful stained glass reduced to glittering shards on the floor. Henry fell back a step with a gasp. The angels weren't outside, or in the heavens at all. They had somehow gotten past him and into the church, hovering above the grisly murder scene.

These weren't Trackers, though. They wore no armor, only robes, and they were barely visible through the radiant gold nimbus around them. Two dozen angels, male and female, lingered beneath the ceiling, held aloft by giant wings of feathered light.

Henry stared, frozen as the angels gracefully floated over the crowd, staring at the people below. Though he couldn't see much of their faces, he could feel the love and concern for the dead radiating from their beings. Even scared of discovery, Henry couldn't bear to look away. He was drawn toward their beauty, their overabundance of love. So pure, so strong, so raw. It rivaled the euphoria he'd felt from misery tenfold.

He needed to get closer.

Henry surfaced from the shadows and went straight toward the entrance. Staying in shadow form, sneaking past the cluster of cops by the door, He found himself inside. Once the angels were out of his line of sight, his head seemed to clear. Sam was either among the dead he hadn't seen or in the bowels of the church with Pastor Owen.

He stopped in his tracks, paralyzed by the angels' splendor. They hovered with yawning arms, as if welcoming the dead below. All at once, colorful lights in the shapes of the fallen rose from their corpses and floated toward the ceiling. Bright colors met the gold of God's hosts as the heavenly beings seemed to absorb them. An incredible warmth wafted through the room. Henry fell into a deep sadness knowing others were unable to witness the glory and had no way of knowing their loved ones were being ushered into something so pure.

Henry wondered if this was the way death greeted good people on their way to Heaven. He remembered nothing of his death until waking in Purgatory. Were all souls carried by angels? Did they simply not remember the journey once they reached their destination? Or did some people just wake in an abyss? Now that he was a demon, doing demon shit, Henry was certain he'd *never* know God's grace. Or had earned it as a *man*.

Had Amélie had been carried by angels only to be deposited in Nowhere for Judgment?

Heaven intoxicated the room. The angels hummed louder as souls seeped inside them, like a soft current through the air. Another child's tangerine-and-rose-tinted soul was swallowed by brilliant gold. It turned the angel white hot. For one amazing moment, she turned every color in the universe, then she erupted into a white glow so soft, the lack of color must have been like the first spot of nothing the universe had ever seen.

The brilliance was overwhelming, mounting on top of too many things at once. Cops, mourners, bodies, angels in the sky, and most importantly, finding Samantha. Unable to keep up with the stimuli, Henry began to lose grip on his shadow form.

He flickered.

While half in and half out of the shadows, doing everything he could to stay within them, Henry saw Samantha, beside the pastor, walking from his office hallway.

She's alive!

Tears streamed down his face as Sam walked into the nave. There was blood on her blouse. Her hair was a mess, her red eyes stared, but she didn't seem injured.

The pastor wrapped an arm around her as they passed a pair of officers. They stopped for a moment, speaking with a paramedic as the angels floated up and out through the roof, vanishing into the night.

As the angels left, so did the pastor and Sam, leaving Henry alone with a room full of death. He felt an immediate deep and stinging loss and wanted to race after Sam.

To hug her tight and let her know how much he loved her and how glad he was that she was still alive.

The room's turmoil shook his concentration. And he was finding it nearly impossible to slip back into the shadows. Despite the energy he was feeling from the misery and death, something else had drained him almost entirely. He was weak and uncertain how much longer he could hold on to the darkness.

He had to reach the exit before he lost them.

Between Henry and the door stood a large cop with a bushy mustache speaking to a man with bloodshot eyes. The man was distraught, his gaze darting back to the pulpit, unable to stop looking.

One of the fathers, poor bastard.

Henry finally had the strength, or urgency, to cross from one shadow into the next, aiming for the one beside the open doors. Without enough muscle to make it, he crashed into the cop, then the grieving father, before falling to the floor.

Henry flickered as the officer looked down. Their eyes met.

Something went bright in his eyes. Maybe he'd seen inside the hoodie to the monstrous face within.

Henry scrambled to his feet and ran out the door.

The officer grabbed at him, his hand catching the back of Henry's hoodie and yanking it back. As the hood fell, he spun around and growled instinctively, forcing the cop to release him.

Henry ran into the night.

The cop, after a shocked pause, gave chase.

Henry's fatigue forced him to abandon the shadows. Despite his best efforts, he was barely faster than the cop. He raced through the crowded lot, desperate to find Sam and the pastor. But with the cop hot on his heels, he knew he had to first get away from the church, then double back after he had regained some strength, assuming he was able to. He sprinted from the lot, the cop following. Thankfully the officer wasn't shooting.

But he was yelling, "Hey! Stop!"

That was the *last* thing Henry was going to do.

He kept running, turning down a side street full of closed storefronts, panting with cramping legs, pushing himself as the cop pounded the pavement behind him, closing in thirty yards back.

Henry remembered Boothe telling him that as long as he had a breath inside him, the shadows were his friends. But when he could barely draw breath, he didn't dare stop to try and hide. Not until he was able to put more distance between him and the cop.

He grunted with effort, pushing himself to go faster. He gathered speed as he turned down a residential side road, congested with a full row of cars parked on either side. Temporarily clear from the cop's line of sight, Henry dove behind a truck beneath a giant maple and into the deep shadows, becoming one with the darkness.

The officer's footsteps slapped around the corner and stopped a few feet away, in the middle of the street.

Keep going, keep going.

The cop paused, whispering his disbelief. "Where the Hell?"

The cop moved toward the truck.

Shit.

Henry's head grew heavy as he struggled to stay buried in shadows. Another flicker would destroy him, and yet the focus was draining his body. He was on the brink of passing out. Then he'd either be found by the cop or ripped from Earth by an angel. Either way, his time was almost up.

Henry kept holding his breath through the final few seconds of a world he'd barely been able to know.

A sudden sound from behind tore at his focus.

He turned, bracing for impact from an unseen assailant. And then Henry saw the old, familiar face.

"Come," Randall held out his open hand.

"Hey!" the cop shouted.

Without even looking Henry took Randall's palm.

A second later, they blinked away, twisting into the folds of space and time.

On the other side of wherever they went, Henry passed out.

Chapter Twenty-Six

HENRY WOKE in a graveyard with Randall sitting in the grass beside him, the moon a smudge behind thick clouds above.

"What happened?" Henry asked, still feeling weak and now dizzy, wondering when the crazy transporting and endless nightmare would finally end.

"You were nearly caught. I kept you safe."

"How did you find me?" Henry tried to stand, but couldn't. "Where's Boothe?"

"I've no idea where he is, but I don't feel him anywhere near. We're safe, at least for now."

"Safe from what?"

"For now, everything."

"How did you find me?" Henry repeated.

"I didn't. We're connected. I had to *reach you*, not find you."

"What do you mean, we're *connected*?"

"When you arrived in Nowhere, Boothe and I were the first souls you met, correct?"

"Yeah." Henry nodded, trying to stand again. He

almost managed to get both legs straight the second time, but halfway up he fell back down, head spinning as he spilled into the cool grass.

"You saw us first because we are your custodians, as we are for *many* who find themselves at the root of the Tree."

"Custodians?"

"We are the caretakers of your soul, Henry. Black and white, if you will. When you passed, your fate was undecided. You lived a gray life. Mostly good, but with an unfortunate number of sins. Not enough to send you to Hell, but your transgressions, when added to your lack of faith, were enough to deny your soul immediate entrance into Heaven. You fell to us instead."

"Why you? Who are you and Boothe?"

"Who we are doesn't matter. We're two of a countless many. We don't control your fate. That is and always has been yours to manage alone. *Your* choices pave the path in one direction or another, and sometimes in a circle. My way leads to Heaven. Boothe's ... well, you know."

"You're saying I chose wrong?"

One of Randall's eyebrows lifted. "What do *you* think?"

"So why are you here? Why are you helping me?"

"Because I don't believe you're lost, Henry. I still have faith in you."

"Faith? To do what?"

"To see the right path and find salvation. To turn from Boothe and reject him before it's too late."

"But I've killed so many people, Randall. Are you saying *that* doesn't count against me? That God will forgive *those* sins?"

Randall shrugged. "God does as he pleases." He fell quiet, as if weighing his words, then, "The people you killed were evil, right? All either hurting you or in the act of hurting others?"

"I think so," Henry said, trying to remember. Most of the mayhem was more haze than memory. Only when questioned by Randall did he realize how little thought he'd given to murdering people. He'd been so enthralled while killing that he'd never stopped to regret, or consider, the lives acquired.

Henry's humanity was as broken as his life.

"Not sure," Henry said, finally able to stand with wobbly legs. "I sensed them at first, these people doing shit. Like God, or someone, pointed me toward them, wanting me to intervene. They were evil, Randall. All of them deserved what they got."

"Led by God? So, you believe *God* told you to commit bloodshed?"

"I don't know if it was God, but I do know the victims weren't exactly members of the choir. All of them were in the middle of some shit when I found them. That's why they're dead."

"You mean that's why you *killed* them."

"Hey, I didn't make them assholes. *God* did. They don't deserve headstones, much less sympathy. I'm glad I did what I was supposed to do."

"How did it make you feel? And how are you feeling now?"

Henry paused, smiling. "I won't lie, Angel Cake. It felt pretty damned good then and not too bad right now."

Randall returned Henry's grin, though it seemed less than genuine. "That's because you feed from the misery, Henry. You're a demon. Like all demons, your fuel comes from the wretched."

"I'm saving people," Henry insisted. "*Ending* misery."

"Yes, but you're still absorbing the anguish around you, feeding from the sorrow. If you think you're helping anyone but yourself, you're a liar. You're no hero, Henry."

Henry said nothing.

"What about the men who broke into your house?"

"I've killed two of the fuckers who took my daughter from me, who raped my wife. Ask me to feel guilty about *that*, and I'm gonna tell you where to shove the guilt."

"Those were your tasks. Revenge murders, right? Those are the *only* men Boothe has directly asked you to kill. Correct?"

Henry nodded.

Randall shook his head. "Don't kill the third man."

"What?"

"You heard me, Henry. Reject vengeance, starting now. It isn't too late to turn from the darkness."

"But he's still out there. The bastard who shot me. The one who killed my daughter!"

"Of course he is," Randall said. "But what about the one who commanded him?"

"What?"

"Who ordered them to kill you and your family, Henry?"

"I don't fucking know. Maybe it was just these three assholes."

"That you have agreed to kill in a deal made with a demon."

"What, you're saying there's more of them?"

"If they are part of a larger organization? Yes, that's what I'm saying."

"Yeah, but where does it end?"

"That is precisely *my* point, Henry."

He shook his head, slicing the air with his hand. "Don't confuse the issue, *Randall*. I got this one last asshole to kill, and that's it."

"But what will killing him solve?"

Henry's anger was bubbling lava, about to erupt. "He

deserves to die!" His voice rolled through the graveyard. But it was dark, and they were far from any curious ears. Not that Henry cared. He was in too much of a lather to consider his volume. "He's responsible for murdering a child. If God can understand the rest of the people I killed, like you said He might, then surely *He* would understand me killing a child killer!"

"It's not as simple as you make it sound."

"So, what?" Henry paced. "I'm supposed to throw up my arms and stop looking? Return to Purgatory? Oh, excuse me, *Nowhere?* Then what? All is forgiven? I stroll through Heaven's gates and order a hoagie and a beer, maybe hang out with the Big Man himself?"

"There are no guarantees, but you *will* have your moment before God. Before you are Judged, you will have a chance to plead your case."

"So you don't even *know* if I'll be forgiven? Why should I come back with you, Randall? What's to say God, Judge Judy, whoever or whatever, is gonna overlook all the shit I've done? How do you know I'm not already past the point of no return? Because if so, then Hell's bells and Heaven's whores, I'm gonna break some fucking faces."

Randall's expression went from tart to angelic. "Because once damned, a soul is past redemption. It's *marked*, and there's no mistaking the stain of damnation. And I don't see that on you. *Yet.* You're still clean, Henry. There's hope if you're not wasteful."

"But he's still out there! The murdering fuck."

"What happens when you kill him, Henry? What then? Do you have a plan, beyond revenge? Do you just follow him up the chain of corruption?"

"Why do I need a plan? He's dead. The fucker's off the streets. His Christmas is canceled, and he can't hurt anyone else."

"But who are you to judge him? 'Judge not, that ye shall not be judged. For with what judgment ye judge, ye shall be judged. And with what measure ye mete, it shall me measured to you again.'"

Henry said, "Don't *even* go there."

"Go where?"

"With the Bible shit. Sorry, Randall, never been one for fairy tales."

"So even after everything you've seen and suffered through, you still don't believe?"

"Oh, I *believe*. But not in the Bible as God's Word. The book was written by men, and correct me if I'm wrong, but holy shit, men are pretty much responsible for every atrocity in our long and miserable history. So forgive me if I'm a bit skeptical about these men who claim to be speaking on behalf of *God*."

Patiently, Randall said, "So when will it be enough, Henry?"

"Enough what?"

"Killing. When will you have killed enough to sate yourself?"

"When the last murdering fucker is dead. Then I'll quit."

"Why stop there? Why not continue, kill all the bad guys in the big wide world?"

"Sounds good to me," Henry growled. "Maybe if someone from your team had been doing this from the get-go, bad shit wouldn't be happening to innocent people."

"No." Randall shook his head. "That is the wrong answer, Henry. Besides, you can never kill them all. Nor can you calculate the costs of your deeds. Every action has an equal reaction. This is an immutable law, whether or not you realize it."

"What sort of reaction? One less asshole in the world?

Maybe a mom or kid goes to bed without a bruise? Whoa, big loss. The universe couldn't possibly give a shit. Way I see it, I'm scrubbing the world shiny."

"Is that what you'd say to the families who lost their children at the church tonight? That you're turning the world into a better place?"

Henry *flared* and flew toward Randall, surprising himself with a sudden swing of his fist.

The angel blurred into motion, dodging Henry's blow. He sent an arc of bluish-white light from his hands which slammed Henry back to the grass.

Lying flat, though not wounded beyond his pride, Henry yelled, "The church wasn't my fucking fault!"

"You can lie to me, but you can't lie to yourself, Henry. Even if you did nothing directly, you *know* it was connected. You feel it inside, no different than *I* do. You killed two of their men. Did you really think they would have no *response?*"

"Like *that?* Shooting up a fucking church? Killing innocent children? No." He shook his head. "I never thought any terrorist shit would go down. You can't lay that at my feet."

"You've no idea what you're dealing with. The hornet's nest you've disturbed."

Henry stood. "You're right, Randall. I don't have a fucking clue. Maybe that's because no one tells me shit! So why don't you be an angel and tell me what in the Hell I'm involved in?"

"I can't do that."

"Why not? Oh, wait, don't tell me. There are *rules?*"

Randall looked at him with a maddening calm, smoothing his skin and making Henry want to punch the serenity from his face.

"What good are you?" Henry shouted. "You could've warned me about all this before I went off with Boothe."

"I tried. I told you not to trust him."

"You didn't explain *why* I shouldn't trust him, though! Context, Randall! How am I supposed to make the right decision with nothing to go on? You could've given me an idea about what he was planning, or let me know I'd wind up looking like a freak show! That I'd become a monster! That I'd …" Henry stopped, unable to continue.

Randall looked down at his folded hands. "That you would cause a massacre?"

Henry's air left his lungs in a rush, and he fell to his knees, crying into his hands as images of dead children stared back from the memory.

Randall rested a hand on Henry's shoulder. Henry wanted to shake it away and tell the old man in white to fuck the Hell off. But his touch was as comforting as if it had been his father's. He might have lost it all, broken down and sobbed into the man's chest, if the sting of shame didn't prohibit it.

"It isn't too late, Henry."

Henry looked up, meeting the angel's eyes. "Tell me what I'm up against, Randall. What sort of monsters would shoot up a church? Who are these people targeting my wife? And don't you fucking dare tell me that you can't say."

His eyes filled with sympathy, Randall pulled his hand from Henry's shoulder. "I'm sorry. I can't."

Henry screamed into the night, letting what was left of his rage consume him. He stood, glaring at Randall. "Why? Why any of this? You said you're looking out for my soul, but you won't give me the basic information I need to make the *right choices.*"

"I've told you enough to make a decision. That is all I *can* do, and all you truly need."

"No," Henry roared. "It's not enough!"

"It's enough to decide whether you want to take the road to Hell or Heaven."

"It's not enough to save my family! I have to stop these people!"

"You'll never bring her back," Randall said.

"Bring who back?"

"*Her.*"

It was then that Henry realized Randall hadn't brought him to just any cemetery, for the angel was pointing to a headstone freshly engraved with his daughter's name.

"Is she still in Purgatory?" Henry said, barely holding his voice steady. "Have you seen her?"

"I've seen her, yes," Randall said gently. "Would you like to go back, Henry? Would you like to return, so you can spend some time with Amélie before she is judged, just the two of you together?"

Henry knew what Randall was doing but would've agreed, anyway. He wanted to scream with a deafening *Yes!* at the angel's offer. He longed to be with Amélie, to close his eyes here and open them wherever the angel was willing to take him. If only he could get the image of Burg Spires littered with the broken bodies of its children from his mind.

Children.

Crying parents.

A river of honest blood.

All because of me.

"I want to," Henry confessed. "But who will protect Samantha?"

"Trust in God."

Henry looked back at Amélie's grave. "He's done a bang-up job so far."

"I can have her protected, Henry. Boothe has his minions, but I have resources of my own. Let me help you. Don't let him force you to do something you can never undo. Save your *soul*, Henry."

Henry turned from the headstone, his head swimming in indecision and bearing the weight of the world's woes. He began to walk away from the angel.

Randall asked, "Where are you going?"

"Home."

"Consider my offer, Henry. Reject Boothe while you still can."

Henry longed to lay his head somewhere and sleep through this latest nightmare.

He felt inches from death on his way to the apartment, so spent he could barely slip through the shadows. He ambled across darkened alleys, wondering how long it would be before he finally found his way uptown.

Hours seemed like days before he feebly climbed the side of his building, collapsing onto his fire escape as the sun lit the early morning sky.

He crawled into the loft, then over and into the California king. He didn't even bother to undress, but simply pulled the covers up to his chin and tried not to think of Samantha in danger, Amélie finding insanity in The Forgotten, or the atrocity he might have caused in pursuit of those that brought harm to his family.

He closed his eyes, fell asleep, and for the first time since his death, Henry dreamt of nothing.

Chapter Twenty-Seven

HENRY WOKE TO DÉJÀ VU.

Boothe was back in the apartment, sitting at the edge of his bed, watching TV in his bedroom while balancing the remote on the end of his finger. The demon popped the remote into the air, caught it, muted the volume, then turned to Henry.

"Good morning, *Hooded Angel*. Did you have sweet dreams?"

Fuck you.

Henry said nothing.

Boothe shrugged and turned the volume back up. "Ooh," he said, pointing the remote at the TV, airing someone's cellphone video footage of Henry, running without his hoodie like an animal into the dark. "That's a terrific shot of you, Henry. Makes you look a little like Gollum, minus the charm."

Henry was surprised by the familiar face on-screen, the man with the tear-swollen eyes the cop had been speaking with at the door when Henry made his escape. He was being interviewed, seemingly on location, at the police station. He wore a dark jacket and tie. His look said *cop* in neon.

Why are they talking to him?

The reporter introduced the man as Detective Michael Stone. He'd been off-duty at the church when the three assailants stormed inside. Gunfire erupted while he was in the restroom. He came out too late. The gunmen, which witnesses said were dressed in black hoodies and dark jeans, had killed twenty-six people in less than a minute before escaping.

Dark jeans and hoodies? What the hell? They tried to set me up?

Stone emerged from the bathroom to find his seven-year-old son, Stephen, dead. As his story ended, Public Information Officer Nanette Ramirez joined the interview, discussing a *person of interest* they were looking for. The screen showed a few photos of Henry, stills from the cell phone video shown a moment before. Ramirez stressed that the police would not elaborate if they suspected that the man in the hoodie was also the Hooded Angel, or if the church massacre was tied in any way to the vigilante attacks throughout the city.

Boothe clapped his hands in mock applause.

"Person of interest, Henry. You've gone from Hooded Angel to Person of Interest! Congratulations. This might be the most attention you've ever managed to nab. Far better than that execrable *Sitting at the Back of the Bus*."

Henry finally said what he'd been thinking since opening his eyes. "Fuck you."

"Don't be upset with me, Henry. You're the one who allowed yourself to be seen."

"I didn't do anything, Boothe. And I didn't *let* anything happen! Those fuckers went to a place of worship to kill Sam, then shot up the entire church! Is that what you wanted, why you set me down this path of revenge?

Because you're a goddamned demon who feeds on creating as much misery as possible? Who the Hell are these monsters, and why are they targeting my family?"

"Disgruntled fans of your work?"

"Seriously." Henry ignored Booth's attempt at humor. "Who are these people? Right after I killed the second fucker, he laughed and straight-up told me they were hitting the church. Oh, and I might add, this was right before he went all suicide on himself. You know what sort of sick fuck it takes to do something like that? Who are these people? Mobsters? Terrorists?"

Boothe shook his head. "Sorry, Henry. I can't help you there."

"Can't or *won't?*"

"Does it really matter?"

"Of course it does!" Henry stared at the demon, sick of his bullshit and the endless death. Done being manipulated. He thought of Randall's offer again. Reject Boothe and he would protect Sam.

Would he, though? Could he?

Well he can't do worse than Boothe is doing. She was almost killed at the church!

"I'm finished," Henry said, making his decision before he'd had a chance to think too much more about it.

Get out now. Get out fast. End it now.

Boothe smiled as if Henry told a joke. "Finished with what?"

"Finished with killing. I'm done doing your dirty work."

"Henry, Henry, Henry. It's not *my* dirty work. These men killed you and your sweet Amélie." He stood from the bed and dropped his voice to a whisper. "They *raped* your wife."

Henry snapped, leapt from the mattress, and shoved a

finger in Boothe's face. "Don't you fucking talk about them, ever again!"

Boothe took a step back, his smile never faltering. "You're much too close to quit."

Henry pointed at the television. "I've had enough death. Those bodies in the church. The families slaughtered. That's on *me!* Randall was right."

"Randall?" He didn't sound surprised. "Ah, I see. The angel's been churning your guilt."

"And what are you churning?"

"Me?" Boothe feigned offense. "I churn nothing, because I don't need to. Our goals are the same. I want what you want. There's no need to manipulate you, Henry. As far as those people in the church are concerned, all I can say is, get over the guilt. This isn't your fault, Henry. It was their time. Everyone dies, some earlier than others. If you want someone to blame, blame your benevolent God."

Henry had a hundred questions, all different versions of the same thing. *What in the Hell do we have in common?* or *Why should I trust you?* Instead, he simply said, "Get out."

"What?"

"Leave. I'm done, so that means you're finished."

Boothe's gentle laugh slithered under Henry's skin.

"No, Henry, you're not. Being nearly finished and entirely finished are not the same thing. You are *nearly* finished. Besides, you can't very well kick me out of *my* loft."

"You said it was mine, and you owe it to me for bringing me back in this." Henry waved a hand across his twisted body. "Like I said, I'm done."

"No," Boothe said, still smiling. "You aren't."

"Yes. I. Am."

"You'll come around, Henry. I know you. Better than

you do, since I'm not afraid to look in all the darkest corners."

"No, Boothe, I'm finished! Done with you and everything. Find someone else to do your killing."

"Why would I do that when you're so good at it, Henry?"

Stop saying my fucking name!

"Fuck you, *Boothe*. I'm done."

"Henry, stop denying what you truly are. Embrace it. Allow yourself to thrive on the power. We both know you want these men dead, so why do we dance? Even Randall knows it, for Heaven's sake, and he's dimmer than a ten-watt bulb. You, Henry, were *meant* for this. Delight in the experience."

Randall's words echoed through his head. Henry wondered if he could truly trust the angel. Could Randall protect Sam? Could he reunite Henry with his daughter, and would they be together in Heaven? It seemed too good to be true, yet, the man was an angel.

An angel wouldn't lie, would he?

"I reject you, Boothe."

The demon laughed, throwing his head back and clutching his stomach. "Ah, Henry, that's rich." Boothe cleared his throat, straightened his raspberry tie, and said, "*I reject you, Boothe!*" The same voice that Eddie Murphy used to impersonate uptight white guys. He laughed again, shaking his head, practically begging Henry to punch him in the face.

Henry nodded and crossed his arms. "I don't know what happens next, and I don't care. I don't need your apartment, and I don't need you. Return me to Purgatory or send me to Hell, I don't fucking care. I'm done dancing."

The laughter finally died on Boothe's lips.

"And what about your poor suffering Samantha? Shall I call Ezra home? Tell him his services are no longer required because you decided to roll the dice on your beloved's safety?" He paused and pointed his index finger in the air, as if conjuring a spark of brilliance. "Or perhaps I can tell him it's finally fine to go inside. He does get so very hungry."

Henry wasn't buying it. "Bullshit. I spent time with Ezra. He may be a monster, but he's not *that* kinda monster."

"You willing to bet what you *think* you know versus what I am certain of?"

"I'll trust God to protect her."

Boothe laughed yet again, his eyebrows rising in surprise. "Why don't you ask Officer Stone how he feels about God? On second thought, maybe you want to stay away from him at the moment, as he's busy forming a lynch mob to find you."

Henry said nothing.

"How long do you think you can stay out of sight, Henry? How long before the cult strikes again? Maybe next time they won't miss your pretty wife."

Cult?

Henry's heart stopped mid-beat, frozen in his chest. "What?"

"What 'what'?" Boothe repeated, seeming confused.

Instinct said Satan's Little Helper had suffered a slip of the tongue in mentioning a cult. But Henry's cynicism said that Boothe had dropped the word intentionally, playing Henry like he had from the get-go, trying to draw him back. Henry felt like a rat drawn to cheese despite the trap. "What do you mean *cult*?"

"Did I say 'cult'?" Boothe shrugged. "I'm sorry, I've no idea why I said that."

"What aren't you telling me, Boothe?"

"No, no, you don't *want* to know, remember?" A wave of his hand. "You want to *reject* me. So go ahead and do that, Henry. After all I've done for you. Risking my eternal soul to save you from Trackers. You reject *me*? Fine, but stop pretending you're better than me. We're one and the same, Henry, and no lies you tell yourself will change that fact. So you go on and pretend you're this perfect little angel. But you *feed* on death. Cease your murders and you will die. Again. And this time you'll go straight to Hell."

"What?" Henry said.

But Boothe had vanished.

One day, I'm going to kill that fucking demon.

"I don't care, Boothe! Do you hear me? I don't FUCKING *CARE!*"

Henry screamed until there was nothing left inside him. He collapsed onto the bed then looked up at the TV. Pastor Owen was on the screen, speaking with the news anchor, Bonnie James, from inside his church, loudly declaring he would not allow fear to win.

"What's next for the church? How do you recover from something like this?" the anchor asked from her comfy seat in the studio, far from the misery she covered day after endless day.

"I'm not sure what's next. We're taking things a step at a time and doing what we can to help the community heal," Pastor Owen said, looking right into the camera. "Time, and our Lord, heals all wounds."

Henry glared at the TV. "Except exit wounds, Pastor. The Good Lord doesn't do dick about those."

Chapter Twenty-Eight

HENRY WAS LEADING a symphony of pain played by an orchestra of murder inside him. Clawing, biting, and tearing the flesh from one innocent victim after another, drinking their rage and misery as if lapping from an endless fountain of death.

And then he woke up, his body throbbing with the ache of withdrawal. It had been two days since he had left the apartment, and he hadn't killed anyone since Bulldog.

Henry thought that once he rejected Boothe, Randall would come and return him to Purgatory. But the angel had yet to arrive, and every hour that passed without feeding was another eternity. To make matters worse, his ability to sense the world's suffering had heightened to the point where he could feel, hear, and taste every whiff of pain within a half mile. The world called with its banquet of misery, and Henry could no longer avoid it.

He had to feed.

Covers hit the floor as Henry crossed the apartment to the kitchen. He drained four tall glasses of water. Then he dressed in a rush and ran to the window. He opened it and leapt into the night, chasing his body's bellowing instincts.

He was a half-dozen rooftops from his apartment when the painful ripping inside him intensified, dragging him in a fresh direction. He went deeper into the city, following the scent. Minutes later, he found himself staring down through the large glass windows of a convenience store at the something horrible happening inside.

He looked around, watching as cars passed on the street, oblivious.

No pedestrians. No cops.

Shit was about to get bad. A tiny part of him whispered to turn, go home. Anywhere but down the side of the building and into the convenience store. It was drowned out by his larger need, and he ignored the whisper, scampering down the fire escape of an old abandoned apartment building across the street from the store. He hit the ground and paused to get a better look. Through the window, fifty yards away, Henry spied a pair of gunmen in mid-robbery.

The sudden buzzing surprised him. It was either a new ability or one he'd not noticed before. A talent he hadn't been able to use until desperate. He could sense the victim inside, terror like heat on his back. But for the first time, Henry also sensed more. Everything from gender, to the old woman's fear that she wouldn't make it out alive, to the sorrow that she would miss her granddaughter's Ballet Folklorico performance the following Friday.

And nearly drowning out her emotions was the raw violence fuming from both men. The taller of the two was named Alex, a rail-thin fucker with a buzz cut and a misshapen nose from too many fights. Clearly itching for a reason to shoot.

Henry tasted, and could almost feel, the murder. Seconds from happening.

Get away from here.

Stay out of it.

Don't give in.

Henry flipped the bird to the whisper, ran toward the store, and screamed as he exploded through the glass. The second, shorter gunman, whose name Henry hadn't sensed, turned his pistol on him. But he couldn't manage a shot before Henry was on him, grabbing the gun from the fucker's clenched fist.

Henry wrenched the weapon from his fingers, twisting them in the process, and swung the handle into the man's skull, sending him to the floor.

Alex moved his aim from the cowering grandma and centered it on Henry's chest.

The muscles in his forearm bulged, and Henry leapt on the gunman before he could pull the trigger. He had the barrel of the pistol in one hand and Alex's thin wrist in the other. Henry planted his feet and leaned back into a spin. He pulled Alex into his rotation then tossed him across the store.

His body slammed into a shelf full of candy. Rattling boxes flew, and the display crashed to the floor. Alex swam through the mess, trying to get to his feet, screaming in terror as Henry moved in a flash, shoving the punk's own gun against his cheek.

"Give me one good reason not to kill you!" Henry roared. He wasn't sure if he would even pull the trigger, but he pulled back his hood, revealing his face to the wide-eyed man.

Alex slung his head from side to side in denial, tears flowing down his cheeks.

Henry felt the punk's fear rise against his face. Tasted it

as it filled his nose. Ignored his own sympathy poking through, like a seedling struggling for sun. He threw the gun behind him, then brought his fist back on the rebound, pounding the guy in his temple.

Alex's head rocked back, and his eyes fluttered closed. He body relaxed, the fear leaving his face. Receding from Henry's senses. Grandma stopped cowering behind the counter, standing to look at Henry. He turned to her with a growl.

"Go! Call the police!"

Grandma ran outside as Henry stood over Alex, fighting the urge to murder him. The fallen men's fear, along with the raw violence still floating in the air, surged through him. Like the sickening sweet scent of the iced cinnamon rolls at the mall. Henry wanted more.

Henry squatted down over Alex. Examined him from head to toe.

Why the Hell should I spare his life? Or the other man's?

They were thugs. Wastes of humanity, preying on those weaker than them.

No different than the men who broke into his own house and murdered his daughter, raped his wife, and killed him. If Henry allowed them to live, it was only a matter of time before they harmed or killed someone else.

Is it not a kindness to take out society's trash?

These are the monsters, not me.

Nah, I don't need to kill them. Randall will come soon.

Don't give in. He's probably testing you.

To see if you can go without killing.

A thunderous gunshot, and the window in front of Henry exploded. He spun around to see the other robber had gotten up and recovered his gun. He held it out in his left hand, the barrel jittering as it shook with his fear and anger. He held the broken fingers of his right hand in front of his chest, curled against his jacket.

The thug steadied his aim and fired. This time, the bullet slammed Henry in the chest.

Henry fell back, pain splintering through him in a spreading fire as he struggled to recover his breath.

He laughed, stumbling forward, sliding on scattered candy. "What the Hell are you?" The thug asked. He was three feet from Henry and unlikely to miss, even disoriented and using the wrong hand.

Henry's heart raced as he stared down the barrel of the pistol. He tried to stand, but fear wouldn't let him. What if a headshot could kill him?

"I asked you a question," the thug said, sneering down at Henry. "What are you?"

Should have killed the fucker while he was down. Mercy was wasted on trash like this. How long did he have before the man fired again? He clutched his chest where he'd been shot, even though he could feel it already healing. Pain lanced into his breastbone, and the twisted bullet pushed from the wound into Henry's hand.

He gasped, and the thug came closer with a smile. "I'm …" He let his voice trail off and hung his head, panting with feigned exhaustion.

"What?" The man moved closer, his legs now inches from Henry's feet.

That's it. Come closer.

As if he heard him, the thug took another step, bravado outweighing his caution. He leaned over to get a closer look at Henry's misshapen face.

His eyes shot open and met the thug's widening gaze. Then he swept his feet and brought the man to the ground. He fired as he toppled, throwing his broken hand out for balance. The bullet whined past Henry's ear. He leapt up and pounced on top of the thug with a roar.

The thug raised his gun, dazed eyes tracking his prey's descent.

He growled, and his black nails extended into claws, sinking into the man's wrist as Henry grabbed his pistol hand. Henry jerked his fists apart, wrenching the thug's gun hand from his arm in one sickening pull.

Blood spurted from his stump as he screamed. Henry felt an invigorating rush at the man's horrified reaction. He couldn't imagine losing a hand, but he could taste the man's screaming denial. He wanted to finish him off right there. More than anything.

But he thought of Randall again. And his chance at redemption.

Do I want it more than my family?

"What the fuck did you do?" the man screamed in a high-pitched shriek, clutching his stump with mangled fingers.

He looked down, then back at Alex, still on the ground in a heap. He tried to convince himself that he shouldn't kill them, frozen with indecision until forced into motion by a siren screaming in the distance.

Henry fled the store, racing back into the night, running near top speed without stopping or slowing until he found himself in a huddle of shadows.

Back in front of Burg Spires.

He felt like a junkie calling his sponsor. He hoped Pastor Owen would say something to make the cravings go away. Henry slipped from one shadow to the next, then inside the church. The pastor dragged a worn broom across the cold floor, cleaning dirt tracked in from outside. He'd yet to scrub the bloodstained wood. Broken glass glittered in the corners.

Henry stayed buried in the shadows, wondering if the pastor knew he was there, and more importantly, whether he would blame him for what had happened on his hallowed grounds. The pastor couldn't possibly know that the men were connected to Henry's victims, but he had surely put two and two together with the *Hooded Angel* sightings.

"Pastor." Henry stepped out from the shadows.

The pastor turned, startled, though his kind eyes suggested he was genuinely happy to see Henry. Yet, behind his smile, Henry sensed a definite anxiety. He seemed nervous, almost skittish, though it was probably impossible to stay unfazed when your church was host to a massacre.

The pastor shifted on his feet. "One moment, Henry."

Pastor Owen went to the wall and leaned the broom against a wood panel, then to the front door, locking it then before returning.

Henry stood at the pulpit, looking up at the giant wooden crucifix he'd looked at so many times over the years from the pews. He stared at the fine details etched into Jesus's face, the frozen anguish as if He had witnessed the massacre beneath him.

"It's good to see you, Henry. I'm sure you've heard about the tragedy, yes?"

"Yes," Henry said. "I'm sorry."

Silent discomfort passed between them, with neither man speaking until Henry finally said, "How is she, Pastor? Sam, I mean. I saw her arrive."

"She's okay. Shaken, of course, but otherwise unharmed."

"And you?"

"I'm fine." He looked down.

Henry followed his gaze to the bloodstained floors.

"Jesus." The pastor winced and he added, "Sorry, I didn't mean to take the Lord's name in vain, especially in church."

The pastor said nothing, pulling them deeper into shared silence.

Henry was hungry to scream but spoke in a whisper. "Why would your God allow something like this to happen, Pastor? Something so horrible?"

"*My* God?"

"Well, he isn't *mine*. Not that He wants me. Even if He did, I don't know that I'd worship a God who was responsible for all this."

"He *does* want you," the pastor said, sparking to life. "And He isn't responsible, not for *any* of this. Your question is as old as religion. Why would a loving God bring misery to so many? That's an obstacle of faith for even the most devout among us, and always more so during moments of tragedy. God may *allow* horrors to happen, Henry, but He does not *cause* them."

Henry shrugged. "Potato, pa-tah-toe."

"No, Henry. Not quite. Bad things happen because God gives freedom to his people. You are free. Not a puppet on a string. No different from the monsters who did this. Yes, they were able to do so because God gave them the gift of choice, deciding between good and evil. But He grieves loudest when man chooses evil, like a parent weeping for a prodigal child."

"I don't know, Pastor. Seems like there's as much bad in the world as good. Sometimes even more. You've gotta wonder what sort of God would allow evil to thrive. He gives us choice, and this is what we decide?"

"Sadly," the pastor said, "there will be more. Much of the world's suffering stems from our separation with God. He is all that is good, yet everyone on the planet, including me, does things to move further from Him, day by day and inch by inch. When I sin, I worsen our global relationship. The more I separate myself from Him, the more likely I am to hurt others. The same holds true for the rest of the world. He has set us as the caretakers of the reality he created."

Henry wondered which sentence to challenge. The pastor, though, kept him quiet by finishing his sermon.

"We are separated from God. Apart from Him, there is suffering. When we use our time to answer His call, He will deliver eternal peace. We are all given choice, Henry. We *choose* to live by His word, or we *choose* to reject Him."

"It's bullshit. Sorry, Pastor. But that's my take. No God worth believing in would let evil exist in such abundance. There's an entire group of fucks, all sharing the same bullshit tattoo, doing everything from beating their women to murdering my family. I can see why God would want to look the other way on that crap. After all, it's not *His* problem. But He better not expect my worship. It turns praying into begging, and I ain't begging for shit."

Henry expected the pastor to argue theology. Instead he said, "A tattoo?"

Henry nodded.

"What did it look like?"

Henry thought for a second, then said, "It's ornate. And specific. The fuckers probably bought 'em in bulk, all at the same place. There's a twisted vine as a circle, with an *F* and *C* inside it. The letters are made of vines too, and they're sorta jagged, with roots at the bottom and a bunch of shit coming out of the top."

Pastor Owen's eyes said he knew something horrible.

Then he proved it.

"I've seen that tattoo."

Wow. So shit can still get weirder.

"I visit Dodd Prison, two Saturdays each month," the pastor explained. "Several of the men at Dodd have the same tattoo you're describing."

"Because they saw it in a Calvin Klein ad?"

Pastor Owen answered Henry as if he wasn't responding to sarcasm. "No, the men in Dodd belong to a religious offshoot calling itself *Order From Chaos.*"

"Order From Chaos?" Henry repeated. "How clever. What the Hell is Order From Chaos?"

"The organization was big a few years back, at least for those in the twelve-step and prison communities living in Burg. It was underground. No single official meeting place. Consisting of broken people trying to piece their fractured lives together. Members of the Order were always overcoming *something.* Addiction, abuse, all the usual bad stuff. It wasn't a cult with Kool-Aid or Satan worship or anything like that. Mostly just a sad assembly of harmlessly confused individuals with lives so desperate that the Order's mantra was their only way out. They saw themselves as pulling order from their chaotic lives, with God's help, of course. Like I said, they seemed more or less harmless, save for a few who used their positions to exploit others."

"These aren't people trying to piece their lives together, Pastor. They're trying to tear lives apart. Assholes, murderers, and rapists."

"Weeds grow in every garden, Henry."

"Could the Order be tied to this?" Henry waved his hand across the empty church. "To what happened to me and my family?"

Henry then told the pastor how he'd found the second of the three men, and the man's warning that his people were gonna strike the church. He told him how Randall said Henry had sown the seeds, that this was all some sort of cosmic payback.

The pastor stared at Henry, his eyes finally registering shock. "The killer told you they were going to strike here?"

"Yes. And then he killed himself. If that's not fanatical, I don't know what is."

"Did he say why he was targeting the church? Did he say he was after Samantha?"

"He wasn't too talkative after slitting his own throat. Do you think the Order did this?"

"They haven't been active since their founder passed a few years back. A man named Darryl Scott. They weren't terribly organized to begin with, and many of the original members quickly fell back into their old habits without his guidance. Still," the pastor shook his head, "I don't see them doing something like this."

"But two of the men who broke into my house had the tattoos, and I'm willing to bet the third does, too. Could that *really* be coincidence?"

"Two or three of the men might've met as part of the Order and teamed together to commit robberies. So in that way, yes, the Order could be loosely related, but that's petty crime. To do something like *this*, well, it makes no sense. The group wasn't violent. *At all.* And I doubt you'd be able to find three members still in touch with each other, much less staging attacks on a church."

"Maybe even five. Remember I killed two. So I'm back to hunting at least three people, assuming there aren't more."

"I don't think you should be hunting *anyone*, Henry. I believe you're far better served by surrendering the pursuit. Let the police handle it. Let them do their jobs."

"But the cops don't have *shit*. They think *I* had something to do with it!" Henry was suddenly angry, as if everything was the pastor's fault. "Haven't you been watching the news?"

"I've been busy," he said, impressing Henry with unwavering patience.

"Can *you* go to the cops? Tell them you saw a tattoo? Give them some clue to the real killers."

"But I didn't. They were in and out so fast I couldn't see much beyond the masks under their hoodies. And I refuse to lie, even if I do believe you."

Henry sighed.

"You must let it go, Henry. Allow God to do His work, so you can find the justice that you, and the many families victimized at Burg Spires last night are seeking."

"Last I heard, God wasn't in the justice business."

Pastor Owen ignored him. "Lay low, Henry. Don't go to Samantha. She can't handle anything else right now. And don't come here. At least not for a while. The police will probably be coming and going, asking follow-up questions of me and my staff."

"I can stick to the shadows. I'll be fine."

The pastor smiled, but Henry could see it was only there so they didn't argue.

"One of the poor souls taken in cold blood was named Shane McGuinness. Shane was born to Ryan and Molly McGuinness after nine years of trying. Yes, Henry, nine years, with only a few flickers of wavering faith. They were as committed a couple as I've ever seen, hopelessly devoted to finding their best possible life together. I had the privilege of helping them through their early years of marriage and many unsuccessful attempts at conception. At four years old, Shane was the youngest of our boys here at Burg Spires. Now he's dead."

Henry wanted the pastor to shut the fuck up. "Why are you telling me this?"

"Because, Henry, when we give into darkness, that darkness feeds and grows, destroying everything in its wake. Your actions are not happening in a vacuum. If this *was* retaliation, then you've set something into motion which you cannot hope to stop. I suggest you surrender before they kill again, or Heaven forbid, hurt Samantha."

"You sound like Randall. He told me to turn back now, while the gates of Heaven were still open to me. So what am I supposed to do? Walk away from everything? No." Henry shook his head. "This won't end unless I end it."

"It only ends when you walk away. Trust in God. It seems as if Randall has offered you a way back. Take it. Go. Be with your daughter."

"What about Sam? If they did this and they're still going after her, then she's in big-time danger. These monsters don't know how to stop and seem willing to do anything."

"God has spared her twice. Do you think that's an *accident*? For whatever reason, He has allowed your wife to escape two terrible tragedies. *Two!* You must have faith that He will continue to keep her safe."

"Well there's the problem. I'm fresh out of faith."

"Then what about mercy, Henry? Remember, blessed are the merciful, for they will be *shown* mercy."

Henry turned to leave.

"What are you going to do, Henry?" Pastor Owen asked.

"Pray for mercy."

Chapter Twenty-Nine

HENRY RETURNED to his former home, trying to keep his mind from cycling through worst-case scenarios like it always did. One of the things he hated most about himself was the near-crippling insecurity that came from simply being him. Ugly and fat and no good in school, awkward and bloated with a stuttering confidence that stumbled and fell and rarely stood up for itself. Worse than a monster, Henry had been a loser. At least monsters had power over the fearful. Losers had power over no one and nothing.

Unless they were funny, which Henry didn't learn until he was older and taking the stage in smoky clubs.

If you were a loser who told the truth while making people laugh, you could do it while standing at least a foot higher than the rest of the room. Then being a loser might be money in the bank. Girls who wouldn't have fucked Henry for money a decade back would've fallen to their knees and taken it on the face before the ink was dry on his deal, just for the privilege of being backstage with *His Royal Chuckles* for fifteen minutes.

But Henry had never said yes. Not once. Not even when high.

He had Samantha. As hard as it was to love her sometimes, and as much of a mess as she'd been during their early years, Henry had never wanted anyone else since the day she sat in one of his acts, yelling for him to speak louder because she wanted to hear what he had to say. Then, sitting at an outside table of a restaurant a few blocks from the club, Henry had told one story after the other for forty minutes. Not one had passed without her laughing.

She loved him because he made her laugh, and for Sam, that was as good as salvation from the rough life she'd had.

Henry approached his house, wondering if Ezra had been pulled from duty.

"Hello, Master Henry," the goll said a second before he saw him, as if to answer the unspoken question. Ezra dropped from the roof, quick and alert, like he'd been snorting Pixy Stix all night.

"Hey Ezra." Something about his subservience made Henry want to kick him. Something he'd never felt before, at least not for someone who wasn't an arrogant asshole. "See anything tonight?"

"Not tonight, Master Henry."

Henry hoped Ezra would say something else, anything, so he wouldn't have to. But the goll stayed silent.

"Aren't you gonna tell me I'm not supposed to be here?"

"No, Master Henry. Master Boothe said you might come and to let you do whatever you wanted."

"Really?"

"Yes, Master Henry." Ezra looked at the house rather than him.

Henry felt bad, wondering if he'd somehow offended the goll. "Thank you," he said after a few seconds of silence. "For protecting Sam."

"It is my privilege to serve you and your beautiful wife."

"Hey, Ezra, mind if I ask you a question?"

"Of course not, Master Henry."

"Did Boothe say anything about me not helping him or you no longer coming here?"

"No, Master Boothe has said nothing. Only that you were having doubts."

Henry snorted. "Doubts. That what he's calling it?"

"What do you doubt, Master?"

"It's complicated. I don't want to do the wrong thing."

"I understand, Master Henry."

"Tell me, Ezra, do you trust Boothe? Has he ever lied to you?"

"No, Master Boothe has never lied. He is the most honest man I know."

Henry stared into the moon's bright light, wondering if golls were like humans. More loyal than honest.

"He's a good man. He's only trying to get her back."

"Who?" Henry asked.

"His love. Maria."

Henry couldn't hide his surprise. "What do you mean, get her back?"

The goll turned his eyes to the grass. "Ezra said too much. Please, Master Henry, ask Ezra no more."

A crimson fear of disappointing Boothe dilated Ezra's eyes, along with something else. Henry thought the goll wasn't afraid of punishment, so much as scared of letting Boothe down, as though he genuinely cared what the man thought of him. Fear born from respect. Or love.

Boothe? Who the fuck is this guy, really?

It didn't matter. Henry had decided, and there was nothing Ezra or Boothe could say to change it.

"So, Master Boothe said I could do whatever I wanted?"

"Yes, Master Henry."

"Then I'm going inside."

"Good luck, Master Henry." Ezra bowed.

"Anything I should know? Anything changed? The code to cut the alarm still the same?"

"No, Master Henry. Nothing has changed. You should have no difficulties if you stick to the shadows."

Henry nodded his thanks, then shadowed his body to the porch. He unlocked the door and slipped inside the house. He silenced the alarm like a blade to the throat, crept up the stairs, then slunk through the hallway until he found Sam sleeping on the gym floor, her hand resting on the treadmill beside an empty bottle of her favorite wine.

Samantha's mouth hung open wide enough to drive through as she snored. Henry longed to touch her again. He reached out, caressing her raven hair, staring at her for what would likely be the final time.

"Henry?" She stirred in her sleep, mumbling.

He fell back into the shadows, his heart pounding as she went back to snoring.

He pressed himself to the wall and sank to the floor, breathing in harmony with Samantha, in and out, until he was strong enough to stand.

Henry was too hungry for sorrow to stay. Her sadness was horrible, practically saturating the air even as she slept. And he felt like a *vampire* feeding from her sadness.

Everything inside him, outside of his instincts, begged him to scoop Sam into his arms and carry her across the hall to their bedroom where he could lay her down on their bed. Instead, Henry wiped his eyes, flew to a shadow in the hallway, then went down the stairs and out the front door.

He felt naked, knowing Ezra could see him slipping from the house to the carport, smelling the city, begging him to greet it. The city's pain wanted him to kill.

He felt weak and murder meant survival.

I can't allow Boothe to win.

Henry climbed inside his Lexus then pulled out and into the street.

Time to end it all.

Henry once had a friend, Janine Novak. Funny. As. Shit. Even though he could tell she was dying inside since the day they met. There was something inside her, blacker than a missing moon. Pure anger, for what, he never knew. Over a shared bowl of some of the best weed Henry had ever smoked, Janine said that most days she fell asleep hoping she'd never open her eyes and woke up pissed as shit she was still breathing without any easy way out.

He asked Janine if she ever thought of ending it all. Henry thought suicide was crazy, even for a crazy person, since no matter how bad shit was, it was better than being dead with no shit at all. She'd said, "Yeah, all the time," then proved she could drive thought to action by jumping from the Vincent Thomas Bridge after a show in LA just one month later.

Four years passed before Henry finally understood. He was ready to die. Right now. A true death, whatever that meant.

Whatever it took not to dance like a monkey for Boothe, so fucking be it. Maybe he would meet Amélie on his way to wherever he went and, hopefully, God and his merry band of fucking angels would find a way to protect

Sam in his absence. If not, maybe she was good enough to wind up in Heaven with her daughter. And maybe, if it wasn't too late, with him, too.

First, he had to get away from Boothe. That meant going someplace where the demon couldn't. Henry remembered him saying the only place he couldn't blink to was a place he'd never been.

Henry hoped like Hell Boothe had never been in the Burg City lockup.

He entered the police station in shadow, trying to summon the courage to leave it, and stared at the woman behind the desk, studying her movements while inhaling her sorrow. Divorced twice, one son from each marriage, each too much like his father in all the wrong ways. The first asshole cheated on her seven times, with nine different women. The second never cheated at all, unless you counted the trannies, and she did. The light wrinkles under her eyes might as well have added a hundred pounds to her figure, the way they hung, warning the other sex to stay the hell away. Most mornings she woke up thinking she would be better off dead.

He marveled that his powers, or abilities, or whatever they were, now allowed him to see so much deeper inside the most miserable souls. He wished he'd had the same abilities when growing up. He could've verbally torn his life's assholes to ribbons by slicing right into their deepest insecurities.

Henry stepped from the shadows, appearing in front of the woman, his palms splayed flat on the desktop. He smiled from behind his hoodie as she shrieked, dropping her pen onto the desk. It fell to the floor as she cleared her throat.

"Can I help you?" she asked, trying to stitch her cracking voice together.

Henry lowered his hood and leaned across the desk. "I'm the man you're all looking for."

Chapter Thirty

HENRY WAITED in a box for fate to seal itself around him. It had been ten minutes since he had been led to the interrogation room.

He sat at a table, gray concrete walls on either side, a heavy and presumably locked door in the wall to his right. The only way out of the room. Mirrors bookended him in front and behind. Henry avoided the mirror, not just because of the monstrous man reflecting back, but more for the people *behind* the mirrors. He felt the cops, watching and judging every twitch as he shifted in his seat.

Their thoughts flooded his brain, as if he were plugged into their minds.

Guilty.

Killer.

What sort of horrible monster does this?

One of the cops thought of Mike Stone, the officer who lost his son in the massacre.

Wait until Mike sees this fucker. This freak just signed his death warrant.

He wished someone would hurry up and come question him. Get on with the process of arresting him. The sooner he was in a cell, unable to get out, the less likely he was to change his mind and flee.

But Henry still wasn't cuffed, though he had no idea why not. Seemed to him the police would have wanted to beat him bloody if they thought he had anything to do with the church massacre. And because he matched the description of hooded shooters and ran from the scene of the crime, he *had* to be a suspect.

So why am I just sitting here in a room? What the hell are they waiting for?

Then he considered that perhaps he wasn't a suspect in the church shootings. Only a 'person of interest', as he'd heard on the news. Someone the cops only wanted to speak with. But they *were* after the Hooded Angel for his string of vigilante murders, and he was turning himself in, ready to confess to what he'd done. That should get him locked up for a good long time.

He formed a circle with his arms on the table and lay his head in the center. Shrouded under the hood, he was reminded of his *blankie* from when he was four years old, the one he'd wrap himself inside while hiding from *monsters*. Between the mirrors and people staring from the other side, Henry had never felt more like a carnival freak.

Hear ye, hear ye, come one and all! Get a glimpse of the Hooded Angel! Just one dollar! Arrive curious, leave in terror. This abhorrent freak of nature will chill and thrill you!

The door begged him to use it.

Get out before it's too late!

Even if it was locked, Henry was reasonably sure he still had enough power to break out. For now.

Because the longer he waited, the weaker he grew. His body drained, as if in concert with his plan. To deplete himself fully, and ensure his imprisonment.

Still, the door begged.

Leave now before it's too late.

Before they lock you up and throw away the key.

Think you're a freak now? Wait until they get you in a cell, Henry Boy. You are fucked!

Henry closed his eyes, squeezing the reflection from his sight so his mind could focus on the streaming thoughts from staring men. He sensed five officers, all men. Then a sixth man joined.

Oh, hell yeah. Now Mike's here! Get a look, Mikey, there he is!

Henry felt a sudden and overwhelming surge of hatred with Mike's arrival. A raw, repellent stew worse than anything Henry had ever felt on stage, all directed at him from the other side of the mirror.

He's right to hate me.

I'm a fucking monster.

I killed those kids! I killed his son!

It was my fault.

The mourning cop's radiating hate revealed the flaws in Henry's strategy. He wanted to get locked up, somewhere where the demon couldn't reach him. Boothe said he was limited to only blinking into places where he'd previously been. Henry figured the police station was a safe bet, especially given its recent construction. Henry could fade from life in peace, assuming he *could* die. He never intended to force a grieving father into further agony by making him look upon the man he thought responsible for his son's senseless murder.

For a man like that, forgiveness was only a word.

It meant letting go of a fucker's throat, even after your fingers were sunk into his flesh. Like the grieving officer, Henry would happily murder whoever hurt, or even tried to hurt, his baby girl.

Though time fuzzed for Henry, he figured he spent

another twenty minutes alone in the room before the door finally opened to Halle Berry. At least the officer *looked* like Halle Berry, if she had ever been cast as a woman waging war in a pair of horn-rimmed glasses, a year of exhaustion clinging to her face. She carried a stack of paperwork and a video camera on a tripod.

She approached Henry's table, removed her glasses, and wiped the back of her hand across her tired eyes. She replaced the frames on the bridge of her nose and turned to Henry. "Hello. I'm Detective Rivera. And you are?"

"John," he lied. "John Hicks."

Henry used the same name that had helped him anonymously check into a hundred hotels. The dead-legend blend of John Belushi and Bill Hicks.

"Well, Mr. Hicks," Rivera said, sitting in the chair on the table's opposite end. "Thank you for coming in."

Rivera avoided direct eye contact, instead looking down at the stack of bulging manila folders. Henry wondered if they'd really compiled a ream of paper in such a short time, on what must be minimal sightings, or if the folders were props, used to make him squirm under the weight of what they might know about him.

Rivera's eyes held the table as she stacked folders in a neat corner to her left, then looked up at Henry as if she'd suddenly remembered something important. "Can I get you a drink? Something to eat?"

Her hospitality seemed almost genuine. Henry wondered how much of his freaky face she could see beneath the hoodie. He had been focusing on the shadows, drawing them toward his face. Being around an attractive woman made him want to crank the shadows even higher.

"We've got a snack machine full of great junk food," she continued.

Even starving, Henry wasn't looking for nourishment.

He wanted his body weak, so he wouldn't resist when they threw him in a cell. He was thirsty, though.

"Got Coke?"

"There's a Pepsi machine down the hall. Will that work?"

"Yeah," Henry said. "Sure."

Rivera stood, walked to the door, and left Henry alone again. The stack of manila kept him company. He bristled at the officers still staring from their side of the mirrors. He pretended not to give a shit about the folders, keeping his chin down and eyes hidden within the shadows of his hoodie.

Rivera returned with two Pepsis, a diet for herself and a regular for Henry. She set up the tripod and camera in front of Henry, put her thumb on *record*, and started the video. "Standard procedure."

"No problem." He couldn't shake the feeling that they'd been recording him from the moment he entered.

Henry cracked the can and drank deeply. It had been too long since he'd had a soft drink. Carbonation and sugar, both better than he remembered.

"So, Mr. Hicks, do you know why we wanted to speak with you?" Rivera popped her can and took a drink. Her voice was calm and kind. Henry figured she was probably an effective interrogator with most criminals. He would be her easiest interview ever.

"You want to discuss the people I killed," Henry said, as though noting nothing more than the gray of the walls. He was pleasantly surprised by a startled jolt as both Rivera and the watching men seemed to swallow their shock.

Rivera peered into the cavity of Henry's hoodie, maybe wondering how it could be so dark inside. "Could you be more specific?"

Henry lifted the Pepsi to his lips, took another drink, followed the sip with a deep breath, then recounted each of the assholes he had ended. From the muggers in the alley to the vermin at White Trash Castle, from the man beating his girlfriend and the robbers at the liquor store, to both men who'd broken into his home, along with every other passage in his book of violence written since his untimely death. He actually wasn't sure how many of the murders the cops already knew about. Regardless, Henry narrated his crimes in full detail, leaving out only what might lead to Samantha, or life lived before he lived it no longer.

He concluded his brief but sordid recounting with, "Sorry, I didn't catch their names, but I'll answer any questions you have."

Rivera juggled surprise and suspicion, as if she'd been handed the basketball under the basket, but thought it might explode. Her face was missing its smile, but Henry had felt her fighting its presence as he emptied his memory's violent contents into the room.

Rivera leaned forward when he finished. "Burg Spires Church of Hope. What happened there?"

Henry shook his head. "That wasn't me."

A blaze of anger burst from the other side of the mirror, followed by a thud against the glass, and a flash of excruciating pain. As the dead boy's father punched the wall, Henry winced at a phantom pain in his knuckles. Agony floated on a current, tempting Henry like freshly fried donuts.

He swallowed more soda, holding the can to his lips as Rivera spoke.

"But you were at the Spires the night of the massacre, correct?"

"Yes, ma'am."

"Why were you there?"

"When I killed the last man I told you about, he told me I was too late and that they were gonna hit the church."

"Too late? For what?"

"He only said they were gonna hit the church and that I couldn't stop them."

"Why would he think you'd want to? Did you know this man?"

"He took something from me."

"What did he take from you, Mr. Hicks?"

"My family." Henry had considered lying, but figured there was no way they'd know who he was, even after he showed his malformed face. His fingerprints weren't on file, even if they were unchanged since his transformation.

"What do you mean they *took* your family?"

"He and the man in the van, they killed my family."

"When?"

Rivera wanted specifics, but Henry had to pull back, be less candid. "It doesn't matter. They must've known I was the so-called *Hooded Angel* from the news, and that I was onto them."

"*Who* were you onto?" Rivera asked.

"The people who shot up the church."

"Do you know who they are?"

"No."

"Yet, they hurt your family, and you somehow found them. Something's not adding up, Mr. Hicks."

"I don't know why these people targeted me."

"So how did you come to find them?"

Henry smiled, though he didn't think Rivera could see it in the shadows. "*They* came looking for *me*," he said, though in truth only one came looking, and for Samantha rather than him. "But I was waiting this time. That was only two of them, though. I'm not sure how many more there are."

"Did you see anyone suspicious at the church? The men responsible for the Burg Spires massacre?"

"No, ma'am. Once I arrived, the cops were everywhere. I was too late. Like the killer had said."

"So, why did you run when you bumped into one of our officers?"

"I watch the news. I know you're after me, about my other … *activities*." He let the word crawl smugly from his mouth, so they'd smile even wider when locking his ass in a cell.

"We wanted to speak with you."

"No. You want to arrest me. And I'm fine with that. I'm here, after all. So please, let's get this over with. Is there something you need me to sign?"

Rivera's cell phone vibrated from her pocket.

"Hold on." Rivera stood, taking her Diet Pepsi, and approaching the door. "I'll be right back."

Rivera left Henry alone with the folders on the table and the camera's red light. Officers stewed, angry and certain Henry had something to do with the Burg Spire shootings. Blinded by rage and hungry for an arrest that would stick. They wanted *John Hicks* to pay and settle the debt in their heads.

Henry would have loved to ease their minds, especially Mike Stone's, but he wasn't willing to make a false confession. The fuckers who did the killing had to be found and brought to justice. Surrendering his pursuit of the third murderer was bad enough. He had to give the police a chance to find the cult raining chaos on the sane.

He wanted to help, and considered telling the cops about the tattoos, or maybe some of the shit Pastor Owen passed to him back at the Spires, but Henry had no idea how to steer the police so they were tracking the right cock-suckers inside the cult, rather than some poor fucker trying to recover from meth. Or worse.

As Henry waited, wondering about the folders' contents and fighting everything inside him not to grab them before anyone could stop him, he heard a familiar, impossible voice.

"Master Henry! Master Henry!"

Ezra?

Henry looked around the interrogation room, but as expected, found only his reflection and a closed door.

"Yes, it's me, Master Henry," Ezra repeated, as if answering his thought.

Henry slowly realized the voice was only in his head.

"Master Henry?"

What?

If Ezra was in his head, Henry figured the goll must be able to hear his thoughts. Henry remembered Boothe telling him that Ezra could instantly reach him if something was wrong. Perhaps he and the goll had a similar bond.

A sudden chill froze his insides.

Why are you contacting me, Ezra? Did Boothe tell you to?

"No, Master Henry. It's your wife, Samantha. She just went away in an ambulance."

Chapter Thirty-One

"WHAT?" Henry said, this time out loud, so startled that he forgot about the listening cops until after the words were already out of his mouth.

Oh well, they'll think I'm crazy.

"What, Master Henry? Who will think you crazy?"

What happened to Sam?

"She took pills. Lots of pills. I felt her slipping away."

What?

"She was trying to die. But Boothe called ambulance. She's on her way to the hospital."

Ezra's voice sounded different in his head, more clipped and *foreign*, like someone struggling with English. He wondered if Ezra had somehow regressed, since he didn't seem to speak this way before, or if it was a limitation of their telepathy, offering a rawer version of Ezra in person. Or perhaps the goll spoke differently when scared. And he seemed *terrified* at the moment.

How is she? Is she okay?

"I don't know, Master Henry. You need come home. Where are you?"

Jail.

"What? Why?"

No reason, Ezra.

"Boothe said you have to come home."

Why didn't he contact me?

"He can't, Master Henry. Only I."

Henry was sick to his stomach. Sam clearly didn't see recent events as a "darkness before the dawn," but rather a permanent midnight. And one she might never wake from.

I should've done something sooner. I should've seen this coming!

Now he had surrendered himself to the cops. Trapped, worn, and stuck inside an interrogation room.

Fuck! Fuck!

"What, Master Henry?"

Tell Boothe I'm in jail. I turned myself in and can't get out. I need his help.

Henry strained to hear something more from Ezra, but the connection was dead and the goll had fallen silent. The door to Henry's room opened. A man entered, his eyes swollen and bloodshot.

Mike Stone.

Fuck.

"You son of a bitch." He quietly closed the door behind him.

Then he went straight to the camera and killed the red light.

Henry raised his hands. "I didn't do it, man. I swear."

The officer was stocky. He looked strong, with short brown hair and a square face reddened from anger. He slammed his palms on the table and growled, "Cut the shit!"

Ezra's voice wormed back into Henry's head.

"Master Boothe said you're on your own. He can't help you."

Fuck! Tell him if he doesn't, they're gonna kill me.

The cop's eyes were on Henry's. "You're gonna talk. And you're gonna tell me everything you know."

Henry's heart pounded in his chest, raw anger stirring inside him. Responding to the man's rage. A familiar hunger urged him to murder the man. Inhale his sorrow and leave him for dead.

Kill him, and I'll have the power to get out.

No reason to wait.

I gotta move before they lock my ass in a cell.

Henry shook the urgency from his mind.

No, I can't kill him. He's a victim, too. He's been through so much, already.

Whatever Stone had been through was replaced by the officer grabbing Henry's hoodie and yanking the fabric back, exposing his misshapen head. Stone flinched, but just barely. Henry could feel the watchers recoil in a wave of shared disgust. They'd seen the pictures, but nothing prepared them for the monstrosity up close.

The cop pressed an index finger into the table, tapping to punctuate his words. "Tell me, now, Hicks. Who's responsible for the shootings?"

"I swear," Henry pled, his voice growing brittle. "I'm telling the truth. I don't know who these people are, or why they did it."

Ezra crackled back into Henry's head.

Master Boothe said he can't help you. He said you're on your own.

Goddammit.

Henry sighed even as the cop paced the room, either trying to intimidate him or control his own anger. The officer's aura was dark. Black, with deep-blooming reds, almost purple, churning in a billow around him.

Kill him. Kill him now. Find Sam.

Then what? So what if I find Sam? How can I possibly help her?

I'm gonna stick to the plan and stay put.

The cop stepped behind Henry, then leaned forward, close enough that Henry could smell his hot coffee-breath and feel his boiling rage as a physical sensation. Stone probably meant to intimidate. He didn't realize that was feeding Henry instead.

"You've already admitted to enough murders to earn the electric chair three times over. What's another few?"

"Nothing, if I had done it." His voice trembled as he tried controlling hunger and anger in unison. "But I didn't."

Kill him. Kill him and bust the fuck out. Now!

The cop stepped away from Henry, moving around the room until he was back in front of the table. Stone struggled to look calmer, smoothing his shirt and nodding his head. "Okay, let's say you had nothing to do with this, and maybe, *maybe* I can believe that. But I'm not buying you don't know who did. There were three people dressed in black hoodies and dark jeans. Same as you. So, what the fuck is that, some sorta freaky coincidence? Because in my line of work, the most obvious assumption is almost always the right one."

"I have no idea why," Henry said. "These fuckers, the same fuckers who killed those people in the church, killed my daughter and raped my wife. They deserve to die. I want to end every last one of them. Why in the fuck would I join them and murder more innocent families? Why would I help them kill other children?"

Henry realized he'd said too much as the cop's eyes met his. There were a finite number of recent crimes that fit those parameters, especially where one of the victim's bodies went missing. Details like that couldn't, and *wouldn't*, be ignored. How long until they realized it was the supposedly dead Henry Black who was sitting in their interrogation room?

He could imagine the media trumpeting the story. One of the country's most famous comics, now a hideous freak with a bottomless appetite for murder.

The door opened and Rivera entered.

Go. Now! This is your chance.

Henry leapt to his feet, shoved Rivera into Stone, and raced out the door.

"STOP!" Rivera screamed.

Henry had no intention of stopping, even though he was weak and slow. Even though he couldn't shift into shadow form — something Boothe had promised he'd be able to do with barely a breath left.

Fucking Boothe!

Henry raced down the corridor toward the lobby. He'd have to flee the station, run out into the parking lot, and hope like Hell they didn't seal the exit gate before he could flee.

The door at the far end of the hall shot open. Three officers spilled into the corridor, blocking his path. Behind him, Henry heard Stone and Rivera fast approaching, followed by more from the viewing room.

He was trapped.

He had to move.

Henry ran at the three cops, reaching out to shove them aside. Instead, he was sent to the floor under strong arms, fists, and then, intense pain as one of the officers tasered him.

Henry screamed. If this was phantom pain, his brain still needed the memo.

The officers on top of him let loose a station's worth of fury — fists and feet in a violence that only seemed encouraged by Henry's hideous form.

He could feel their hate, anger, and fear soaking into him. Horrible … but wonderful, too. Like freshly grilled meat for a famished body. Even as the pain increased, so did the ecstasy, making for a bizarre but beautiful blend. Confusing, yet empowering. Making Henry stronger.

"Stop!" Detective Stone shouted. "Secure that suspect."

Not a single cop stopped, or even slowed their assault. They kept hitting and kicking, as if every officer had lost someone in the church and he had personally pissed on their graves.

"I said *stop!*" Stone repeated, pulling one of the three officers off and away from Henry. That left two more, one with a knee in Henry's back trying to put a cuff around his wrist, the other holding his face to the floor.

He felt another surge of energy, stronger than the first. He pulled his hands free, twisting his body. He grabbed one of the officers, a pudgy crew cut with a pug nose, and slammed the man's head into the drywall. The cop slid down the wall into a boneless heap.

Henry felt like someone had shot adrenaline-laced cocaine straight into his veins. He was far from full strength, but he suddenly had the energy to fight back. Maybe even escape.

White powder from the dent showered the officer's face. The remaining cop fell back, open palm reaching for his pistol. Henry lifted the first officer off the ground and over his head, then tossed him into the others, knocking them back like bowling pins.

Then he spun around, kicked open the lobby door, and raced toward the exit.

Henry hopped over a bench, pushing a hobo to the side, racing into the night with the grieving voice of Mike Stone shouting behind him, angry and pleading. "Stop!"

Henry ran until he was again one with the shadows.

Chapter Thirty-Two

HENRY DIDN'T STOP RUNNING until he was rounding the corner toward La Paz, the street where his mansion sat in darkness. He called for Ezra the entire way home, but heard nothing in response. When he reached the house, the goll was nowhere to be found. Instead, Boothe was sitting cross-legged on the roof, as if calmly waiting for the world to end.

Ezra! Henry tried, calling for the goll a final time.

Of course Boothe was there. Fucker always knows everything.

For the first time since fleeing the station, Henry thought he might be walking into a setup. Was Ezra's call meant to lure him back to Boothe? If so, he was going to lose it and kick the demon's ass. He raced up the side of his house, leapt to the rooftop, and yelled, "What the fuck happened, Boothe?"

"Where were you, Henry?"

"You want answers from me, Boothe? You start first. Where is Sam? Is she okay?"

"Relax," Boothe said, rising from his cross-legged spot

249

on the roof. "Samantha's fine. She's at Mercy Hospital right now. Ezra is with her."

"I'm going," Henry said, turning to leave, hoping to get answers from Ezra.

"No, you're not." Boothe pulled Henry toward him. "Samantha's in intensive care. And it is impossible for you to reach the hospital's interior unseen. Ezra can stay invisible far longer than you."

"Then *you* take me. Make us invisible." Henry thrust his hand out, hoping Boothe would accept it.

He laughed in Henry's face instead. "No." He turned his nose up at Henry with the same cool indifference countless women had shown Henry during his teens and twenties.

"What?"

"*No.* I'm not taking you anywhere or doing *anything* for you. You need help, you call Randall. I'm sure he'll be happy to oblige. You and me, though? We're done."

Henry stood, snarling. "So why are you even here, then?"

"I wanted to see the look in your eyes when you realize that your supposed savior had abandoned you. Hurts, does it not?"

Henry inhaled and exhaled, trying not to give into the anger. But even as he struggled for control, the moments since his death bubbled inside him. Anger, fear, hate, and sorrow, all rolling into a furious boil.

Henry erupted, launching himself at Boothe.

The demon laughed, stepping deftly out of the way. Henry was overconfident, used to dealing with slow humans, and flew past Boothe before landing chest and palms first onto slate shingles.

Boothe laughed louder. "Really, Henry? Is that all you can do? I thought you had learned more than that."

The demon had said the wrong thing if he was hoping to calm Henry down.

Henry leapt to his feet, screaming through his rage toward Boothe, surprising himself. Maybe even the demon. He scored with a solid blow to the side of the head, knocking Boothe back to the rooftop. Henry jumped on top of him.

Boothe was stuck, pinned beneath Henry's legs. He leaned forward, shifting his weight to hold the demon in place as he launched one fist after another in a frenzied assault. Just like the cops had done to him.

The demon took the beating for several seconds before his eyes turned to rubies and his face shifted, twisting away from the handsome well-coifed man he'd always presented and into a demon. Though *still* better looking than Henry.

Boothe was a snarling monster beneath him, hissing and spitting as he shoved him away with a thrust strong enough to send Henry flying from the roof and sailing through the air to land on a patch of brickwork beside the pool. Boothe leapt from the rooftop, shattering brick as he landed next to Henry and slammed a fist into his forehead.

Pain erupted in his skull. *Real* pain. Not that *in his mind* shit he could push past with focus.

Henry rolled away, the spinning twisting nausea into his stomach. He pushed to his feet and staggered toward the water, staying upright and struggling through a sudden dizziness and shrill ringing in his ears. He spun from the pool and took a swing at the other demon, missing with a whistle of his fist through the air. The same for his second and third tries. On Henry's fourth swing, Boothe ducked under the blow but kicked Henry's feet from beneath him, sending him onto his ass.

Boothe's demonic appearance faded, replaced with his

sharp nose, perfect skin, and neatly-slicked dark hair. He pressed the heel of his shining loafer into Henry's chest.

Henry squirmed beneath the pressure. He snarled and beat at Boothe's leg with weakening blows but could only sip at the air beneath the demon's weight,. His vision dimmed with his struggles. "I wish you'd never brought me back! You should've left me dead."

"Boo-hoo," Boothe taunted. "You're a *child*, Henry, incessantly whining. What about me? *I* wish you'd not strolled into my corner of Nowhere. I expected more from you. I thought we would do great things. Go places. Together. I *believed* in you, and all I or God ever asked was for you to believe in *yourself.*"

Boothe lifted his foot and kicked Henry in the stomach, like a period punctuating his sentence. Then he straightened his tie and buttoned his jacket. "But how can you see value in anyone or anything, when you can't even see your own." He set his heel back on Henry's chest, grinding it down as Henry started choking, gasping and struggling to free himself from the demon's hold.

Boothe continued the hectoring. "You're a disappointment to me, Henry. Maybe I should have expected that. You were a disappointment to your teachers growing up, and, of course, your parents before they died. Your grandparents after that. Your new money means nothing. Your grandfather thought you were an idiot for trying to make a living talking like a vulgarian on stage, and your grandmother thought you married a harlot. You're a disappointment to me like you're a disappointment to Samantha. Which is what she thought every time she had sex with you for pity."

Lies!

Henry gathered everything inside him, and launched his anger at Boothe, twisting himself from under the demon's heel before grabbing him by the ankle and spinning his body back to the ground. Henry was on his feet first, using the moment to do the only thing that might keep him safe from the demon's rage long enough to think of something else.

Henry threw his arms around Boothe's waist and drove them both into the pool.

They crashed into the water. Henry kicked, pushing himself away and sending the demon toward the bottom of the deep end. Henry aimed for the surface, headed for the edge, gripped the pool's lip, and brought his head above the water, gasping for air.

Boothe surfaced with a roar.

Henry pulled himself out, rolling to his knees on the concrete apron then charging toward the copper gate. He had to get to the hospital. To Samantha. Away from Boothe. Unfortunately, he was only ten feet from the exit when the demon appeared before him in a shower of pool water and bellowing rage. His clawing fingers dug into Henry's throat. The demon lifted them both high into the air with a giant leap, past the treetops, before launching him to the ground.

More decorative concrete crumbled beneath him. Boothe landed seconds later, his hands back on Henry's neck.

He gasped for breath, spitting and sputtering but unable to die.

Boothe shook his head, disappointed. His sopping hair fell over his eyes. "Do you know why you're so mad at me, Henry?" Boothe waited as if Henry wasn't sucking for air and might respond. "Because *you* are the liar, Henry. You act like you're a saint who's been thrust into doing horrible things against your will. We both know that's a lie, don't we?"

Henry struggled to cough out an answer, but Boothe kneed him in the gut to make certain he wouldn't.

Then he pulled Henry closer, until their noses almost touched. "You're so set on what you think I am and what you think *I'm* trying to do to *you*, that you've ignored *your* part in all this. You didn't come back because I brought you back. You came back because you had hate in your heart and *wanted* to return. You *wanted* to kill the men who did this to you and your family. I merely helped you achieve your goals. *You* did this, not me. *You* are the monster, not me. *You* are responsible for the church full of dead children, not me. So take your hate and either make the most of it, or return to Purgatory and wait for Satan to come collect your soul."

A blinding light beamed from overhead. At first Henry thought it was a helicopter. Then, he heard the music.

A Tracker!

Boothe opened his hand, and Henry fell in a pile at the demon's feet, gasping for air, his stomach cramping from panic. The Tracker, bathed in brilliant light, was larger than the one he'd seen outside Burg Spires. Its body seemed to block the entire moon as it descended. It hovered above, looking down with kind eyes as it unsheathed a glowing blade from its scabbard. The sharp edge crawled with sparkles of light.

Its voice boomed in Henry's mind, and he winced beneath its weight.

I am here to ease your pain.

The air swelled with its music, lulling Henry into peace. A motionless glaze of surrender.

Boothe looked down at Henry, his lips peeling back in a sneer of disgust. He wiped water from his face and straightened his tie. "Well, you wanted your misery over. It was almost nice knowing you, Henry."

Boothe's body blurred and was then gone.

Henry lay by the pool, soaking wet, yet still on fire from the angel's proximity, inches from what would surely be his true death. According to Boothe, an everlasting nothingness where he'd never see his wife or daughter again. He wondered if he could roll into the water, and if that would keep him safe.

He tried to move but his limbs barely twitched.

Henry cried as the Tracker drew nearer, paralyzed by the song. The voice like a trumpet. Like a thousand bells echoing from the hills. It wasn't that Henry *couldn't* move, but that he didn't *want* to. He was drawn to the angel's infinite beauty and the sprawling majesty of the music, floating through the evening air like a promise.

Every wrong will soon be righted.

Suffer no more.

The voice was intoxicating. The lyrics to Pink Floyd's *Comfortably Numb* ran through his mind. Henry smiled at the thought, even as death descended in all its statuesque glory. The angel looked like a gladiator. An angular face and square jaw. Huge muscles under flowing robes. Armor polished to shine like the sun. Henry stared with strained eyes, listened with tired ears. Hypnotized, yet grateful for the trance. His world was slipping, and Henry had no way to hold it.

A net woven from golden strands of light spread wide above his body, fluttering down like an autumn leaf.

He thought of all the death since that horrible night.

Sam and Amélie.

The bodies in the church. Henry could feel the Tracker rummaging through his catalog of sins, figuring him out. Appraising him.

Was the angel his judge and jury? Did the huge sword make it his executioner?

I'm ready. Take me.

Once dead, Henry would be where he was supposed to be.

The melody in his head told him that everlasting peace awaited. Henry wondered if Boothe had been lying all along. Perhaps the Trackers delivered salvation, not the endless nothingness Boothe had claimed. As the sweet song grew sweeter, Henry didn't care if the promise of peace was a lie. It was a *beautiful* lie. All he needed to do was relax and surrender.

The Tracker hovered a few feet above, promising with his song that Henry was seconds from his happily-ever-after. He would be taken away to somewhere beautiful.

Somewhere without pain. Without darkness. Without death.

Relax.

Welcome the light.

The net would become his shroud.

Everything would be perfect.

Better forever.

The net was an inch above Henry's eyes when Boothe blinked back into existence between Henry and the angel. He held a large black spear with a glowing spiral of darkness circling its tip.

No! Don't stop it!

Boothe spun away from the Tracker, swiping his spear across the net.

It dissolved into wisps of light, scattering like confused fireflies. Booth continued his turn, lifting the spear to his shoulder. He hurled it into flight.

Henry cried out, wanting to grab the spear before it destroyed such beauty. But he was too late.

The Tracker dropped his sword into the spear's path, and the weapons collided in front of the angel's massive chest. Lancing light and snakes of black smoke erupted from the impact.

Then it fell back, still floating, opening his mouth wide, venting a shriek that rang so loud that Henry thought he might not ever hear anything again.

Impossibly, the scream grew louder, splitting into shards of agony as the Tracker was swarmed by the wisps of unspooling darkness. It fell to the ground, the song and light falling with it.

You killed it!

Boothe looked down at Henry, his eyes swirling with dark energy.

Before either spoke, Henry passed out.

Chapter Thirty-Three

HENRY WOKE in what he had started to consider his bed. Bright daylight streamed in from the apartment's large windows as the twenty-four-hour news channel screamed from the living room.

At least he's not in my fucking bedroom again.

Henry sat up, swinging his legs over the side and throwing the sheets back. He forced his aching body into the living room. Boothe sat on the couch, wearing a silk robe and drinking a martini. An odd sight for the demon. Henry had yet to see him in anything other than his black suit or robes. Henry ignored him, going to the kitchen and pouring himself several glasses of water. The demon ignored Henry right back.

With his final glass empty on the counter, he glanced at the silk robe again. "Been hanging out with Hugh Hefner?" Henry crossed the apartment and stood at the end of the couch.

Boothe turned his head and looked up with a sour face. "No, Henry. Such trivialities don't interest me. I'm a romantic, not a pervert."

"Yeah, and I read *Playboy* for the articles." Henry plopped down in the overstuffed chair across from Boothe. "Any word on Sam?"

"She's recovering. In Room 741, in case you'd like to peer through her window like a Peeping Tom. I'd wait for nightfall since apparently you now have angels, a cult, *and* the Burg City Police Department searching to kill you. Very well done, by the way." Boothe sipped his martini.

"Where's Ezra?"

"Nearby, looking out for your wife so you don't have to, like always." Boothe pursed his lips. "So, now that last night's scuffle is history and you've another bandage on your boo-boo, would you like to tell me what you were thinking, getting yourself thrown in jail?"

"I didn't *get* thrown. I threw myself. I'm sick of the pain, the murder, the *everything.*"

"So, what? You were going to leave Samantha defenseless against these crazy maniacs who shot up a church? Really, Henry? I pegged you as smarter than that."

Henry rolled his eyes. "Randall said I still had hope of salvation. That I could reject you, and that if I did, he'd make sure Sam was protected."

"Well," Boothe said looking up with a condescending grin, "Where is Randall *now?*"

Henry wondered if his loyalty to Randall had been misplaced. Demon or not, Boothe had saved him twice and Samantha once. While Randall had blinked him away from being caught by the cops, that was all the angel had done for him besides fill his head with confusion.

"Randall!" Boothe shouted in an exaggerated fashion. "Don't keep Henry waiting!"

Boothe looked around for any sign of the angel. Then he laughed, a large deep guffaw that made him nearly choke on his martini. "So, let's get this straight. A fallen angel promised you salvation, and you believed him? I suppose you thought the pearly gates might swing wide the second you rejected me? Maybe God Himself would welcome you with a guided tour?"

"Well, no," Henry said. "But Randall promised a shot at redemption, but only if I didn't listen to you. Is that true, Boothe? Do I still have a chance?"

"I've yet to lie to you, whether you choose to believe that or not. Have I obfuscated the truth in a dressing of light fog? Of course, we all do what we must when shoving someone off the fence toward where they're meant to go. But I've *never* lied. Yes, there's a slim chance you can still be saved. But … cross my heart and hope to die, Randall was the one lying to you. About Sam, no less. Once you went wherever you're going to go, *he* couldn't stay and protect her."

"What do you mean?"

"Randall said what he had to say to get you to turn against me. Return to Nowhere, and he has no link to Earth. Not through *you*, anyway. He couldn't protect Sam, no matter what he promised."

"I thought you could travel to Earth whenever you wanted."

"We *can*, so long as we're connected to a soul in our care. Right now, you are that soul, Henry. Sure, we'll be guardians of another, and the new soul will provide us with a way back, but we'll be too busy working with them to see after Sam."

Henry shook his head, trying to sift through sense and logic to determine whether he was hearing more of Boothe's manipulations or the truth.

Did the angel lie?

"He lied?"

Boothe said, "You sound shocked."

"But he's good. He's an angel, right?"

"A fallen angel, Henry. Good, yes, but not perfect. He's trying to earn his way back into Heaven. That means he must convert enough people to earn his return."

"Fuck, if I can't trust the *good* guys, who *am* I supposed to trust?"

Boothe's massive grin said it all. *Why not me?*

Henry's eyes fell to the TV screen, and a familiar pair of photos, Tiny Eyes and Bulldog. A third photo appeared, a man Henry hadn't seen before. Under the photos were the words, *Suspect in Henry Black Murder Case Arrested.*

Henry stared at the screen, at the man with longish hair framing his pretty boy face. At least ten years younger and a few zip codes away from the first two killers. Everything about the asshole screamed *rich kid*. Under his photo, a name: Patrick Harrison.

"What the fuck?"

"Looks like the cops just found your third man," Boothe said.

The photos transitioned to a shot of Henry and Amélie, taken at Disneyland two years before. He swallowed, thinking of his baby girl only for a second before the image blurred to a picture of the trust-fund asshole. That photo went to archive video of Patrick Harrison walking out of the courthouse surrounded by reporters. Beside him stood what appeared to be three hundred and fifty pounds of sweaty, sleazy lawyer. Or maybe a mob bodyguard in a fifteen-thousand-dollar suit.

"Harrison, son of Harrison Tech president *Alfred* Harrison, a high-level donor in last year's re-election of Mayor Lucius, bonded out this morning and is expected back in court in two weeks," said the female anchor, beaming.

Henry found the remote and rewound the story, starving for details.

The police tied two dead men to the murders at his house, then somehow linked one of the men to Harrison, though they weren't detailing the connection or ruling out additional suspects.

"Bonded out?" Henry shouted as the story repeated. "The trust-fund fucker *bonded out?*"

Boothe shook his head, folded his fingers on his stomach, and said, "Well, Henry, I'd say that's the best news we could've hoped for, yes?"

"What? That fucker is out of *jail!* How is that *good* news?"

"It means that the window to get him is now open. And now you have a name and face. All you need to do is find him and kill him. That shouldn't be too hard."

Henry thought of Randall's offer.

Boothe must've read his eyes. "Don't even tell me you're considering *rejecting* me again, Henry. Pretty soon you're going to start hurting my feelings."

"I don't know. Why are you so hot for me to kill this fucker? What's in it for you?"

"I said our interests are aligned. That's all you need to know."

"No," Henry said, jabbing his finger at Boothe. "I wanna know what happens *after* I kill this fucker. You said Randall's trying to earn his way back into Heaven, so what the fuck are *you* trying to earn? Your way into Hell?"

Boothe shook his head. "Forget it, Henry. I'm not telling you."

"Then tell me what happens to *me*."

Boothe stared, as if weighing how much to say.

"Okay, Henry. I'll tell you what happens. Kill this man, and your soul is turned for good. Or bad, as it were. You stay a demon and don't go to Heaven. You're either stuck in Nowhere forever, like me, or you go to Hell."

Henry stared. "So you're saying I *could* go to Heaven if I turn my back on killing this guy?"

Boothe said nothing, not even with his eyes.

"Don't lie."

"Like you could tell if I *was* lying," Booth snorted. "But, yes, it's *possible*. The real question you should be asking is, *Do you really want to let your daughter's murderer go?*"

"I sure don't want to spend a fucking eternity in Hell!"

"Hell's not as bad as you think, Henry. Nothing like the fire and brimstone in your storybooks. Of course there's *some*. Hell *does* have a reputation to live up to. But some parts of Hell are quite exciting, especially if you're well respected, or an excellent earner. With your thirst, you surely will be."

"'Earner?'"

"If you convert enough souls in Purgatory."

"So, that's what this is about? You're converting me to do what? Get a corner office in Hell?"

Boothe laughed. "Henry, Henry, Henry, it's not about *me*. It's about *you* protecting your wife. Ask yourself what would've happened if Ezra had *not* been watching when Samantha wanted to end it? What would've happened if *I* hadn't called the police?"

Henry said nothing.

"Don't worry, Henry, I'll tell you *exactly* what would have happened. Samantha would've died. By suicide. You know what happens to suicides, right? They go straight to Hell. No Purgatory, no judgment, amen and hallelujah, Brother Henry. Believe me, that's not what you want for her."

Something shifted in Boothe's tone. In his eyes. Subtle, but enough to suggest that he was speaking from painful experience. It was too much for Henry. He had to ask the question burning his tongue.

"Who's Maria?"

Boothe, without missing a beat, asked, "Did Randall tell you about her?"

"Yes. Well, sort of. Randall told me to ask you."

Boothe shook his head. "Maria was my Samantha ... except she succeeded."

"You mean ... she killed herself?"

Boothe looked down at his martini glass, then out the windows. "Yes, Henry. She killed herself. Now she's in Hell."

Something clicked for Henry.

"Wait. So, you're doing this for her, right? You're trying to earn your way to Hell so you can be together again?"

"No, Henry. I'm trying to get her *out* of Hell. And that's all I'll say about this. My troubles aren't something I wish on *anyone*. You have a chance to protect your true love. Kill these men so nothing bad happens again. When I see how little you must do to keep Samantha safe, and see the pitiful size of your sacrifice alongside the heft of your complaints, it sickens me. I'd slap the Devil on the back while handing him my soul for the opportunity you seem so eager to fritter away."

"What about the angel?"

Boothe sighed. "Why are you so keen on Randall?"

"Not Randall. The Tracker you killed."

Boothe's face blanched. He took a slurping sip of his martini, looking at Henry from the corner of his eyes. "I didn't kill him, Henry. I'm not a fool. I expended a significant amount of power in obtaining that spear from an old friend and bringing it to your defense. I don't expect you to thank me, but neither will the Tracker. He's probably sitting on a couch of his own, nursing a drink." Boothe stared into the swirling liquid of his glass. "He *will* be watching for me."

Henry stared out the window, joining Boothe in his absent gaze, feeling a sudden fraternity with the demon. Boothe was right. Henry should be willing to do anything to protect his family, eternity be damned.

He had a chance to avenge his wife and daughter. One chance to put down an enemy that seemed determined, for some reason, to kill his wife.

"Okay," Henry said. "I'll kill him."

Chapter Thirty-Four

THAT EVENING, Henry went to Mercy Hospital, well-rested and rather strong. Surprising, since he hadn't killed anyone since Bulldog and had been running on fumes back at the police station.

Was sleeping last night really enough?

Henry barely slowed on his way to Mercy, at least not until he slipped beneath the fluorescent glow bathing the hospital lot. He crept around the building, searching for where he thought Room 741 was. He scampered up the side to a wide ledge circling the seventh floor, where he went from window to window, searching for his wife.

He wasn't alone. Ezra appeared on the ledge, turning visible from his hidden guard position in front of a window two from Henry. He moved to join the goll, then glanced into the room, seeing his wife in bed, tubes running into her arms, nose, and mouth, hooked up to God knows what kind of monitors and IV bags.

But still alive.

"Hello, Master Henry," Ezra said with a slight bow.

"Hey, Ezra. Since we're away from La Paz, you think

there's any way you could see to dropping the Master stuff? Just Henry is fine."

"No, Master Henry. I'd not disrespect you. You are my Master. There is no shame in that for me. It is my honor to serve you."

"Okay, Ezra," Henry said, noticing that the goll's weird-speak in his head had cleared to normal. "Thanks for being here. For Sam, I mean. I know you've kept her safe."

"You're most welcome, Master Henry. I am glad I could help."

"Hey, Ezra?"

"Yes, Master Henry?"

"Would you mind if I asked for a little privacy? I'd like to look in on my wife, and I don't really wanna worry about what you're thinking or what I'm not saying, or anything. I just want to *be*. That okay with you?"

The goll nodded. "Of course, Master Henry. I will wait on the roof. Keep a look out for Trackers up there. Master Boothe said they almost had you. Twice, that was."

"Yeah, I'd appreciate you looking out for them so that doesn't happen again. Thanks."

Ezra bowed, folding his hands as he looked up at Henry, as though he would do anything in the world to please his master. Then he left with a *POOF!*

Henry stared through the window, watching his wife lying in bed. He knew things were often dark for Sam. Before they met, a few times during their marriage, and definitely after his death. But not so dark that she never wanted light again.

Maybe losing Amélie was the beginning, and this was the end. Perhaps the shootings at the church had hurled her over the edge. So much death, brought to children she'd known, no less. That would ruin *anyone*. But what would it do to someone who had already lost so much?

Things were awful after they lost Avery, the first of two miscarriages. The last time they had been willing to name a child before she was brought breathing into the world.

Samantha had cried for weeks, rocking in a chair they couldn't afford while staring at the empty crib from page forty-seven of the Pottery Barn catalog. Bought on a maxed-out credit card. Sitting in the small writing office that was supposed to be the new nursery in their tiny apartment. She might have circled the drain into forever, but dawn cracked through the blackest night and Sam got pregnant with Amélie.

Amélie changed everything. She was healthy, smart, happy, and exciting. Able to keep Samantha company during the many long nights when Henry was touring. She was a living, breathing token of their trajectory. From not having enough money for clothes that weren't worn by another kid first, to letting her wear things just once if she wanted. A career set aside for a child she'd dreamed about her entire life.

Yet, Amélie was unaffected. A beautiful girl who understood her world should never be taken for granted. Part Henry, part Samantha, and every ounce amazing.

Henry stared through the window, wishing Sam could see Amélie again, as he'd seen her ghost. He gasped. As if she had heard his thoughts like a call, his daughter appeared, standing next to her mother's bed wearing jeans and the long purple sweater that she often let drape over her hands. She looked down, smiling, stroking her mother's hair.

At least, sort of. Amélie's hand was transparent, and fell through Sam's skin as though sinking into a river. She kept smiling, though, and tried tucking the blanket further up under her mother's chin, even as her fingers slipped through the fabric.

Henry watched, guilty like a spy, standing in shadows outside the window, looking in and saying nothing. Amélie had somehow escaped Purgatory, but he wondered *how* she had escaped, and if she had managed to flee with her full mind intact.

It was the first time the three of them were so close together since dinner the night that he and Amélie were killed.

How did she get out of Purgatory?

Does she know I'm outside?

Amélie turned from her mother, looked up at her father, and grinned from ear to ear. "Hi, Daddy!" she mouthed, then kissed her mom on the cheek, sinking through Samantha's skin, before heading his way.

Walls meant nothing once you were dead. Amélie moved from one side of the glass to the other, as if there was nothing in between them.

"Hi, Daddy." She sat on the ledge next to Henry, swinging her legs high above the parking lot. "Mommy's going to be okay, right?"

"Yes." Henry nodded as he sat.

After a long moment, he caught a look in his daughter's eyes. That one which said she wanted to ask something but was afraid to bring it up. She knew something was wrong. He couldn't *not* talk about the elephant in the room.

He cleared his throat and said, "Mommy has always been very, very sad."

"I know."

Henry turned to Amélie, surprised. "You know?"

"Of course," she said, as though it were a matter of public knowledge.

"How do you know that?"

"Because I saw it in The Forgotten."

"Oh," Henry said, trying to figure out what she meant. "What else did you see?"

"Everything." Amélie laughed, sounding nervous.

"How did you get out?"

"By being okay with whatever I saw."

"Oh." Henry fell silent.

Into his quiet, Amélie said, "Are you going to take care of the bad man who killed me?"

"You mean kill him like he killed you?"

Amélie nodded.

"You think I should?"

"I think he deserves it. It's fair. But Randall said if you kill the man, something bad will happen, something that can never be taken back."

Randall!

"Do you know what that something is?"

Amélie shook her head. "He didn't say."

"Didn't or wouldn't?"

"Wouldn't."

Henry laughed humorlessly. "Well, that sounds like Randall. Did he send you here to stop me?"

"No. I heard Mom crying and found my way out of the scary buildings. It took a while, but I finally found her, just like I found *you.*"

"I'm glad you're here." Henry put his arm around his baby girl, surprised when he could feel her physical form. Maybe demons and ghosts could connect.

"Me, too." She leaned on his shoulder.

Her touch melted his insides. He wanted to hug her forever. He put his arm around Amélie and drew her closer.

My girl is here with me.

They shared the silence. Henry swung his feet, matching Amélie's rhythm. Finally, she pulled away from his embrace. "You shouldn't kill him, Daddy. I don't want you to do something bad that can't be taken back."

"But I have to protect, Mommy. That's my job."

"You don't have to kill him."

"I might," Henry argued. "And there's more than just one man left. There's at least three who are trying to hurt Mommy. What if that's the only way to keep her safe? These men are bad, *super* bad, and I don't know why, but they want to hurt our family. Since Mommy's the only one left, you and I have to do all we can to protect her. That means you being okay with whatever I have to do. What do you think?"

She shook her head, growing more insistent. "No, Daddy. You *have* to find another way."

"There isn't one." Henry held her eyes, quietly begging his daughter to believe him, if only so it would be easier for him to believe himself. "I have to stop them."

Amélie pouted. "Randall said there's another way."

"Maybe. But if there is, I don't know what it is."

He looked to Amélie for the answer, but her quivering lip had nothing to say. Her face was about to crack into a cry … and then she was gone, as suddenly as she had appeared.

"Amélie?" Henry cried out, searching the ledge, before peering through the glass, back inside the hospital room.

His daughter was gone.

And again he was alone.

Chapter Thirty-Five

HENRY PRACTICALLY FLEW on his way to kill Patrick Harrison, leaping from the hospital ledge to the parking lot, racing through the night and gliding from one shadow to the next until reaching Boothe's apartment. He went straight to the computer, looking up everything he could on the rich fuck sucking at the teat of Harrison Tech.

He couldn't find a direct route, and ended up hopscotching all over the Internet for twenty minutes, eventually finding the fucker's address in his public arrest report.

Time for justice, motherfucker.

Twenty-one minutes after memorizing *82734 Ariel Way,* Henry dropped into the shadows on the other side of the long retaining wall surrounding the compound bought by Daddy. Probably with kickbacks and tax incentives paid out by the mayor after a landslide victory. Harrison Tech didn't donate. They invested.

Henry skirted a pool, water glowing like an invitation in the cool night, and passed a half-dozen cabanas. He climbed the Spanish tile steps to the sliding glass door where he sensed activity at the edge of his awareness. He dropped into the darkness, and slid inside.

Three rooms later, Henry walked in on Patrick Harrison under a blanket of naked women. The room had barely any light, though he doubted either Patrick or his invoiced companions would've noticed him, even with a bank of fluorescents on the ceiling. Lines of coke, loud music, and dripping sex. Patrick's senses were indulged to overwhelm. The music was loud, but Henry was louder. He dropped into a crouch and roared.

Seven whores rolled toward the front door. Half were naked, but there wasn't time for modesty when you were hauling ass away from a monster.

Patrick froze, blinking the daze and confusion from his eyes. For Henry, nothing else mattered.

The trust-fund fucker stood, as if waiting for Henry to start talking, his hard-on still raging as Henry flew forward with a punch. Patrick ducked, but Henry ducked lower, his fist connecting with Patrick's jaw.

His head whipped around, his knees wobbling as he threw his arms out to keep himself upright.

Henry stepped in and wrapped his arms around Patrick's shoulders and slammed him onto the floor, his forehead driving into Patrick's nose. A crunching squish, and the asshole's blood dribbled into Henry's eyes. Henry tasted it as it dripped into his mouth. Delicious.

Patrick said nothing. He didn't cry out or beg or even laugh. He growled like an animal and lashed out at Henry. The monster ignored the ineffectual blows.

Henry picked Patrick up by his hair and stood him against the wall. He wouldn't stop swinging, so Henry drove a boot into his balls, smashing the flopping erection into his gut.

Patrick's breath exploded out of him. Blood coursed

from his crushed nose as he tumbled to the floor. He landed with a thud and a wheezing gasp. Henry stomped on the killer's back.

Once Patrick finished gasping, He stomped again, another whistling from his body each time Henry's heel landed on the asshole's back.

Henry stomped one final time and hooked his toe under Patrick's arm. He kicked him over onto his side.

The man curled forward, hands cupping his balls. "Why are you doing this?" he whined, blood spilling into his mouth, staining his teeth. "Whatever you want, it's done. It's money, right? I've got plenty. Let me take you to the safe."

I fucking wrote that line.

He flashed back to his own pleas the night Patrick and his buddies broke into his home. The night they murdered his daughter, raped his wife, and sent Henry down his highway to Hell.

"There's not enough in your safe for absolution," Henry growled.

Patrick rolled over, and Henry allowed him to get up, watching him carefully. He bawled like a child. Giant shuddering sighs, weeping and begging, "Please."

Henry grabbed a fistful of hair on the back of the man's head and yanked him so they stood face to horrible face. "Make this quick," he hissed. "Your two partners gave you up in seconds, without crying like pussies. Tell me who else is in your cult."

"That's what you want? A handful of bums who like to get wet? No problem, I'm happy to help. The Order means *nothing* to me. Same safe, different prize inside. I've got documents in the safe that'll tell you everything."

Henry looked at Patrick, like he knew he was lying. "No fucking bullshit."

"Hey, man. I pay for some of this shit. That doesn't mean I'm willing to give up my life for it."

Patrick turned and stumbled toward the same black hole the whores had run through before. Henry followed, down one long hall, then another to the left, up a short one, and through a doorway on the right. At the room's far side, on the opposite end of a long and handsome desk, Patrick stood by the wall, looking over his shoulder with a bloody smile.

Though the wall looked like nothing but wood, Patrick swiped his thumb on the surface. There was a *beep* and a *click*, then a large painting of a racetrack slid three feet to the left. Patrick entered a code and the wall safe sprang open with a flash. Henry watched carefully, in case the man had a gun waiting in ambush. But it was just a wooden box, approximately ten inches by fourteen inches, perfect for a stack of documents. He brought the box to his desk.

"Here you go." Like a carnival barker, he grinned and spread his hands. "It's all yours. Order From Chaos!"

Henry approached the desk, leaning to the side for a better look. He'd managed two steps when Patrick opened the box. He spun it, sliding his fingers under the edge of a neat pile of papers. The box faced Henry, and he bent to study the evidence Patrick was offering.

But instead of lifting the papers out, Patrick flung the stack into his face. Henry ducked, knocking the fluttering papers from his line of sight, and Patrick lifted an onyx blade from the bottom of the box. He pulled back, but faster than his eyes could follow, the blade crossed the space between them, and it slid deep into his chest.

Henry screamed and fell to his knees. Patrick released his grip and danced back to avoid the gush of black blood that splashed at his feet.

"Fucking Christ!" Henry roared. A sun burned beneath his skin. "The fuck is this?"

Patrick laughed. "A blessed knife, specifically designed to kill dumb fucks like you."

Like the Tracker's net, the blade held him paralyzed. He couldn't move, not even when Patrick punched him in the face, walking around his frozen body and kicking him in the balls. An echo of Henry's earlier beating on him.

"I know who you are and why you're after us," Patrick whispered. He launched another kick, this one to Henry's side, right over his liver. After landing the blow he leaned in with his bloody lips next to Henry's ear. "Mr. Punchline. Henry Black."

If he hadn't been worrying about whether he was bleeding inside or out, Henry would've wondered how in the fuck Richie Rich knew his name.

"Why?" Henry gasped, crying in pain, certain he was minutes, if not seconds, from death.

"He told us your family would make an ideal target," Patrick said, ignoring Henry's question.

"Who told you I was coming for you?"

The man laughed with a shrug. "God."

"Fuck you," Henry hissed. "What the Hell would you know about God?"

Patrick smirked, happy that Henry wanted to play.

"You know," Patrick said, circling Henry, "We hadn't *planned* to rape your wife. With no idea what was behind Bonus Door Number Four, I just didn't see it coming. But damn, that black hair, man, hanging just above those perfect tits. Shit." He kicked Henry in the back.

Pain flared in his kidneys, but he couldn't even control his muscles enough to properly fall.

"Don't get me wrong, brother. I get it. Sad sack of shit like you couldn't get a fine bitch like that without the money and fame. So I get why you'd be mad that we came and took her. Like I said, we never planned to stir that honeypot, but the way your lady wiggled it … fuck, man, I couldn't help myself."

I'm gonna kill this fucker the minute I've got breath in my body.

"Shame about your little girl, though. While my man was finishing your old lady, I went up to get a piece of your daughter, but she was too *little* to fuck." He shrugged, looking down at Henry with a shake of his head. "There are some places even *I* won't go. I *did* have second thoughts after she was dead, though."

"You sick fuck!" Henry groaned, struggling against the blade's hold.

I give up.

Help me if you're there, and I'm yours forever.

Boothe, Ezra, Randall, someone. Anyone! I NEED YOU!

Patrick went to the desk, but Henry couldn't see what he was doing. He turned back toward Henry, cell phone to his ear. "Yes, Father, I've got him here … don't worry, I'll take care of it. He's as good as dead."

Father?

What the hell does his rich dad have to do with this?

Patrick left the den, laughing at Henry's writhing as he disappeared into the hall.

Henry wondered if he would die before Patrick returned. He kept blinking, unsure if his life, along with his blood, was seeping out between blinks. A side effect of the onyx knife in his chest.

Amélie appeared in front of him, bursting into his sight like a flaring match. She looked down with wide, terrified eyes and a question on her lips.

"Are you okay, Daddy?"

He couldn't tell if she was real or imagined. He would accept her even as a dream.

Henry swallowed the blood flooding his mouth. Clenching against the cough threatening to take his breath. "Please, baby girl. Pull the knife if you can."

"I don't want to hurt you," she said, staring at the knife, her hand hovering inches away.

"Please, you won't hurt me. Just pull it out, or I'm going to die."

Her hand circled the hilt, and their eyes met, hers on the verge of tears. "Are you sure?"

"Positive." He looked at the door and hoped like Hell Patrick wouldn't return at that moment. He wasn't sure if she could be harmed, but he didn't dare take a chance. He whispered, "Just please pull it out before he comes back."

She pulled in a swift motion he didn't think she could have managed alive. As the blade slid out, strength and anger coursed through him, fueling Henry like fire burning hotter by the moment. Anger descended into rage, and his vision turned crimson.

"Come on," Amélie said, trying to pull her father to his feet. "Come back with me. Randall is waiting."

"No. I have to finish this now."

"Please," Amélie begged. "Don't do this, Daddy. Let's just go. We can be together, forever! Just take my hands."

He thought of all the offers he'd received since death. An angel, a demon, and now his daughter, all tempting him with a deal. An open hand, to join them on one path or another. This was the first one he truly wanted to take. Her tears pecked at the edge of his anger. He hated to see her cry, and would do anything to halt her tears.

He reached out for Amélie's hand and was about to take it, but Patrick returned, shaking his head and laughing as he walked through the door.

Henry couldn't tolerate sharing a planet with the monster for six seconds longer.

Henry smiled as Patrick froze. His shocked eyes narrowing, his brain puzzling out how Henry was no longer incapacitated. Patrick sneered in confusion, his eyes darting from Henry to Amélie then back to the demon. "What the fuck?"

Henry leaped across the room, landing against Patrick and driving him to the floor. With his hands at the fucker's throat, Henry growled, "Who did you call? Who else is involved in this? Is it your father?"

Patrick laughed. "I called someone that's going to kill you, dumbass. You fucked with the wrong person, Henry Black! I suggest you leave before it's too late."

Either in his head or right beside him, Amélie yelled, "Don't do it, Daddy!"

Everything else in the universe, including every cell inside him, screamed for Henry to tear the fucker's face from his skull. He asked again, "Who did you call? Why are you people fucking with my family?"

Patrick said nothing, meeting Henry's eyes with a glare. "Kill me and you'll never find out. Or stick around. They'll be here soon." Then Patrick looked at Amélie, and back at Henry with his eyebrows drawing together. "What is it with your family that nobody wants to stay dead?"

Then Patrick grinned.

And in that smile, Henry's life with his family flashed before his eyes. From when Samantha discovered she was pregnant, to when Amélie was born, to a hundred other tender moments. They all flew by even faster than they had in real life. Gone and never to happen again because Patrick Harrison and his stupid fucking cult ended everything.

Henry's hand shook around Patrick's throat, even as he squeezed tighter.

"Tell me why. Why us?" His voice was nearly dead with calm.

"Please, Daddy," Amélie said, now standing beside him, tears streaming down her face. "Please, just come with me. He's not worth it."

Patrick's eyes met Amélie's, his face shaking and red, drool spilling from his mouth as Henry continued to squeeze, his nails pushing into the skin as they became claws.

Henry leaned in. "Don't you fucking look at her."

Patrick kept looking, his smile creeping wider.

"Stop fucking looking!" Henry screamed, squeezing tighter.

"Please, Daddy!" Amélie cried out.

Patrick stared at Amélie, even as his face turned purple. This was the last man who had touched his daughter. The man who had stolen her life.

He gritted his teeth and growled, his voice cracking and desperate *"Stop looking at her!"*

"Daddy!" Amélie cried out as Henry's claws shot through the bastard's throat, meeting through his spine and ending him in an instant.

Amélie's scream echoed against the polished walls.

Henry spun to her, but his baby girl was gone.

"Amélie!" he cried out. He screamed a hundred times but heard no response. He closed his eyes, trying to squeeze away the emptiness. Then he opened them on a crumbled road at the edge of The Forgotten.

Oh, God, please don't let Amélie be here. Please, God!

"Henry?" someone said from behind.

He turned to find Boothe and Randall standing behind him, both in their robes.

How did I get here?

He turned back around, surprised to find himself out

of The Forgotten. Back in the garden, in front of the table, beneath the giant Tree. Randall seemed especially sour. Boothe looked mostly relieved, though the corners of his mouth appeared heavy.

Henry looked from one to the other. "What the Hell happened?"

Randall said, "Go ahead and tell him."

"Tell me what?"

"He's going to be very, very angry," Boothe said, unwilling to meet Henry's eyes.

"What did you expect?" Randall looked disgusted. "Everyone knew this would happen."

Henry felt sick. Or rather, sicker than usual. He didn't know what they were hiding, but an ugly truth bubbled under their skin hot enough to burn him where he stood.

Henry's voice cracked. "What don't I know?"

Boothe turned to Henry and finally met his eyes. "Amélie ... she's in Hell."

"What?" Henry took a step back, clutched fists shaking at his side. "How?"

Boothe said nothing.

"*How?*" Even as he yelled, Henry's mouth fell open with the dawning realization. "Oh, God. You tricked me."

Boothe's eyes were the most genuine Henry had yet seen, but his words held no apology. "You really trusted a demon, Henry?"

"I warned you," Randall said.

Henry fell to his knees. His palms slapped the ground.

"I'm truly sorry," Boothe said. "I had to lie. You never would've ..."

Henry went from kneeling to standing without transition. Maybe demons wielded less power in Purgatory, but Henry was a fat guy who'd had to stand up to bullies all his life.

He swung at Boothe repeatedly, rage fueling him even as he felt a sharp pain in his shoulders and gasped for breath as exhaustion claimed his bones. Not a single blow landed. He stopped, wrapping his hands around Boothe's neck instead, his hands still sticky with Harrison's blood. He squeezed, glad he could finally choke the fucker to death.

Agony rolled across his forehead and into his eyebrows. From his temples to his cheeks. Fire against his skin, rage boiling him from the inside out. His claws sprang out, curved and sharp. They pressed into Boothe's skin, but didn't break through. His vision blurred, and Henry drew a breath that sent a spear of pain through his lungs.

"You fucking lied!" Henry screamed, eager to end the demon's life with his own two hands.

Randall cried behind him, his plea like a bee in the wind.

"Please," said a woman's voice, floating through the mist behind him.

Henry stopped, looked back. Blood dripped into his eyes, burning his vision away. He wiped at it absently, and his fingers caught against the horns blooming from his skull. He looked down at the black blood pooled in his palms. He dropped to his knees and looked up as the fog parted, lit by brilliant light. And from that light, gliding across the grass, came a beautiful woman with long dark hair. Judging from the way she looked at Boothe, then down at Henry as if he were a monster, he knew in an instant who she was.

Maria.

She looked at Boothe, her eyes wide and filling with tears. "Walden, is that you?"

"Maria!" he rasped.

Henry sat back, staring up at the woman, bathed in

light like the angels who'd taken the souls from the church massacre. Henry could only shake his head and stare.

Boothe spread his arms. He smiled, running to greet his love. He pulled her into his body, sweeping her up and spinning her in a circle. Kissing and crying and calling her name.

Henry turned to look up at Randall. "This is why he betrayed me?"

Randall nodded. "Wouldn't you have done the same thing?"

Henry glared at the reunion, feeling sick and murderous like never before. Poisoned by betrayal.

"I warned you," Randall said again.

"Yeah, well you could've fucking told me the stakes! You could've told me it wasn't *my* soul I was damning, but my daughter's."

Randall said nothing, casting his eyes down.

"Oh, yeah. You and your fucking rules!"

Boothe was suddenly walking toward them, Maria standing behind.

"I'm so sorry," Boothe said.

He shook his head. "No! Fuck you, Boothe. And fuck you, Randall." Henry pressed to his feet, swaying with dizziness as he stared up at the swirling clouds surrounding them. "And most of all, fuck God."

Henry turned and staggered toward The Forgotten.

Randall called out, "Where are you going?"

"To forget. All of you and all of this!"

Henry stumbled into a run, ignoring Randall and Boothe until he hit the crumbled edges of The Forgotten.

Chapter Thirty-Six

HENRY WOKE in the last place he ever thought he'd see again — Boothe's sprawling apartment.

The clock read 5:12 a.m.

How the hell did I get here?

No TV or sirens outside.

"Boothe?"

No response.

He rose from bed and looked down at his naked body.

Where are my fucking clothes?

Something seemed off, though he wasn't sure what.

Henry went to the kitchen, drank water straight from the pitcher, then went to the bathroom to piss. He remembered nothing since leaving Randall and slipping into The Forgotten. That felt like a day ago, and forever. He could feel the passed time. Just not how much.

If Henry had seen Boothe, Randall, or Amélie, his mind had no mementos to show him.

He flipped on the light and turned to the mirror, seeing what he hadn't been able to in the dark. His body was different. Shifted closer to a purpose. He was bulky, his muscles more defined. Black horns rising from his puckered forehead. Dark, shaggy hair. Fangs and claws.

He felt as powerful as he was hungry. And then he saw her face in his memory.

Samantha!

He had to know if she was still alive.

Henry went back to the bedroom and half-smiled at the jeans and hoodie lying by the bed. He dressed and crossed the apartment to the wide window looking out over the harbor. He slid it open and leapt outside onto the fire escape, then from rooftop to rooftop and alley to alley, quickly making his way through The Burg to La Paz.

Ezra wasn't on duty, and Henry surprised himself by missing the little guy.

He was shocked to find the front door unlocked. The alarm not set. He swallowed his uncertainty and crept up the stairs, down to the bedroom he once shared with the only woman he had ever loved.

He wanted to cry, seeing Sam lying naked in bed. It had taken five years of marriage before she would do that every night. Henry loved skin-to-skin, but it made Sam feel like her brittle shell would break. At least at first. As much as she loved to peel her clothes to nothing, she wanted them back on when finished.

Sleeping naked meant Sam was content. Happy.

How long have I been gone?

Henry could smell her jasmine-scented shampoo and conditioner. He inhaled deeply. Longed to touch her. Let her know he was there,

He halted in the shadows, unsure.

Is this why I'm back?

Henry moved from the shadows and out into view, but then he paused in confusion. At the sharp aroma of rosewood and leather. A *man's* scent.

A sudden sound from the bathroom sent Henry back to the corner. His heart raced, sorting through a hundred thoughts, each bleeding into the biggest one.

She isn't alone.

A tall man stepped from the bathroom and slid under the sheets.

Henry choked his own throat to silence the scream.

In bed with Samantha was the cop who'd lost his child.

Mike Stone.

TO BE CONTINUED...

A Special Request

Thank you for reading *Monstrous*.

If you enjoyed this book please consider writing a review of it on your favorite bookseller site so other readers can enjoy it too. Just a couple of sentences would mean a lot to us.

Thank you!

SB & DWW

About the Authors

Sawyer Black writes dark and violent fiction for people who secretly love puppies and rainbows. In addition to being a U.S. Army veteran, he's also a beardsman. In fact, that's where all his ideas come from. The beard. Speculative stories about struggle and triumph and brutal emotion, written mostly for his ideal reader, his wife of nearly twenty-five years. He's an independent woman who likes cigars and margaritas, and he holds the deep belief that the earth is round.

David W. Wright is the co-author of edge-of-your-seat thrillers including the best-selling post-apocalyptic series *Yesterday's Gone*, the paranoid sci-fi *WhiteSpace* series, and the vigilante series, *No Justice*, as well as standalone thrillers *12*, and *Crash* which was recently optioned for a movie.

David is an accomplished, though intermittent, cartoonist who lives in [LOCATION REDACTED] with his wife and son [NAMES REDACTED.]

He is not at all paranoid.

He is "the grumpy one" on *The Story Studio Podcast* with fellow Sterling and Stone founders, Sean Platt and Johnny B. Truant.

You can email him at david@sterlingandstone.net

We swear, he almost never bites. Unless you feed him after midnight.

~

For any questions about Sterling & Stone books or products, or help with anything at all, please send an email to help@sterlingandstone.net. Thank you for reading.

Also By Sawyer Black

The Monstrous Series

Soulless

Monstrous Book One

Monstrous Book Two

Monstrous Book Three

Stand Alone Novels

Zoomers vs Boomers

Analog Heart

Born To Die

Also By David W. Wright

Cold Vengeance

Cold Vengeance

Cold Reckoning

Hidden Justice

Hidden Justice

Hidden Honor

Hidden Shame

Hidden Virtue

No Justice

No Justice

No Escape

No Hope

No Return

No Stopping

No Fear

Karma Police

Jumper

Karma Police

The Collectors

Deviant

The Fall

Homecoming

Yesterday's Gone

October's Gone

Yesterday's Gone Season One

Yesterday's Gone Season Two

Yesterday's Gone Season Three

Yesterday's Gone Season Four

Yesterday's Gone Season Five

Yesterday's Gone Season Six

Tomorrow's Gone

Tomorrow's Gone Season One

Tomorrow's Gone Season Two

Tomorrow's Gone Season Three

Available Darkness

Darkness Itself

Available Darkness Book One

Available Darkness Book Two

Available Darkness Book Three

WhiteSpace

WhiteSpace Season One

WhiteSpace Season Two

WhiteSpace Season Three

Stand Alone Novels

Crash
Emily's List
Threshold
The Secret Within

www.ingramcontent.com/pod-product-compliance
Lightning Source LLC
Chambersburg PA
CBHW010535100726
47903CB00011B/3015